V

Grace Thompson was born in Barry, South Glamorgan, and apart from a few childhood years at school in Luton, she has lived in South Wales virtually all her life. She trained as a Nursery Nurse once her two children were at school, and has worked with children in care. Recently she moved from Wales to Chesham in Buckinghamshire to be near her daughter and her two grandsons. She is currently working on a third book in the *Valley* series.

Also by Grace Thompson

A Welcome in the Valley
(previously published as *Dirty Nelly*)

Valley Affairs

Grace Thompson

KNIGHT

First published in paperback in 1990
by HEADLINE BOOK PUBLISHING PLC

This edition published 2000 by
Knight an imprint of Caxton Publishing Group

10 9 8 7 6 5 4 3 2 1

ISBN 1 84067 261 7

Printed and bound in Great Britain by
J. H. Haynes & Co. Ltd., Sparkford, Somerset

Caxton Publishing Group
20 Bloomsbury Street
London
WC1B 3QA

To all my friends in Swansea

Hen Carw Parc

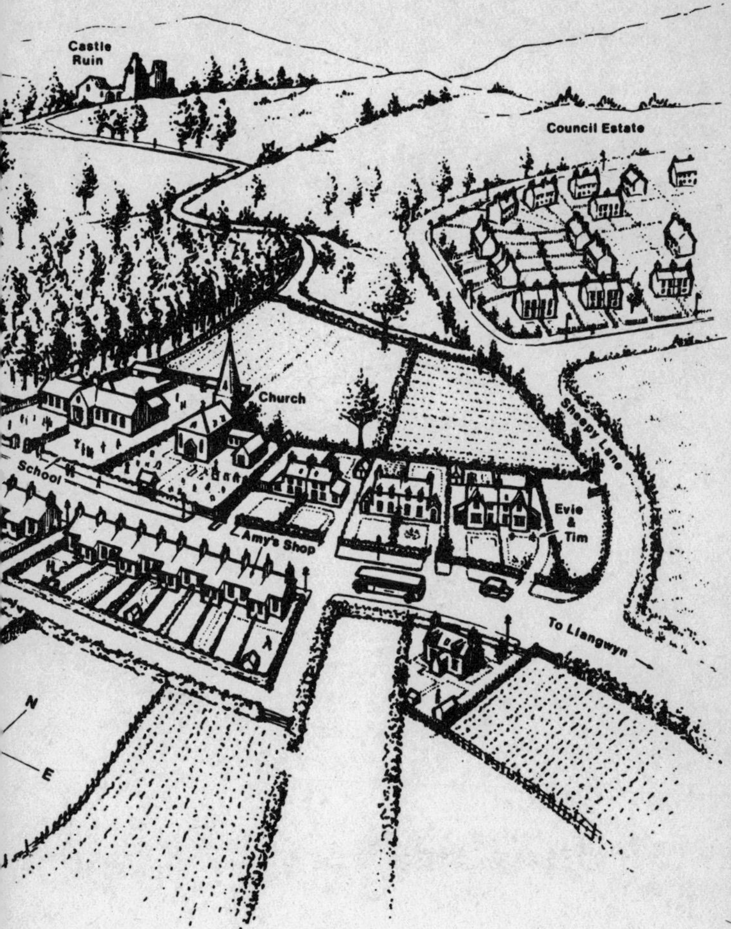

Castle Ruin
Council Estate
Church
School
Sheepy Lane
Evie & Tim
Amy's Shop
To Llangwyn
N
E

Chapter One

The cottage was silent in the early morning. No light showed and the incipient dawn added to the blackness. A fox sniffed around the edge of the chicken run and drooled as the disturbed hens clucked nervously. He tried the gate of the run, pushing it with a paw experimentally in the hope that it would be open, as he did every morning, but he was unlucky. The catch slipped at the last push but he had given up and failed to notice the gate give slightly.

He found a few pieces of bread that Nelly had thrown out for the birds and a few discarded apples that had fallen from the old gnarled tree. He ate half-heartedly, the act of chewing gave him the appearance of a smile, as he watched the run. He trotted around to touch the nestboxes with his nose before departing up the cinder path and off through the woods.

A shrew ran across his path and the fox jumped and landed almost playfully on the shrew with his two front paws, like a kitten with an innocent ball of wool. He chewed the morsel before disappearing into the silent darkness of the trees.

It might have been the anxious clucking of the chickens which disturbed Nelly, for although it was still dark outside, when she opened her brown eyes and peered at the battered alarm clock on the table beside her bed she did not settle back into sleep. She rose and stretched, sighing like a child at the pleasure of the lazy wakening, and felt for her clothes on the old army greatcoat which covered her bed.

She dressed, smiling at the sound of the dogs whining below, waiting to greet her. She knew that even this early on a chilly October morning they wouldn't refuse a walk in the woods. They would have to wait while she attended to her toilet first though. They were never included in her private moments.

She didn't go far into the trees. So early and in such an isolated spot it was unlikely someone would see her lifting her skirts. She went back to collect Bobby and Spotty and she watched them playing, wishing she knew what their noses told them about the activities of the night.

Nelly had put the kettle over the fire, low after the night, but she didn't go back to wait for it to boil. Sometimes the mornings were irresistible and even the thought of the first cup of tea could not persuade her to hurry home. She went past her gate and down the narrow lane to the main road of the village.

The houses were swathed in an early morning mist and she watched in wonder as it slowly lifted and revealed the moist hedges and the shining wet road. The cottages looked dazzling white and, as the outlines became clearer, she smiled as lights appeared in several windows.

Johnny Cartwright was up, and in the next house Phil Davies the postman was already opening his door to get started on his round. He waved and she shouted a greeting, breaking the silence.

'I 'opes you're comin' out an' not creepin' in!' she laughed.

'No chance of any secret love affairs in Hen Carw Parc,' he replied. 'Not with you and that nosy old bugger up by there.' He pointed into the mist to where Prue Beynon lived. 'I swear she never leaves that landing window of hers.'

Nelly watched him cycle away then she turned to see lights going on above the general stores owned by Amy Prichard. She would be rising now and getting Margaret ready for school and Freddy up to help her in the shop. The street was empty of people and cars passed only occasionally, hissing through the surface moisture, lights making the road gleam like metal.

The groan of a heavier engine slowly approached and the forestry bus loomed out of the mist. In the steamy windows Nelly saw the distorted shapes of faces. The bus slowed, its horn sounding impatiently, calling for Archie Pearce who lived near Phil Davies and worked at the forestry.

His door didn't open and the driver of the bus hooted again. Still the house was dark and the driver jumped down and strode to Archie's door, anger bristling visibly even at the distance that separated Nelly from him. She chuckled as he banged and rattled the door and window, and threw grit up at the bedroom, shouting as some fell back on his face.

The door finally opened and Archie stumbled out, clutching at his half-fastened trousers and carrying his coat and food box. The driver, shouting insults at him, climbed back into his cab and started off, determined to make Archie stumble to make up for the irritating delay.

'Every Thursday it's the same,' he shouted, more to himself than in the hope of an interested audience. Nelly chuckled. On Wednesdays Archie played darts at The Drovers and the excitement and the few drinks made him sleep through his alarm the next morning. The figure faintly seen in the opaque windows of the lighted bus staggered and laughter filled the air but was quickly lost as the bus noisily increased speed.

She walked on past the row of small cottages, past the school her grandson attended, and the church, and the house where her daughter Evie lived, and then turned up Sheepy Lane which led back to her cottage. It also led to the council houses and was wide enough for traffic, although it had once been used to bring sheep down from the hills beyond the woods.

In the field below the trees several rabbits sat or wandered around casually, but as soon as the dogs pushed through the fence they disappeared as if by magic. She wondered if Phil had been out with his nets recently. He hadn't brought her any for a while. She would have to drop a few broad hints. Meat was a luxury and rabbit made a good casserole.

When she went back inside the warmth hit her and she loosened her coat and went to the now steaming kettle to make a pot of tea. She breakfasted off some home-baked bread, made in her large oven range, and some cheese made from sour milk and celery seed, then dozed contentedly in her big armchair while the day gradually woke up. The dogs slept across her feet and outside the mist finally gave way to autumn sunshine and the promise of a warm day.

'Gran, Gran, the gypsies are back!' Oliver ran down Nelly's path, scattering the startled hens and sending discarded feathers into the air. 'Can we go and see them, Gran, can we? I've finished my homework.'

'Give 'em a chance, why don't yer? Leave it 'til tomorrer then I'll take a fresh baked loaf and a few carrots I've got left from me garden.'

'Talk to them you mean?' Oliver, a serious-faced eight-year-old, looked horrified.

Nelly put down the fork with which she had been clearing the weed-filled vegetable patch. 'Course talk to 'em!

Friends of mine they are, 'specially Clara.'

'I don't think Mother would—'

'Then don't tell 'er. Not 'til after we've seen 'em!' Nelly said firmly. She scraped the worst of the mud from the fork with her shoe and propping it against the straggly hedge, scraped her shoes clean. She knocked the mud from the fork for a second time and Oliver laughed.

'This could go on for hours, Gran.'

'I gives up in the end. I can't be bothered with them fancy foot-scrapers meself. I'll leave the fork there 'til it dries, then a good clout against the shed an' it'll be as clean as it ever is. Come on, I've got a couple of cakes left in the tin.'

After checking that the hens were safely inside, she banged the fork enthusiastically against the wooden coop to demonstrate her theory but failed to notice that the catch had slipped from horizontal to vertical.

'Go on, you know where I keeps 'em.' She gave Oliver a push, kicking off her shoes before following him.

Oliver went to the tin with the picture of the Queen and Prince Philip on it and helped himself to a date slice.

'All right, I suppose we could just slip up there an' say hello,' Nelly smiled. 'Take another piece of cake, why don't yer, can't 'ave you collapsin' with hunger half way up Gypsy Lane, can we?'

Oliver still looked rather doubtful.

'They don't eat little boys!' Nelly snorted in exasperation. 'There you come, peltin' down me path full of excitement sayin' the gypsies are back, and now you don't want to meet 'em.'

'I thought we'd just have a peep through the hedge,' her grandson said in a small voice.

She laughed, showing the gap in her mouth where a blow

from a swing, many years previously, had knocked out three teeth, giving her a lop-sided grin.

'All right. We'll just 'ave a peep, but I'll 'ave to say 'ello, me bein' a friend. You can hide an' only come out if you want to.'

She called the dogs, who had run to greet Oliver but then settled to lie down near the back door. 'Better leave Bobby an' Spotty 'ere. In you go, boys.' She pulled ineffectively at the door to close it. 'Damn door,' she grumbled. 'I can only shut it from inside where I can get me bum be'ind it.'

Nelly and Oliver set off, leaving the dogs whining their disappointment and peering through the partly closed door.

Turning left at the gate they walked down the lane to the main road. Right then, past the small estate of large houses, where Mrs French and Prue Beynon lived. Nelly 'did' for Mrs French twice a week and she looked up as she passed the house, ready to wave if Monica French was looking out of the window. She sat there a lot these days, Nelly thought, dreaming about the son who had survived the war and died a late victim of it, eight years after the fighting was over. The hedge was high and Nelly stretched her plump body and waved but only caught a glimpse of the sad figure half shaded by the curtains. The last house was where Prue Beynon lived and Nelly poked out her tongue as they passed.

The lane into which they then turned was called Gypsy Lane and it led up between high banks and hedges to Leighton's farm. They saw smoke rising from the fire before they turned the final bend in the lane and Oliver grasped Nelly's hand tightly.

The small encampment was in a place where the grass verge widened. There was a gate close to the solitary caravan which led into a field and on hedges either side of it, branches had caught wisps of straw from the waggons as the field had been emptied of its harvest. Birds'll be glad of them come the spring, Nelly thought as she pulled one off to chew.

Two horses were tethered further on, held by a metal stake knocked into the ground. The caravan, or *vardo*, was canvas-topped and rounded, the cart and supporting posts beautifully carved and painted maroon and yellow. The wheels too were cut and patterned and painted in the same colours. The panels on either side of the front opening had a more elaborate scroll design and behind them were shelves and cupboards built to hold the family's possessions.

From the rounded canvas roof a tall chimney rose, but the smoke they had seen did not come from there. Some distance from the *vardo* a fire burned brightly, a black cooking pot hanging over it on a tripod and chains. A thin, dark-haired woman was dropping pieces of meat into the pot, humming quietly to herself as if unaware of the approaching visitors.

To Oliver she looked oddly dressed, and his heart began to beat faster. Her long black skirt hung half way between her knees and the ground, and a dark floral overall covered most of its length. A cardigan came next, shorter than the overall and adding another layer. Then a bright scarf around her neck and another holding back the long hair. On top of all this was a fringed shawl, draped around her shoulders and tied loosely near her waist. Large gold earrings glinted when the gypsy's head moved and on her fingers shone several rings.

Oliver stared in amazement, but hid behind Nelly as the woman raised her eyes and looked at him. When the dark eyes crinkled in a smile he was so relieved he thought his legs would give out. She dropped the ladle into the pot and stood with her arms wide in welcome. She hadn't spoken and the dogs, who watched them from a corner of the *vardo* were silent, waiting for the woman to give a command.

'Nelly Luke!' the woman said at last. She turned her dark eyes on Oliver, who looked away from her. 'And who is this?'

'Me grandson Oliver. What d'you think of that, eh?'

Oliver continued to stare unseeing into the stubble of the field beside him. The two long, thin dogs relaxed, reassured by Clara's acceptance of the strangers.

'Come on, Ollie, come an' meet Clara.' She tugged the boy closer.

'How d'you do?' he whispered.

The gypsy woman held out her hand and when Oliver slowly raised his, she took it and turned it over to examine the palm. Then she lifted the other hand and studied them both for a while in silence. Oliver's legs began to shake nervously.

'What d'you see then? Clever boy, ain't 'e?' Nelly knew her friend would say nothing to frighten the boy.

'*Cushti*,' Clara said, nodding approvingly. '*Cushti*.'

'That means good,' Nelly whispered, smiling proudly.

'You've got a clever boy there, Nelly my friend.' She smiled into the boy's apprehensive face. 'Quiet, kind and gentle and a good scholar.' She glanced at Nelly then added, 'Books. Lots of books. A good scholar he'll be.' The wise old woman had seen from Nelly's slight reaction that 'scholar' pleased her and had repeated it.

She let Oliver's hands drop and gestured with her head towards the *vardo*. 'Would you like to see inside? Me and your grandmother, we have some talking to do. A lot of news to exchange. Go on, there's no one there.' She smiled at Nelly as Oliver, whose curiosity had driven away his fear, went towards the gaily painted steps.

Nelly sighed as she settled her stiff hip to sit near the fire. The pot was beginning to boil and she watched as Clara adjusted the chain to raise the pot until it was gently simmering.

'What's been happening since we last met, my friend? From the smile of contentment on your face it has been nothing but good.'

'Marriages, ghosts from the past and even a murder, an' worse than that, Clara. My Evie's come back 'ere to live an' she's drivin' me to drink with 'er fussin'.'

'You don't take much driving from what I remember,' Clara smiled. 'But is Evie worse than a murder?'

'The things I 'ave to do to stop 'er from runnin' me life you'd never believe.' She patted the gypsy woman's shoulder. 'But tell me how you are first.'

'My boys have all gone now. Married. Gone into houses. There's but me and Ivor, and the girl. We're doing nice enough.'

As they exchanged news Oliver climbed the steps and looked inside the neat *vardo*. Mirrors gleamed from several places. Shelves and cupboards hung on the walls, all neatly fitted to use every inch of precious space. There was a long seat against one wall, which left only a small area of floor on which there was a thick, colourful rug. The covering on the long seat was an exact match.

He marvelled at the beautiful painting which decorated everything in the small room. The china, the long line of tins and bottles, and the kitchen utensils that hung on hooks in small gaps between shelves were all covered in scrolls and flowers. The mirrors were patterned with cut-out designs which caught the light and added sparkle to the scene.

At the opposite end of the *vardo* a window was open and a curtain swung in the breeze. He looked out and for a brief moment imagined the freedom of a life continually on the move. If he lived with the gypsies no one would force him to learn to read. There were no books to be seen.

'What d'you think of our home then, boy?' Clara asked him when he stood again at Nelly's side.

'Where's the bed?' he asked.

'Did you see that long seat?' Clara asked. 'Well, that opens out and holds the bedding and at the same time 'tis the bed. The girl sleeps across the end below the window.'

'Thank you for letting me see it. It's a lovely place to live,' he said in his awkward, formal way. The laughter which had accompanied the women's conversation had ceased and he felt he had interrupted a discussion which would not be for his ears.

'Who is the girl Clara talked about, Gran?' He asked as they walked back home.

'Clara's son had a wife who died when their little girl was born. The son went away and Clara has brought up her grandchild as her own. So it's like you an' me, Ollie.'

'Can we go and see them again tomorrow?'

'O' course. You ain't scared then?'

'Clara is a bit scary, the way she stared, and looked at my hand pretending to see something. It isn't true is it? I'm not a scholar.'

' 'Ow d'you know what you are? You ain't nine yet! She saw only good things. So what's scary in that?'

'Nothing, Gran. It was—*cushti*,' he said with a shy smile.

It was Saturday and Nelly had done a few hours' housework for Mrs French. The rest of the day was to have been spent digging the garden and clearing the last of the cabbage stumps and the bedraggled lettuces which had shot up and gone to seed. Now she had lost enthusiasm for the work and she put the fork in the shed and went inside.

The fire was low. The red heart hidden under grey ash was almost beyond reviving. She stirred it gently with one of the long pokers and added some fresh wood. When it crackled into life she placed a few lumps of coal on the wood with tongs and the result was thick smoke. She turned towards the open door, swearing under her breath, and as the room cleared she turned the swivel on which the kettle sat and put tea into the teapot.

She was standing close to the fire, waiting for the water to boil, when she heard the gate click. She stretched and looked expectantly out of the window. The kettle was beginning to show signs of boiling. 'Nice time fer a visitor,' she said to the dogs who were staring through the open door, their long tails tapping the linoleum. Nelly's smile faded and she groaned as she recognised her visitor.

'Evie.'

It was difficult to believe the two women were mother and daughter. Nelly was fat and dressed in ill-fitting clothes, with shoes tilted over and worn, dark hair untidily drawn back from a face in which crooked teeth now showed in an uneasy smile of welcome.

Evie was smartly dressed in a navy suit and a cream blouse. Her neat court shoes exactly matched the small handbag on her arm, and she carried crocheted gloves in the same shade of cream as her blouse. She walked cautiously down the path, concentrating on avoiding the worst of the hen droppings and mud. She reached the door before looking up, her tawny-brown eyes full of disapproval, the bubble-cut hair not moving a fraction as she shook her head.

'Mother, you look a mess! But that's not what I have come to say,' she hurriedly went on, stopping Nelly who was open mouthed and ready to protest.

‘I know what you’re goin’ to say and gypsies won’t do ’im no ’arm!’ Nelly managed to blurt out while Evie took a breath. ‘Clara an’ ’er family, they’re friends of mine.’

‘*That*’s no guarantee of their suitability! Rather the reverse! Please, Mother, don’t take him up there again. There’s no knowing what he’ll pick up.’

‘Pick up? What the ’ell d’you think ’e’ll pick up? Fleas? Poison? Spotless that *vardo* is, and if you don’t believe me, ask young Oliver.’

‘*Vardo*,’ Evie said disparagingly. ‘It’s nothing more than a tent!’

‘You know that, do yer? When did you see inside it like Ollie did? Spotless it is, an’ a lot more than a tent.’ In her anger, Nelly had bent almost into a boxer’s stance, her head low and an aggressive jaw pushed forward.

Evie repeated her complaints, her voice shrill and loud as Nelly argued back. Suddenly Nelly stopped and into the silence, which made Evie feel embarrassed at her shrieking, asked quietly, ‘Come in fer a cuppa, why don’t yer?’

‘No thank you, Mother,’ Evie said in a more carefully modulated tone, ‘I just want your promise.’

‘Encouraging that boy to be dishonest, you are, with your don’t do this an’ don’t do that.’

‘You might have got the better of me in my plan to get you out of this – hovel – but you won’t lead my son away from the decent upbringing Timothy and I are giving him. You or that tramp you married.’

‘George, ’is name is George.’ Nelly smiled as she remembered telling Clara of how, when Evie and Timothy threatened to make her leave her home, she and George had married in secret so she could stay. ‘Good day that was, Evie. I ’ad a letter from ’im once, you know.’

‘He can write, can he?’

'Want to see it?'

'I can't spare the time. I just want you to promise not to introduce my son to any more undesirables.'

'No "undesirables",' Nelly repeated the word, her head on one side, like a bird listening for worms. 'Stay for a cuppa, the kettle's boilin' its 'ead off.'

'No, thank you.' Evie went back up the path without saying goodbye.

'Bleedin' kids.' Nelly muttered. She went in and made her tea and, lifting a cushion, found a bottle from which she poured a generous helping into her cup. 'Enough to drive anyone to drink, my Evie.'

Nelly's cottage was at the edge of the woods and some distance from the road. There were no lights to shine on her home at night and without a moon to break the darkness, her garden was without form. When she woke in the middle of the night with the hens squawking and flying against the sides of the coop, she crawled out of bed and peered uselessly out of the window. The dogs were barking furiously but there was no way of finding out what was wrong without getting up and going downstairs. She pressed her face against the window for one more try.

'Like looking into a cupboard,' she grumbled, feeling for the candle and the matches. 'What's upset them now?'

She knew the fox often rattled the door and sent the chickens frantic, but the noise was different from before. She pulled on the army greatcoat for extra warmth and went sleepily down the curved staircase.

As always her first thought was the fire. It was still red and she threw a few small pieces of wood onto it from the wicker basket nearby. In a corner of the window-sill was the torch. The dogs fussed around her as she tried it and looked hopefully towards the door. The light flickered so palely that she discarded it and stood the candle in the window.

Dragging the door open she let the eager dogs out and, standing on the doorstep, she listened intently, screwing up her eyes in the hope of seeing something to explain the fuss. The dogs growled and gradually Nelly made out their shapes as they sniffed around the garden and the coop and hen run. When she heard them eating something she groaned. Taking the almost useless torch she investigated and found the carcass of a chicken newly killed.

The door to the coop was hanging open and she decided not to look inside. They would all be dead, she was certain of that. With unaccustomed anger she called the dogs from their feast and dragged them inside.

Phil Davies the postman left his house, where he had stopped off to rouse the fire and toast himself a slice of bread. He placed the bag on his bicycle and pushed his way through the overgrown hedge to the gate. A second breakfast was essential these chilly dark mornings, and with a bit of luck he might have a third when he got to his mother's house.

He lived on the main road, in a small row of cottages just down the street from Amy's stores. There were lights on in her flat above the shop and he smiled as he thought of her getting herself dolled up to face the day. Loved fancy jewellery and frivolous clothes, did Amy.

A car whined up the hill and Phil followed, pushing his bicycle when it became too steep to ride. On his left were fields belonging to Leighton's farm and, up beyond, woodland and the ruined castle. On his right were the council houses and more steep hills. He turned into Heol Caradoc and into St Teilo's Road.

Leaving his bicycle on the corner he wound his way around the short roads all named after Welsh saints. St Cenyth's, St Non's and finally into St David's Close. Fay's car was standing against the kerb, right at the end of the Close. So she hadn't gone to work early. What was she doing slumming it in the council houses?

He walked back down Heol Caradoc to collect his bicycle and then through Hywel Rise and St Illtyd's to St Hilda's and St David's Close again. He hurried, and sweat was sliding down his forehead as he peered once again down to where Fay's car was parked. She was just coming out of the house at the end of the Close, facing him. He busied himself sorting letters that didn't need sorting and waved as she drove past.

Climbing on to his bicycle again he rode back down St David's to look at the house she had been visiting. It was empty. He frowned, surely Fay and Johnny Cartwright weren't considering moving into a council house? Not Fay's style at all, that. He rode off down the hill still puzzling it out. He liked a mystery. It helped pass the time and made his job more enjoyable, fitting everyone into their places in his world.

He free-wheeled lazily down towards the village but when he had almost reached the end of Sheepy Lane, he turned into a narrow, unmade track which led to the small cottage where his mother lived. It was muddy after a week of rain and he left his bicycle at the end. He could see the backs of the houses where Evie and Timothy lived, and as far as the church and the school, but the row where he lived was hidden by trees.

Ethel Davies' place was small and lacking in luxuries but it was as neat and orderly as Ethel could make it. The outer walls were whitewashed annually and shone now in the

October sunshine as it glinted on the windows and patterned the spotlessly clean tiled floor. Phil called and went inside. The iron oven range was black-leaded, the fire a welcoming red glow, and the table was set for a meal.

Ethel sat on a rocking chair, carefully crocheting a baby's shawl. She smiled a welcome and pointed to the teapot warming on the brass fender. She didn't rise as he came in, her knees were painful and she had difficulty getting around. She watched him with her dark, deep-set eyes, knowing he had something to tell her, her full mouth widening into a smile. Her hair was grey and held back in an untidy bun from which strands continually strayed, but her face was still youthful, belying the pain she often suffered.

'Hello, boy, there's early you are today. I thought I'd wait and have breakfast with you today and here you are before yourself!' She smiled at him, and added, 'What's happened to make you excited then?'

'Tell you in a minute, got to wet my whistle with a cup of tea first.' He sipped then asked, 'Who's the shawl for?'

Ethel Davies chuckled. 'Secret this one. For a while anyway, even from you, nosy boy that you are.'

Phil watched as she patted the white wool, looking anxiously for signs of knotting or swellings on her hands that he dreaded to see.

He added hot water to the teapot and opening the heavy oven door, took out two plates of eggs and bacon which he placed on the table.

'Mam, where do you get bacon?'

'Don't ask!' she grinned and swivelled her chair around to eat. 'No post for me this morning?'

'Damn, aye, I nearly forgot. It's from our Maurice again. He must be excited about coming home, he's written more in these last weeks than in all the five years he's been in the army!'

They ate and talked for a while then Phil finished the last of his fried bread, wiped his mouth and said.

'Funny thing, I saw Fay this morning looking at an empty house. What d'you think of that? Not the sort to live in St David's close that one, fancies herself. Definitely the *crachach*, our Fay – a bit above the rest of us.'

'Say nothing, Phil. Best to leave them to sort out their own problems. Gossip only makes things worse.'

'Mam!' Phil said with a frown which rapidly turned to a grin. 'As if I'd gossip!'

'Got troubles those two, what with Fay's ex-fiancé turning up the way he did. Let them be, there's a good boy.'

'Boy? It's forty-two I am.' He leaned forward and whispered, 'All right then, tell me who you're knitting that baby shawl for and I promise not to mention the council house.'

'Not yet. I don't think the mother is sure about it herself.' She nodded towards the larder. 'Go and look in there, will you? I was given a couple of rabbits yesterday. Skin them and there's one for you and Catrin.'

Phil collected them and, pushing back the tablecloth, set to work on the well scrubbed board.

Although rationing was still in force, Ethel Davies seemed unaffected by the restrictions. Hanging from the ceiling were two pieces of ham, cured in a farmhouse kitchen, and beside them a flank of fat bacon which she kept to fry for Constable Harris when he called. He loved a bit of fat bacon with some of Ethel's home-made pickles.

A slab of cake was under a glass dome, and a plate of tart sat cooling. Ethel had a constant stream of visitors and they kept her well supplied, so she was used as a sort of café by many of the passers-by. But beside the gifts of illegal food she received, she was an expert at making do; her sponges made without fat and pies which contained not meat but remnants of cheese and onion or leeks, were a favourite with her friends.

Skilfully skinning the rabbits and jointing them ready for the pot, Phil wrapped one and set off to complete his round.

'I'm off to see Nelly now, Mam, any messages?'

'Tell her I'd like some more eggs when she's got some to spare.'

'Right then, I'm off. I'll read Maurice's letter tomorrow. Perhaps he'll give us the time that he'll be home. Funny to have my baby brother back.' He kissed her and went on his way.

Nelly still hadn't looked into the chicken coop when Phil called several hours after she had found the dead chicken. She hadn't gone back to bed but had sat dozing in her favourite armchair. Phil was surprised to see her still in her nightdress.

'Nelly, you not well?'

'I'm well enough,' she said in her coarse cockney voice, 'but I can't say the same fer me chickens.'

Phil looked up the garden and for the first time noticed the dead birds. 'Want me to get rid of them for you?'

Nelly stood up and looked sadly at the bundles of untidy feathers. She gave a big sigh and said, 'Thanks, Phil. Hatched 'em from eggs, I did, some of 'em anyway. Me an' young Ollie got the rest from Leighton's farm and stuck them in with the 'en after sitting 'er on potatoes for a while. Fascinated 'e was, young Oliver. Used to bring all 'is friends to see the 'en cluckin' and chortlin' away, teachin' her babies what to eat and what to leave.'

'I'll come back later with Johnny and we'll get the coop fox-proof. Then you can get yourself some pullets ready for the spring.'

Nelly watched as Phil placed the bodies into a sack. 'Can't blame 'im. The fox I mean. It's nature.'

'What, to go on killing when he doesn't need them for food? Evil they are.'

'According to Clara, she's me gypsy friend, they expect their prey to run away so they only usually get one. But 'ens, bein' locked up, they only fly round and round and the fox gets excited and goes on killin'. Never kills more rabbits or birds more than 'e needs. He don't expect them to hang around and give 'im the chance, see.' She picked up a tail feather and tucked it into the lapel of the army greatcoat. ' 'Ating the fox won't bring me chickens back.'

To take her mind off the disaster, Phil told her about Maurice coming home.

'Been in the army five years. It'll take a while for him to settle back in Hen Carw Parc, won't it.'

' 'E won't be the same boy what went, that's for sure.'

Phil rubbed the side of his nose. A gesture he made when he was about to discuss a bit of gossip. 'Mam's makin' a baby shawl. Know who it's for? She won't tell.'

They discussed the possibilities for a while, Phil drank two more cups of tea and ate a piece of cake, then the sad cargo was fixed to the back of his bicycle and he began to walk away.

'Get some more, Nelly. Johnny and I will make that hen-run safe this weekend. *And* we'll expect some more cake!' Nelly heard him whistling as he rode down the lane to the main road.

Nelly sat for a while thinking about her finances. She wasn't sure she could afford to replace the chickens, yet the place wouldn't be the same without them. She wrote out lines of figures with an old pencil stub and tried to plan a way of buying some replacements. Perhaps Amy would know of someone needing a few hours' cleaning. The other worry, that of not knowing who now owned her cottage, she pushed aside. The loss of the chickens was enough for one day.

It was not one of her days for cleaning other people's houses and she didn't feel like cleaning her own, so she put the dogs on their ropes and walked down to the village street to call on Amy at the shop-cum-post office.

'Got me *Woman's Own* yet, Amy?' she asked, pushing her way through the line of customers waiting at the counter. 'There's a story about Princess Margaret in it this week. Lookin' forward to that I am, cheer me up a bit.'

'What's wrong, Nelly?' Amy Prichard asked, handing the postage stamps to Milly Toogood. 'Not like you to be in need of cheering.'

'Me chickens is all dead. Killed by a fox. It's upset me proper bad.'

'Go through and put the kettle on,' Amy said. 'When things have quietened down we'll have a cuppa and you can tell me what happened.'

But Nelly stayed in the shop, sitting glum-faced on a sack of dog-biscuits and accepting all the sympathy going. It was only when she had thoroughly milked the situation that she sighed and went through to the small kitchenette.

She put the kettle to boil and busied herself setting a tray, helping herself to biscuits and giving one each to the dogs. She opened the back door and pushed them outside.

'Go on, boys, go an' sit in the sun while I have a chat with Amy. If she catches you peein' I won't be able to save you from a clipped ear'ole.'

Amy finished the rush of early morning customers and came through to sit with Nelly. She sparkled with life. Her blonde hair fluffed out like a halo, makeup heavy by some standards but right for her, bringing out the blueness of her beautiful eyes and emphasising the perfect shape of her face. The earrings she always wore glittered in the artificial light in the dark corner of the store room.

'Now then, Nelly, what's this about your chickens? Not all dead, are they?'

'Yeh, every one. Phil says I should get some more, but I don't think I can afford 'em. Not with you movin' out of yer flat and me losin' the mornin's work an' all.'

'But I'll still want you to clean for me. The house I'm moving to isn't that far and as everything is newly done the work won't be hard. You can get there on the bus, can't you? And as for the flat, well, the people who are moving in might want you to do the same for them as you did for me. And there's still the shop. You and I will still have to give it a good do once a week. You'll be better off, the house is an extra. If you can manage it all,' she added doubtfully.

'You mean you still want me to do for yer? Smashin' that is. Gawd bless yer, Amy, you're a real friend.'

Inside, Nelly gave a sigh of relief. She had been afraid that Amy's move to the house left to her by her brother-in-law, Harry, meant a drop in her already low income.

'Would an advance help?' Amy asked. 'You'll want to get the chickens as soon as possible, knowing you. You'll be lost not having them squawking about the place.' She went to find her purse which she always jammed behind the water pipe. 'How much will you need?'

'Thanks, Amy, real pal you are an' no mistake.'

Amy smiled, noticing that as usual when Nelly was upset her London accent was more pronounced. Nelly had lived in Hen Carw Parc more than thirteen years but she was still a Londoner, even though she was as much a part of the village as the oldest inhabitant, Grandad Owen.

* * *

Johnny Cartwright jumped off the bus as it slowed for him. He shouted a cheerio to the conductor and the driver and ran to Amy's shop to buy some sweets. He was a bus driver and had finished for the day. He loved to be home before Fay, washed, changed and ready to make her a cup of tea and listen to her tell him all that had happened that day.

He would hide the sweets under her pillow for a surprise. She always went upstairs to undress early in the evening, and would enjoy the little treat. She would bath, and carefully comb her lovely hair while he looked on and marvelled at his good fortune at being married to her.

Then he noticed that her car was parked outside the house. She must have got back from West Wales early. Fay was a hat saleswoman and worked long hours as her area was a large one. Occasionally, as today, she finished early and was waiting for him when he finished his early shift. He wondered what was on at the pictures, she might like to go out.

'Fay?' he called as he ran upstairs to their room. He pushed open the door and yelled as he caught his shin on a low stool. '*Diawl erioed*, woman! What you trying to do to me? Always changing the furniture around you are. I keep thinking I've come to the wrong house!' The smile faded from his face as he looked at the over-filled room.

'Fay, love, what have you brought this extra furniture for? No room to move now. Pansies in the window box have got more room than us.'

When they had married, Netta Cartwright had willingly emptied a bedroom for them to start their home. A bed, a chest of drawers and a cupboard was all there was comfortably room for, but gradually Fay had been buying extra items and taking a few pieces at a time out of store, and filling the tiny room. Her recent additions had been a table and two chairs. Now there was a second chest of drawers, a table holding a vase of flowers and six hat-boxes.

'What are you trying to do, my lovely, tell me there's not enough room for us? We know that already for sure. But filling us up with all this clutter isn't helping. Why, Fay?'

'I need some of my own things around me, Johnny. I had a whole house to myself before we married and this cupboard of a place makes me so miserable.'

Johnny climbed over the bed, his small figure looking boyish and young as he squeezed past the newly arrived chest of drawers and hugged her. He was shorter than Fay and, in spite of the moustache, looked immature beside his sophisticated wife. Fay was tall, slim and always immaculately dressed. Her blonde hair hung in a neat under-roll on her shoulders, but her blue eyes were clouded and unhappy.

'I know, my lovely. It isn't what you want, nor what I want for you, but our savings are growing and it won't be for ever. Perhaps if they start building the small estate up near the council houses they're talking about, we'll be able to get ourselves a place. But can't we make this more comfortable while we're here? Working hard we are, both of us. A nice place we need when we get home, not a storage shed.' He tried to make her see the funny side of what she was doing, exaggerating the difficulty as he pushed around the room to open the window. 'Send it all back, is it?' He touched the hat-boxes. 'Worse than living above the shop this is.' He piled the boxes up and opened the door. 'Take these back to the car for a start.'

'Be careful with them, they're my new winter models,' she snapped.

'I'll be as careful as if they were babies.'

'Don't start on about babies as well!'

'*Yn wir*, I didn't mean—' He fell silent for a moment, wondering whether to try and explain the innocent remark, then turned to go downstairs. 'I'll take these back to the car. Better get downstairs then, Mam's got supper ready.'

'Dinner,' Fay corrected irritably.

'Dinner, supper, whatever. Only better hurry, it'll be getting cold. Faggots and peas it is.'

'I hate faggots and peas.'

'You said it was your favourite.'

'It was, until we started having it every Friday, week in week out.'

'Mam does her best, Fay, give her that.'

There were only three of them, Johnny's brothers were seamen, going out of Swansea to catch fish and only coming home occasionally. His sister was married and had moved to live near London. The meal was a silent one, Johnny trying to keep the conversation light with talk of the customers he had watched from the cab of his bus, but the stories failed to pierce Fay's uneasy silence and his mother's anxious mood. He volunteered to wash the dishes, glad to escape from the atmosphere Fay was creating. If only they could get a house. He wondered fearfully if the marriage would last for the two years it would take to save up for a home of their own. He had loved Fay for as long as he could remember and the thought of her leaving him was terrifying.

That weekend, Johnny and Phil repaired Nelly's chicken coop and disinfected and dug it over ready for the new arrivals.

'I spoke to Mr Leighton for you,' Phil said. 'He's keeping half a dozen for you. Go up on Sunday, will you?'

'Yes,' Nelly said. 'Oliver is comin' with me. Her ladyship

– my Evie that is—'as given permission for 'im to taint 'imself with me company. She doesn't realise we'll 'ave to go past the gypsy camp to get there!'

On Sunday afternoon, after he had changed from his best clothes which he had worn to Sunday School, Oliver set off with Nelly, dragging her cart, made from an old pram. The dogs were left behind and they could hear them complaining as they walked down the lane to the main road. When they reached the spot where the gypsies were camping, there were three families and seven dogs.

'Thank Gawd we didn't bring Bobby an' Spotty,' Nelly said. 'This lot would've eaten 'em!'

The dogs' barking made a terrible noise and Nelly clapped a hand over one ear, unable to let go of the cart to do the job properly. Faces appeared in several doorways and Oliver hung back while Nelly went to talk to Clara and the new arrivals. People came out and welcomed her. Backs were patted, the dogs fell silent and the chatter of old friends filled the air. When Nelly beckoned him, Oliver went forward and stood close beside her to be greeted in his turn.

'Me grandson Oliver,' Nelly said proudly. ' 'Andsome, ain't 'e? Where's Clara? I got a loaf of bread for 'er.' She handed it to Oliver. 'Stick this on 'er table, will yer?'

Afraid, yet more afraid to show it, Oliver climbed the steps of the *vardo* and reached inside to place the loaf as directed. Suddenly a voice cried, 'What are you wanting?'

A girl rose from the dark interior and came to the door. Oliver was cemented to the spot and he stammered and pointed to his grandmother.

'Gran – Nelly – we brought this for Clara,' he managed to say. He backed down the painted steps, staring at the girl, who was like every picture of gypsies he had seen. She had long black hair held back from her face with a braided band of multi-coloured ribbons, a scoop-necked blouse, embroidered and trimmed with lace, and below it, just visible over the low door, a brightly patterned skirt. He wondered why she wasn't shivering with cold.

'Afraid of me, are you?' The girl leaned closer and smiled.

'Of course not.'

'You look fair trashed for all your denying it.'

'My gran is a friend of your mother,' he ventured nervously.

'Grandmother,' she corrected. 'My father and mother are dead, at least mother is and father might as well be. Your mother dead is she? That why you're living with your old 'un?'

'I don't live with my grandmother! I live at home with my parents!'

'Oh, hoity toity.'

He felt ill at ease but unable to move away for fear of looking foolish. He was saved by the sound of Nelly's loud laugh and the dogs beginning to bark again as loudly as when they had arrived.

'I'd better go back, Gran and I are going to buy her new hens.' He turned and walked carefully down the steps, imagining the girl's laughter if he tripped.

'I'll be seeing you again, I expect.'

'Yes, I expect so.' He walked as far as he could restrain himself, then ran fast back to Nelly's side.

'Come on, Gran, we have to get the chickens settled before it's dark.'

On the way back from Leighton's farm Oliver helped to guide the cart down the lane with the boxes of young chickens on board. He began to feel uneasy again as they neared the gypsy camp, wondering if the girl would still be there in her fancy dress that looked so odd in a Welsh village. But this time the encampment was empty except for two dogs, who growled menacingly as they passed.

'Where will they be, Gran?' he asked.

'Out collecting wood to burn or to carve into pegs and flowers to sell.'

'Why was the girl dressed like that? The others wore dark clothes.'

'She's young and likes to be noticed, and she likes people to know straight off what she is.' She stopped and struggled with the cart, which wanted to go in a straight line into the hedge on the corner. Then, as it began to move easily again, she added, 'I cheated yer mother, Ollie, askin' for you to come to the farm. Don't tell 'er we saw the gypsies, will yer? She finds plenty to complain about without us givin' 'er reasons.'

'What does trashed mean?'

'Frightened. You're learnin' fast, young Ollie-don't-tell-yer-mother!'

Oliver didn't even want to tell his friend Margaret Prichard about the gypsy girl. He wanted to keep her as his secret, but regretfully, he allowed his tongue to slip later that day.

'Did you enjoy your dinner, Oliver?' Evie asked.

'*Cushti*,' he said, not taking his eyes from the comic Nelly had given him.

'What did you say?' Evie demanded. 'What does 'cushti' mean, for goodness sake?'

'Oh, it's a word meaning "good".'

'Where did you hear it? What language is it?' his mother insisted, and when he admitted it was a gypsy word and he saw the look on his mother's face, he sighed and mouthed 'sorry, Gran' behind the pages of his comic.

Chapter Two

As the train pulled into Swansea station, a young man was the first to alight. He carried a suitcase and he slung a rucksack across his shoulders as he shouted good-bye to the people he had travelled with and pushed his way impatiently through the rest of the passengers. After five years of occasional brief visits he was home again and in a hurry to reach his mother's house in Hen Carw Parc.

He wondered if anyone would be meeting him, and when he had succeeded in forcing his way through the crowds to the ticket collector he paused and glanced around at the small huddles of men and women staring hopefully at the barrier. No sign of Mam or any of my brothers, not even Phil, though he could hardly give me a lift on his post-office bike. His good natured face smiled at the ridiculous thought.

He gathered his luggage more comfortably and began to walk to the bus stop for Llangwyn. It would be a while yet before he reached Ethel Davies's welcoming feast. He bent his head against the drizzle, tilting the smart new trilby on top of short, wiry auburn hair.

Maurice Davies was not a tall man, no more than five feet six, but there was a bouncy enthusiasm about him that made heads turn. He winked at every girl who met his eye and promised himself he would enjoy the possibilities their looks offered. His smile widened at the prospect.

At the thought of his mother's food he felt pangs of hunger, but hunger was an almost constant state for him. Putting down his case he fumbled in the pocket of his new brown suit for the last of the chocolate he had bought in Paddington. But he stopped in the act of pushing it into his mouth and, with the chocolate held in his strong white teeth, gave a yell of delight.

'Johnny Cartwright!' he shouted around the chocolate. 'Got your car, have you? Good boy! Here, take this damn rucksack it threatens to cripple me.'

'Not so much of the "boy", you. Even if you are taller than me and twice as ugly!'

The two friends ignored the hooting of impatient motorists and Johnny settled Maurice and his luggage into the car.

'How's married life then?' Maurice asked, poking Johnny in the ribs. 'I heard from Mam that you and Fay nearly didn't make it.'

'Great,' Johnny said. 'You ought to try it yourself.'

'Not me. Still playing the field I am. Got to make up for the girls I've missed being in the army.'

'I bet you haven't gone short.'

'No, but I've missed all the local girls, haven't I?' He smiled at his friend. 'Different for you. Always been soft on Fay you have, even when we were kids and she was too old and too smart for you.'

'She's still too smart for me.' Johnny grinned, 'but everything's fine now.'

He was silent for a while as he negotiated the busy streets, then went on, 'You know that Alan French turned up? He and Fay were engaged, then he went into the army during the war and was reported dead. He wasn't and he came back and that was why me and Fay nearly didn't get married.

But the poor chap is dead now and Fay is slowly getting over the shock.'

'Yes, I heard all about it from Mam. Working is she? Or looking after a helpless male full time?'

'She works. Damn hard. Out all hours she is, selling hats. I'd never have believed there were that many heads to put 'em on. Goes up to Brecon and down as far as Pembroke.'

'Work is something I'll have to find now I'm finished with the army. God knows what, though. School seems a long time ago and apart from the little I learnt there, it's been "Yes sir, no sir" for the past five years, and what does that qualify me for?'

'Helping Mary Brown in the milk round?' Johnny laughed, and they reminisced about the years of helping Mary Dairy to fill bottles and deliver them to her customers, first with a horse and cart and later in a van, to earn extra pocket money.

Johnny stopped at the bottom of Sheepy Lane to let Maurice out.

'I'll park the car outside the house and give you a hand with your case.' He stopped in the middle of the row of small cottages, and leaving the key in case Fay needed it, he ran back to join his friend.

Ethel Davies had a meal laid out that would feed a dozen. She was only expecting her youngest son and possibly Johnny, but you never knew who might drop by. She was always prepared for extra mouths, though food was still rationed even now, eight years after the war had ended. Sugar had been released from restriction only the month before and sweets earlier in the year, but meat and fats were still controlled and, apart from the occasional illegal gift from the locals, were very limited.

In the centre of her table was a plate piled high with bread and butter, its richness shining golden in the light of her oil lamp. Her four sons had shared the expense of having electricity brought to the house, but she rarely used it, preferring the softer glow of her old lamp. They had also bought her a small electric cooker which sat on a table in the back-kitchen, but it too was only used on rare occasions in the summer. 'I have the fire going all day and it seems a waste to burn fuel I don't need,' she had explained, but in truth she was used to the old oven and found it hard to learn the controls on the modern cooker, simple as they might seem.

It was from the brightly polished oven beside the fire that the scones and cakes on the table had come. The bread too had been baked on its spacious shelves. A dish of home made brawn and a knuckle of ham, which represented her bacon ration over several weeks, and the pickles and jams had all been prepared in the kitchen-cum-living room of the small cottage.

Maurice started calling as he opened the wooden gate.

'Mam? Mam, where are you? Damn, it's good to be home.' He picked her up and swung her in delight. 'Mam, are you getting smaller or am I getting bigger?' he laughed.

'Put me down, you daft boy!' Ethel sat back in her rocking chair and smiled at him. 'You've grown a bit,' she said, head on one side, dark eyes examining him critically, 'but it's out not up. Too fat you are for twenty-three.'

'More of me to love then. And the girls around here will soon realise what they've been missing these last five years!' He picked up a piece of bread and butter and began eating it, a look of surprise spreading across his face. 'Real butter? Been saving your rations and going without for me have you?'

'It's from the farm but don't tell anyone,' his mother whispered.

'I heard, Mrs Davies,' Johnny said with a smile.

'Come on, Johnny, sit down and eat before Maurice swallows the lot. The others will be here before you know it. Not a word about the butter, mind!'

'Who's coming, Mam?' Maurice asked as he began slicing the ham joint.

Ethel shrugged. 'Sidney I expect, and Phil and Catrin. Teddy if he can manage it, and there's bound to be a few from the village.'

Maurice passed Johnny a piece of ham. 'Better eat this while we can.'

In less than half an hour the word seemed to have spread on the air and the small room began to fill up with laughing, talking visitors. Leighton, the taciturn farmer, came with Sidney, who worked for him and who had supplied the butter. Phil and Catrin arrived breathlessly, having seen Maurice stepping out of Johnny's car. Mary Dairy and her brother Billie squeezed themselves in, Billie's large frame still in the brown dungarees he always wore. They helped themselves from the loaded table, even the visitors who were not related but had come with friends and were sure of a welcome.

Everyone wanted to say hello to Maurice, who played up as if he were a war hero instead of a soldier who had gone unwillingly from home to wear the King's uniform, choosing five instead of the compulsory two years to get a better deal.

Ethel was a widow and she had four sons. Phil was the local postman and Teddy worked in a factory in Swansea and was rarely home; his wife and three children keeping him busy. Sidney was a farm-worker like his father had been and Maurice, now just twenty-three, was the unexpected surprise, born when Ethel was almost forty.

The table was replenished by packages brought by guests and bottles of beer and cider emptied at an ever-increasing rate. The large kettle on the shining hob worked overtime making endless cups of tea and laughter rang out as tales of adventures long past were told and embellished and repeated.

At eight o'clock Fay arrived with Amy from the shop and Amy's two children. Margaret, at eight, was quite thrilled to come out to a late evening party. Freddy, at fifteen, had come under protest but now chatted eagerly to Maurice.

'Tell me about the army,' Freddy asked. 'I've been to the recruiting office and my name is going forward for selection.'

'You joining the army? Are you *twpsyn*? Daft? Your mother's moving to a fine house and you got a good job with your Auntie Prue's building firm. It's made for life, you are! What do you want to go in the army for?'

'I don't work for Auntie Prue any more,' Freddy muttered. 'Once Uncle Harry died I – it wasn't the same.'

'Miserable old bugger your Auntie Prue, I'll give you that, but you have a chance of doing very nicely there. Don't be soft, boy. Go back and tell her you've changed your mind. Big strapping lad like you, she won't say no, with you being related an' all.' He felt the arms of the young boy and gasped. 'You sure you're only fifteen?'

'It's the army for me,' Freddy said stubbornly.

Freddy couldn't tell Maurice or anyone else the real reason for wanting to get away from Hen Carw Parc. The thought of going far away from everything he knew and loved was frightening, but he had to go. The reason was a secret never to be shared.

It was almost ten when Nelly arrived. She struggled up the lane and along the narrow track, the two dogs pulling her enthusiastically through unseen puddles and past cruelly sharp hawthorn and blackthorn branches which tore at her face and pulled her hair across her eyes. When she stepped into Ethel's kitchen gales of laughter greeted her entrance.

'The *gwrach* of *cwm ych y fi*!' Maurice spluttered, hugging her affectionately. 'The witch of mucky valley. Come and look at yourself. Thank God it isn't Halloween or you'd have scared us all stupid!' He hugged her again and added, 'Nelly, it's good to see you. My welcome home wouldn't have been complete without you, or them damn dogs of yours.'

'I fergot it was today you was comin' 'ome, Maurice,' Nelly wailed in a slightly slurred voice.

He helped her through the crush of knees and feet to where she could see herself in the mirror and teased her as he helped remove the dead crinkled leaves and a few twigs from her untidy hair. 'How did you come? On a broomstick through the wood? It must be almost midnight. Where have you been till now?'

'I come on a dog-sleigh,' she laughed, 'and it's only just gone ten! I dug me 'eels in the mud an' the dogs pulled me right to the door.' She took off her coat and sighed as a cup of tea was handed to her. Maurice suffered a blast of beery breath.

'I've bin to the pictures. *Abbot and Costello Go To Mars* is on at the Albert Hall. I couldn't miss that.'

'That's not the only place you've been,' Maurice said, shaking his head and grinning at her.

'Had to take the dogs out when I got back. Look at 'em now, pinchin' all the 'eat as usual.'

The two large dogs were sprawled across the hearth, pressed up against the fender. Ethel's three cats were sitting further back, their tails swishing angrily at the impertinence.

'Sorry, Nelly,' Amy called across the noisy room, where she sat between Billie Brown and Phil. 'We'd have called for you but I thought you'd be here hours before us.'

'Fergot!' Nelly slapped her head theatrically. ' 'Ead like a bleedin' sieve these days,' she shouted back.

She moved a bit closer to add something more and inadvertently touched Spotty's tail with her foot. He leapt up and growled and the cats, thinking they were under attack, squawked in terror, spat at the dogs, clawed their noses and disappeared in the forest of legs. Spotty was so shocked at this treatment that, supported by Bobby, he began to chase the cats, knocking Nelly on top of Mr Evans who had just arrived. He tried to escape but his chair tilted back against the wall imprisoning them both. To make matters worse, when Billie tried to help he was bitten by one of the cats.

It wasn't until someone had the sense to open the door and allow the animals to escape that order was partially restored.

'Damn dogs,' Nelly said with sombre seriousness. 'You'd think they was pissed not me.'

Maurice laughed and wiped his eyes, '*Duw*, I've missed all this.' He turned and poked a laughing Freddy, 'You won't get this in the army!'

Amy's shop was a miracle of orderliness. Every shelf was packed with tins and packets, bottles and jars containing practically everything the inhabitants of the village could want. Many customers were tempted to buy far more than they intended, due to her skill in displaying the right things in the right places. The variety was endless and yet it took no more than a moment for her to find what was wanted on the closely packed shelves.

A few weeks before Maurice's return, the shop had been

extended by knocking down a wall and combining it with the room at the back that had been a store room. A new store room had been built in the yard and a small kitchenette fitted in beside the door. The result was a well-stocked shop with a separate counter for the post office work, and a little more room for her customers to stand in.

As always in these last moments before she released the blind on the shop door, she looked around and thought of Harry Beynon, who had created the new shop for her out of the undersized and cluttered room she had managed with before. Harry was dead, and every time the thought entered her mind it sent the shiver of shock and horror through her body and a longing for him that never seemed to lessen.

Harry had been married to her sister, Prue, but through the years he and Amy had been lovers. That he was dead, and the death, a blood-chilling murder that had stunned the village for weeks, made it seem like a nightmare from which she would one day wake. She still expected someone to tell her she had been hallucinating and that Harry, strong, lively Harry, who had laughed and loved with such an enthusiastic joy, was not dead, but there, within sight of her doorstep, his hand hovering over the 'phone, waiting for a private moment to dial her number and arrange for them to meet. A thousand times she had picked up the 'phone and fallen into an abyss of despair when the voice at the other end was not his.

She stood for a moment longer, swallowing her grief and patting her fair hair in a nervous gesture, slipped up the blind and opened the shop door. There were a few waiting outside and they began talking as she smiled a greeting and went behind the counter. Her son Freddy ran down the stairs from their flat above as he heard the shop doorbell announce the beginning of the day, and he stood there waiting, ready to fetch and carry as needed.

'Any orders to put up, Mam?' he asked, glancing at the spike on which orders were placed as they arrived. Amy usually had a messenger boy to take customers' weekly groceries to their doors, but now Freddy had taken on the job while he waited to hear from the selection board.

'Can you put these sacks outside first, Freddy?' She pointed to the pile of sacks and boxes which usually stood outside lining the narrow pavement beneath the window.

'Something for Constable Harris to moan about, Mam?' he grinned.

He set about the task of dragging the sacks of potatoes and crates of greens through the doorway. They both knew the policeman would be along soon and they would be told to bring them all in again. But once he had made his official complaint, he rarely bothered to insist. Amy's shop was a necessary part of village life and he knew he would face a storm of protests if she had to give up selling the many items which gave little profit but saved the locals a long haul from the town.

Sacks of carrots and onions, chicken meal and dog-biscuits, barrels containing brushes and mops went out, and, with winter approaching, there was even a basket of daffodil bulbs to tempt the gardeners.

The first rush of customers was over and Amy went to the back of the shop to put the kettle on for a cup of tea.

'Did you speak to Maurice last night?' she asked. 'He was in the army for five years and should know the ins and outs of it all.'

'I still want to go, Mam.'

'But you were so happy with the idea of working for

Uncle Harry. His death didn't change that. Auntie Prue still wants you to stay.'

'I changed my mind. I want to get away, for a while at least.'

Amy handed him a mug of tea. She longed to cry and beg him not to go. She would miss him so much, but she knew it would be wrong to persuade him. Freddy was not yet sixteen but he was a man and had to make his own decisions.

Brought up in a house without a father, he had taken on the role of family head when he was still a child. Now, as she looked at his tall broad figure, and the young face and serious eyes behind the glasses, at the fair hair on his chin and the hint of a moustache, she knew she had to let him go. She would sadly miss his strength and reliability but she couldn't risk swamping him by her selfish need of him.

Children, she mused as she served Milly Toogood with a half pound of biscuits, were only borrowed for a few years, then they had to go, a step at a time, to achieve independence. But for all his size, and the moustache, it was impossible to think of him as more than her baby, and someone who needed her for day to day support.

Freddy found a box in the store room and began making up the order for Brenda Roberts, wife of the bossy ex-sergeant.

'Bert Roberts, he was in the army, I might have a word with him when I take the order,' he said.

Amy began dusting the shelves where she had left off the previous day. 'You haven't quarrelled with Auntie Prue, have you?'

'No, Mam, we haven't quarrelled. Got on all right we did.' Freddy paled at the thought of his mother knowing just how well he and his aunt 'got on'. The affair between him and Prue had been brief and strange, and embarrassing and exciting. Discovering the joys of sex in an unacceptable relationship with his aunt had been a thrill. But Uncle Harry dying in such a horrific way had seemed like a punishment and his muddled feelings of guilt and anxiety were now driving him from home.

'Uncle Harry would have wanted you to stay with the firm he'd built up from nothing. To have a member of his family still involved would have meant a lot to him.' A lump filled her throat as she spoke the name. To lose someone she deeply loved and whom she had been unable to openly mourn was so painful. A mistress was not allowed the luxury of grieving.

She was torn from her melancholy by the shop bell and looking up smiled her brightest smile for Constable Harris.

'Sorry, Amy, but them sacks have got to be moved. You know they're impeding the passers-by.' He smiled apologetically.

'Not impeding!' she teased. 'How can that be? They don't pass anyway, they all come in.'

'Got to tell you to move them. If it was only one or two, it would be all right, but there's more every time I look, it seems to me.'

Amy put her head on one side appealingly. 'They're only there 'til I get the floor washed.'

'Yes, I know that one. And you'll be too busy all day right 'til closing time so you can't get it done.'

Amy smiled, her earrings sparkling as she shook her head. 'You know me too well, Mr Harris.'

'I'll just have an ounce of my tobacco while I'm here.' He carefully counted out three shillings and seven pence, and taking the silver packet, nodded and went out.

'If you don't need me this afternoon, I thought I'd go to the new house and do a bit of gardening,' Freddy said later as they sat eating a snack lunch. 'I miss doing Auntie Prue's garden.'

'The house isn't really ours yet,' Amy warned. She knew that if Prue could stop her from inheriting it from Harry's will, she would. She had tried once already but her sudden decision to withdraw her protest had been a surprise and the reason for the change of heart was a mystery.

'I thought I could start to plan it, and maybe plant a few bulbs so you have something to look for in the spring. I can keep it going when I come home on leaves.'

'Yes, Freddy, that would be lovely.' She hid her face, fussing with the teapot as loneliness again overwhelmed her.

They were sitting drawing sketches of the garden and discussing the plants they would need when they heard the shop door being rattled.

'Nelly!' Amy said, getting up and reaching for another cup. 'I forgot that she's cleaning the flat today instead of tomorrow.'

Freddy put their plates into the sink and went down to open the door, but it wasn't Nelly who had knocked so impatiently. A young woman of about twenty looked at him with growing interest in her wide blue eyes. She was dressed in a trouser suit with the jacket open revealing a red roll-necked jumper, amply filled. The rest of her figure was slim but shapely and Freddy was unable to resist looking her over with interest.

'Sorry if I disturbed you,' she said, her pert head on one side, her body thrust slightly forward. 'I called to see Mrs Prichard. Is she in? I'm Sheila Powell and I'm coming to live in the flat.'

'Be a bit crowded,' Freddy grinned. 'There's three of us already!'

'I mean when you all move out, of course. I wondered if I could measure up for curtains.' She looked up at him and added sweetly, 'You can stay to help if you want.'

'I'll call Mam.'

'Who is it, Freddy?' Amy called.

'So you're Freddy, are you? How do you do?'

'Nicely thanks.' He was a bit confused by the rather blatant way Sheila showed her approval of what she saw, and he was glad when he could leave the interview to his mother and disappear upstairs.

He was washing the dishes when heavy, slow footsteps announced Nelly's arrival.

'Who's she when she's 'ome?' Nelly whispered, pointing down to the shop.

'Sheila Powell. Her parents are renting the flat when Mam and Margaret move to the new house.'

' 'Er and 'er mam and dad, ain't it?'

'I think so. She wants to measure for curtains or something. I'll be off, I'm going to start on the garden at the house when I've delivered the last of the orders.'

'If you was a couple of years older, Freddy me boy, I reckon you'd be in luck there. She looks as if she might be a lively one. Sheila *what*, did you say?'

'No, Nelly, Sheila *Powell*,' he grinned and ran down the stairs to where his carrier bike was already loaded with the full boxes.

When he was returning the bike before setting off to start on the garden, Freddy saw Sheila again and stopped to say hello just as she was about to turn into Sheepy Lane. As he was trying to think of how to begin a conversation, Maurice called and ran down the lane to join them. With regret, Freddy introduced them and left them talking while he went back to the shop. He saw them walk up the lane together as he parked the bike and set off to walk to 'Heulog', their new home.

When Nelly had finished her work she sat on the bottom stair and waited until Amy had closed the shop.

'Thought I might as well stay and give you a hand washing the shop floor before I goes,' she said, picking up the mop and bucket she had filled with soapy water.

'There's no need, but thanks,' Amy smiled.

They worked together while Freddy waited for the floor to be washed and covered with newspapers before bringing in the sacks and boxes.

'Seen the paper today, 'ave yer?' Nelly asked as she poured away the dirty water and washed out the mop-bucket. 'Seems like we're goin' to see an end to the ration books after this one finishes. It says there won't be any more issued. Good news ain't it? I thought I'd never see the day.'

'Thank goodness for that! No more counting up coupons and finding them short, and panicking about being too generous with the fat bacon.'

'And no more pretending you got a bit of meat mid-week by coverin' yer veg and 'taters with Bisto gravy.' Nelly tilted the heavy bucket upside down to drain, then added, 'Ere, Amy, what about comin' to the pictures with me next week? Abbot an' Costello are on again, at the Carlton this time. Good laugh they are. An' there's a Tarzan picture with it. Come, why don't yer? Take your Margaret and my Ollie if you like.'

Amy looked at Nelly's red, eager face and shook her head regretfully. 'Sorry, Nelly, but I'm too busy. What with the move, and renting the flat, there's a lot to do.'

'I'll 'elp yer! An' you don't need to pay me for the few extra hours,' Nelly coaxed.

Still Amy shook her head. 'No, but thanks for asking me.'

Nelly hung her head in disappointment. 'I wouldn't let yer down, Amy. I'd dress tidy.'

Amy laughed and patted Nelly's plump shoulder. 'I wouldn't be ashamed of you! What an idea! Friends, aren't we?'

'I know I'm a bit on the scruffy side. "Dirty Nelly" they calls me when they think I can't 'ear.'

Amy felt guilty. She had used the nickname herself. 'Let me down indeed! All right, sod the work. I'll come.'

Nelly's teeth appeared in a crooked grin. Her ruse had worked. She was very fond of cheerful, kindly Amy and knew how deeply she had felt the death of Harry Beynon. A good laugh is what she needs, she thought, nodding her head wisely.

On Monday morning Nelly helped Amy with some extra cleaning. She scrubbed the wooden floor of the bedroom, which had been emptied of carpet and linoleum ready for the move. She hummed happily in tune with the music on Amy's wireless, wishing she could afford one for herself. Netta Cartwright was very good, inviting her to stay and listen to her favourite *Goon Show* and other programmes she enjoyed, but with Fay and Johnny living there she didn't go as often as she had previously, thinking it unfair to crowd the small room.

Workers' Playtime came on and she tidied up and began setting the table for Amy to eat her lunch, laughing her loud laugh at the comedians and trying to remember the jokes to tell Amy. There were newspapers spread on the floor to keep it clean and when Amy came upstairs she found Nelly on her fat knees, head on fists, reading items she had missed.

'There's a cottage for sale in a small street in Swansea fer a hundred pounds. Couldn't never live in a street meself, but fer young Johnny it might be a thought. Fay 'ates livin' in a small bedroom she does.'

'Most married couples start off living with their parents,' Amy said. 'What's the situation with your cottage, Nelly? I've never known whether you rent it or whether you bought it when you first came?'

Nelly climbed awkwardly to her feet, puffing with the exertion. 'That kettle boilin'? Gaspin' for a cuppa I am.'

'I don't want to pry,' Amy said when she realised the question had embarrassed Nelly. 'Come and have your tea.' She poured water over the leaves and stirred them vigorously. 'But if you have a problem and ever want to talk—'

Nelly was peering at the newspaper again. 'Twinsets thirty-seven and six. Blimey, that's a lot of money!'

Amy chuckled. 'I paid nearly four pound for this one.' She held up the sleeve of the fluffy, aqua-blue jumper and cardigan she wore with matching earrings and a white necklace and bracelet.

'It's worth it for someone like you, Amy. People looks at you. Who'd admire my fat body, even if it was in a fluffy jumper?'

'Yet you're married and I'm not,' Amy said sadly.

Nelly chuckled as she remembered her wedding to George, but added seriously, 'Yes, but you got Margaret and Freddy an' look at what I'm stuck with, Evie!'

They were eating a sandwich when Freddy came in.

'All right if I go fishing with Maurice this afternoon, Mam? There's no room for me here with you two charging about cleaning.'

'Of course, love.' Amy stood up and began slicing more bread. 'I expect you'd like a few sandwiches to take with you.'

Freddy left the two women discussing their plans for the rest of the day and the news items Nelly had gleaned from the old newspapers. He strapped his fishing rod to his bicycle and, putting his bag of tackle and the food Amy had prepared into the saddlebag, rode up to call for Maurice.

'Unpack your bike,' Maurice said with a grand gesture. 'We're travelling in style. Johnny and Fay said we can borrow their car!'

'Great, man!' Freddy helped to load the car and was surprised at what they were taking. A groundsheet and an ancient greatcoat as well as enough food to last them for a week. There were three rods, two bags of tackle and a fork and a spade to dig bait.

'How long we going for?' Freddie laughed.

'Safari this is going to be. I thought that as Johnny generously filled her with petrol, we could go as far as Gower. How d'you fancy a walk out to the Worm's Head? I've checked the tide and it's possible but we'd have to stay there all night.'

'No fear,' Freddy gasped. 'I like me comfortable bed too much for those larks!'

'Just as well I've decided we'll go to Llangenith then, isn't it?' He whistled cheerfully as the last of the baggage was pushed into the back seat.

'Have you ever been on to the Worm's Head?' Freddy asked as Maurice carefully guided the car back down the narrow track to Sheepy Lane, bumping wildly as it hit several of the numerous pot-holes.

'Yes, great fun it is too, depending on who you're with of course.' He winked. 'Went over there early one morning with a couple of girls. *Duw* that was a day to remember. Took fishing rods of course, to reassure their mothers, but we didn't catch no fish. Went out with the same girls in a friend's boat once too. Didn't get any fish that day either, but I learnt a hell of a lot about balance!'

They went first to a beach where there were plenty of lugworms to be found and each set about the task of filling their bait tins. Maurice dug enthusiastically with a fork, turning over the heavy sand and occasionally pulling out one of the multi-coloured worms. Freddy found a pair of holes and, after removing a wedge from behind them with his spade, dug out a spadeful of sand, broke it open gently and removed a worm each time.

'That's the hard way,' Maurice jeered, but Freddy retorted, 'You're sweating more than me!'

They managed to hook several small dabs as the tide turned and the flat fish fed in the turbulent water, then they relaxed for a while before fishing the in-coming tide. When they packed up to drive home their bag was hardly a full one but they had both enjoyed the day; Maurice amusing Freddy with stories of his five army years, and Freddy giving Maurice the contented feeling of being 'quite a lad'.

They came back to the village past The Drovers Arms, and as they left the public house behind they saw a girl limping along at the side of the road. They both recognised Sheila Powell at the same time.

'Come on, let's try our luck, shall we?' Maurice slowed down and called across the road. 'In trouble are you?'

'My heel snapped off my shoe.'

'Give you a lift if you don't mind a few fish for company.'

'I'm going back there, I'm meeting my parents in The Drovers.'

'Come on, I can *turn* the car! I've been driving bigger vehicles than this these past five years!'

'Might as well I suppose, though Mam'll be none too pleased.' Sheila slid into the back seat and, with some struggling which caused her skirt to rise well above her shapely knees, she managed to find room to sit among the assorted tackle. 'Good God, what you got in here?'

'Fish, rods, slimy worms.' Maurice started the car, turned in the road and drove off amid Sheila's shouts of dismay to the car park of the public house.

'What do you do, Sheila Powell?' Maurice asked, while Freddie sat silently, embarrassed and unhappy at the way Maurice was getting to know Sheila.

'I work in a gown shop in Llangwyn, if it's any business of yours.'

'I don't work anywhere. Just out of the army see. Maurice is the name in case you forgot. Maurice Davies.' He held out a hand and the girl touched it briefly and stepped out of the car.

'Don't fancy shaking hands after you've been handling worms, thank you very much. Ta for the lift though.' She waved at Freddy and limped on her uneven shoes through the open door of The Drovers.

'Fancy a drink, Freddy?'

'Not old enough.'

Maurice laughed and drove back to the shop. Freddy was in a less happy mood after the brief encounter. He had no reason to feel proprietory towards Sheila Powell simply because he had met her first, but the way Maurice had flirted with her had raised a knot of anger in him. Still, he thanked Maurice for the day out and went around to the back lane and into the flat. Before he opened the door to greet his mother and Margaret he forced himself to shake off the strange mood and, with a smile set firmly on his face, held up the largest of the flat-fish he had brought home, with a flourish.

'Freddy,' his sister laughed, 'that's kidnapping babies, not fishing.'

'Just for that you can eat it for your breakfast. Or, better still, try some of these!' He showed her some of the worms he had forgotten to throw back into the sea. The shrieks and laughter made Amy chuckle and reflect that it would be strange without Freddy coming in and out, quiet as he usually was. She would have to make sure she kept extra busy in the weeks following his departure.

Outside, Maurice turned the car and once again headed back to The Drovers. The girl was sitting between a rather surly and anxious looking couple whom he guessed were her parents. He went to the bar and ordered a drink, then went to the men's room and washed his hands and combed his wiry auburn hair back into some order after the day on the beach.

He stood at the bar and allowed his gaze to travel slowly over the few customers. When he looked at the girl he saw her blush and look away. Then the father looked up, frowning, and Maurice saw him question Sheila, who shook her head. The mother then seemed to sense the presence of an interested man and she turned so Sheila had to turn also to talk to her. The mother's curls shook vigorously as she spoke to her daughter, as disapproving as their owner.

He watched the trio finish their drinks and, with a hostile glare in his direction, walk out. Parent trouble, he diagnosed. Poor Sheila Powell. He'd have to see if he could rescue her. Something in her eyes told him she would be very grateful.

Chapter Three

Prue Beynon stood at the small landing window looking along the main street of the village. She wondered if she would ever walk along it again without feeling foolish. Anger against herself and a little self-pity made tears threaten and she held them back determinedly.

She was feeling nauseous again, a weakness she could not accept as normal. The doctor had told her she might expect these miserable bouts for a few weeks, but Prue objected to them and tried to think herself out of them.

It was mainly the fear of looking foolish, something she had always hated. That she was pregnant at the age of forty was hard enough to bear, and being a widow encouraged sympathy which she did not want and made it worse. To show herself up in front of neighbours would be too much.

She took deep breaths, held her stomach in, as if by sheer determination she could dismiss the churning and the rhythmical heaving. But she could not, and she ran to the bathroom and leaned over the toilet, tears brimming in her eyes as she was sick.

Lying back on the still unmade bed, she stared at the ceiling and wondered what to do. There was still time to move away from Hen Carw Parc before the news got out. Ethel Davies had guessed of course; she only had to look at the face of a pregnant woman to know. But she doubted if

Ethel would spread the news. People went in and out of that house as if it were a railway station, but Ethel could hold her tongue.

Perhaps that would be best, to leave. Sell up and live on the other side of the town. She could still manage the business from there. The prospect of such an upheaval was not a happy one. There was no one to help her and now that Harry was dead she was on her own with only his ghost to keep her company in the large, over-tidy house. Tears welled again and she brushed them away angrily.

At least there were a few men who worked in the building firm and would give their time to assist her, if they were paid of course. She couldn't think of a single person who would support her for any other reason except money. Amy was her only relative, but the sisters had not been on friendly terms ever since Prue had learnt that Amy was Harry's mistress. Amy's son would have been the ideal one, but now that was out of the question.

There was a knock at the door and she stood up and looked out of the window. Her groceries had arrived from the shop in Llangwyn. She opened the window and called down for them to be left in the porch. Since finding out about Amy and Harry, she no longer bought from Amy.

It was tempting to lie back on the bed but she went instead into the bathroom and ran a bath. While it filled she straightened out the double bed in which she would sleep alone for the rest of her life, still fighting melancholy. She sat in the bath and washed herself, looking at her thin body for signs of the new life within her.

'Life is so unfair,' she muttered. 'All my life I've dreamed of having a child to rear. That it should come now when I am on my own is so—' She scrubbed her body fiercely with a small nailbrush as if to punish it for its stupidity.

She didn't risk breakfast, but drank a cup of tea with lemon juice and, still in her dressing gown, planned her day. A letter from her solicitor was propped against the teapot to remind her to attend to it. She opened it and read it again, not because she had forgotten what it said, but for an excuse to sit a while longer.

It was brief, simply telling her that the house Harry had bought and modernised was ready for Amy and her family to take over. Amy's signature was needed and then the house would be hers. Too weary even to feel the usual anger at the idea of Harry leaving Amy a valuable house, she allowed the letter to fall from her hand, and went upstairs to dress. Better get the visit to Amy over and done with.

Fortunately the shop was empty as it was almost lunchtime for most people. Amy was standing behind the post office counter, her fair hair falling over the counterfoils she was counting into piles and bundling with elastic bands which she had on her wrist in readiness. Prue waited until she had finished the final pile before moving slightly to attract her sister's attention.

Amy looked up and her blue eyes widened warily. Since Harry's funeral she and Prue had hardly met.

'Hello,' Prue said quietly, as if trying to get disapproval even into that short word.

'Hello, Prue, everything all right? You look a bit pale.'

'I'm perfectly well, thank you. I have come to tell you that the solicitor wants to see you.'

'Oh? What about?' It must be to do with the house.

'There's a form of acceptance or something to sign and the house is yours.'

'Oh,' Amy said again. She was relieved to know it was not another delay caused by Prue who she knew would have held it up for months if she could.

'If you give him a ring you can arrange the time between you. It's nothing to do with me any more.'

'Oh.' Amy put away the counterfoils and came to stand nearer her sister. 'Prue, I want to say—'

'You don't have to thank me.' Prue's voice was sharp. 'It was Harry's wish to help you. I only did what he wanted.'

'Well, thanks anyway. I'm sure you could have made difficulties and delayed things if you'd had a mind to.' Amy politely glossed over the way Prue had initially fought against her having the house and the sudden change of mind. She felt deeply sorry for her sister whose prickly, stand-offish ways had resulted in her loneliness and wished there was some way she could open her out to the warmth of friendship.

'Perhaps you'll come there with me one day soon and we can look at it together. You're better at choosing good things than I am,' she coaxed. 'I'd be glad to have your opinion of what to buy.'

Prue wasn't taken in by the attempt to flatter her. 'I'm sure you'll choose to suit yourself,' she said. 'You and I differ so much it would be impossible for me to choose for you.'

Still Prue stood there, and Amy pulled the blind down on the door. She felt in a drawer and brought out a price list she was preparing.

'Look at this then. I've been to see what I can afford in the way of new furniture.' She read from the list, 'A piano. That's a must but please don't tell Margaret, it's a surprise. Monica French is quite impressed with her talent and has been giving her free piano lessons, but she'll have to have a piano of her own if she's to do well.' Still no comment from Prue. 'A very nice bedroom suite will be thirty-nine guineas, but I can manage without that, make do with what I've got.'

She was beginning to feel she was talking to an empty room and embarrassment almost made her stop. But looking at Prue's drawn face and the sad, cold eyes, she forced herself to continue.

'Then there's a three piece suite. Got to have one of those, that'll be about thirty guineas. Leather-cloth and velvet to be practical.' She looked nervously at Prue who seemed not to hear anything she said. She prattled on, her voice sounding strange to her in the silence of the empty shop. 'Dining suite would be nice too, but there again, I think I'll make do, use the old scrub top kitchen table and cover it with a pretty cloth. What d'you think?'

'Amy, I'm going to have a baby.'

'What? You can't be!' Amy stepped back as if her sister had struck her. Harry hadn't slept with his wife for months, even years. He had assured her of that. How could this cold, unemotional woman be expecting his child? She wanted to cry.

'Prue, you must be mistaken.'

Prue, white faced, did not reply.

Someone tried the shop door. Amy saw Milly Toogood's daughter poke her head through and she pushed her roughly out, ignoring the woman's pleading and turning the key in the lock.

'Come upstairs, there's no one in. We can talk.' They hardly heard the angry banging or the complaints shouted at the shop door.

Prue sat on a chair and stared into space while Amy made tea and opened the biscuit tin. Her hands were trembling and she had no appetite for the lunch already prepared and waiting for her. With shaking hands she placed a cup and saucer in front of Prue, who sipped it without speaking.

'How will you manage?' Amy asked to break the oppressive silence.

'The same as always, capably and on my own.'

'You don't have to be on your own, Prue.'

'It's something I've learnt to expect. And accept.' She turned her pale blue eyes towards her sister and Amy tensed for the outburst to come. 'How can you help? You or your illegitimate children?'

'*Because* they're illegitimate of course! I managed alone and without even the comfort of a wedding ring!' Amy snapped. 'Who was there when I needed help? No one.'

'You were young. I'm forty and pregnant for the first time.'

The door creaked and Freddy stood in the doorway, the colour draining from his face as both women watched.

'Go downstairs for a moment, will you Freddy? I'll make your lunch when Auntie Prue and I have finished talking, all right?'

'Don't want anything,' Freddy blurted out, and he ran back down the stairs as if he had seen a ghost.

He felt sick. His stomach churned alarmingly and he put a hand to his mouth in a futile attempt to stop it. He reached the outside toilet, disposed of the curdled mess and stood sweating and shaking, holding the basin for support. He had made his aunt pregnant. How could he walk out of this small room and carry on as if nothing had happened? He wanted to curl up and hide.

The strange affair with his aunt had happened almost without a thought for the wrongness of it. He relived the wonder of it all, the way the stern-faced woman he had always been slightly afraid of had relaxed in his loving. Even her face had changed, become less stony, filled out somehow so the angular lines softened. He thought of her voice when she spoke words of endearment. It was soft and gentle and completely without her usual harshness.

Freddy washed his face in cold water, the skin reddening and intensifying the blue of his eyes. He put his glasses back on but they immediately clouded over so he removed them and washed his face again. He stood for a long time before he felt able to face anyone, then went into the yard.

When Freddy had raced off so hurriedly, Amy was puzzled.

'What's upset him?' she said. 'D'you think he overheard? Young boys are a bit embarrassed at the thought of babies, aren't they?' She stopped when she saw that Prue was shaking and had gone deathly white. 'Prue, what is it? Are you ill? Don't move, love, I'll ring for the doctor.'

'No!' Prue stopped her as she reached the door. 'I don't need a doctor. I – I've just realised what this will mean, that's all.'

'I don't understand.'

'Ridicule,' Prue invented fast, trying to cover the real reason for her nervous attack. She had seen the horror in Freddy's eyes as he had realised what had been said, and she had to prevent Amy from guessing. 'I saw in that fleeting moment what everyone will think. How they will react to the news. Me, cold, unfriendly Prue Beynon conceiving a child. I have to get away from here, Amy. Will you help me?'

Amy stared at the somehow shrunken figure of her sister, but she shook her head. 'No, Prue, the only way is to face it. Believe me, any other solution will bring nightmares of loneliness and despair. If I can't teach you anything else I can teach you that. Face them. People take their attitudes to you from you. You look ashamed and they will treat you as if you're guilty. Walk with your head high and feel proud and you'll attract nothing but good will and kind thoughts. I'll help you. So will others if you only give them half a chance.'

She bent over Prue and touched her shoulder tentatively, unable to show the affection that, with anyone else, would have lead to a hug. 'I'll do everything I can to help, I promise. I owe you that,' she added in a whisper.

Prue stood up to go but Amy pushed her down in her chair. 'Stay. Your tea's gone cold. Put the kettle on, will you, and we'll have another.' She left Prue seeing to the tea and ran downstairs to the shop. In a corner behind the post office counter was a display of wool. Gathering up a handful of patterns and a few skeins, she went back upstairs. At the door to the living room she paused and leaned back against the wall, her eyes closed to squeeze away a tear. 'Harry, Harry my love,' she whispered with a sob, 'how could you?'

Unaware of how the news had devastated her son, she allowed waves of dismay to flow over her, believing she alone suffered the shock of it. How could Harry have made love to two women and tell each that she was the only one? Grief for his death intertwined with anger. She had been his lover for years but she had not really known him. That he was unreliable was something she had learnt to accept. That he was too much the coward to reveal his love for her and leave his wife, she had also admitted to herself, but sleeping with Prue when he had told her he could not, and giving her a child, was a cruel shock. It was the ruin of the pathetic dream of their love and that false dream was all she had to show for the years of loyalty to him.

She ran down to the darkened shop and combed her hair. Then she carefully reapplied her makeup before returning to her sister.

When she had stifled the tears of hurt she went in, talking

as soon as she entered, hoping her moment of self-pity and the feeling of betrayal would not be noticed.

'Now then, Prue. You're a good knitter and for once you can knit for yourself. Made dozens of things for charities you have, now it's for yourself. Here,' she handed Prue a few patterns, 'you look through them and tell me what you'd like and I'll start as well. Then I'll take mine to the shop and leave it on the counter. Everyone who asks will be told with great excitement about the baby and how thrilled we all are that at last you have what you and Harry only dreamed about, a baby to fill your life and bring you nothing but happiness.'

'Harry—' Prue began but the words failed her and at last she cried.

Awkwardly, Amy patted the bony shoulder. 'Come on, love, we both know that Harry was a swine, but we both loved him didn't we? No use pretending. Not now. Let's both enjoy his baby, shall we?'

'But Harry—'

'Harry's gone, and we both have to accept it.'

When Prue finally went home, Amy sat in a chair and shook from head to toe. She had held back from necessity while Prue needed her, but the moment she was alone the trembling shock overcame her. She didn't hear Freddy come in, but felt his hand touch her gently.

'Shall I open the shop for you, Mam, tell them you're not well? It's long past time.'

She nodded, but did not look up.

The world was blanked off for a while as she sat, gazing into space, her mind empty of everything except the memory of Harry telling her he and Prue never shared the same bed, and that she, Amy, was his only love. Yet in this, as in so many things, he had lied to her—unless Prue had a lover, and that thought was ludicrous! Even to pay him back for his unfaithfulness, Prue could never have defied the conventions and found someone else.

Gradually she became aware of the sound of voices, and she realised that the shop was full and Freddy, who could never remember where things were kept, was on his own. She washed her face and spent a few moments putting on the pancake makeup she always used and without which she could not face the public. Cherry lipstick to blend with the rouge and complement her pink jumper, diamanté earrings and a treble row of pearl beads brightened her up. Forcing a smile, she ran down the stairs and began serving.

As the shop closed, at five-thirty, Nelly appeared. She pressed her face to the window as Freddy was about to pull down the blind.

'She 'asn't fergot, 'as she?' she shouted. 'We're off to the pictures.'

Freddy opened the door and Nelly entered. She was dressed in her best grey coat, which she had had to struggle to fasten, and on her head was a grey felt hat with a few paste cherries decorating the brim. On her feet were wellingtons.

'You aren't going to the pictures in wellingtons, are you, Nelly?' Freddy asked, amused in spite of everything.

'Course not. What d'you take me for? These is fer walkin' back up me lane. Full of mud it is, what with Leighton's tractor goin' up and down with muck fer 'is fields and—'

'Would you like to leave them here, Nelly?' Amy asked. She had completely forgotten the evening out and frantically searched her mind for a reason to cancel it. Margaret had come in from school and had run upstairs without mentioning it. If she had forgotten too—but almost as the thought entered her mind, she heard her daughter run downstairs.

'Mam? Is it time to go? I've finished my homework.'

'Yes, love. Just give me time to do the till and we'll be off.' She nodded to Nelly, 'Go on up and make some tea, will you Nelly? I'll only be about half an hour.' She smiled brightly and no one would have guessed her recent shock.

Amy finished the till with Freddy's help and went to change out of the sunray skirt and pink jumper into a princess line dress in pale blue with a set of jewellery in pale green. She tied a green scarf loosely around her neck and was satisfied with the reflection that stared back at her from the mirror. Amy had always considered herself strong; these next few months were going to prove or disprove it. Jutting her chin out in a caricature of determination, she smiled bleakly. Oh, Harry, why did you have to die?

Margaret and Oliver were very excited at the prospect of going to the pictures in the evening. With only Amy and Nelly to look after them they would be able to relax and enjoy the occasion. Evie was forever telling them to sit up straight, and keep their feet down and to stop chattering. How could they not point things out to each other, or share a joke? Talking and joining in each other's laughter was a part of the treat. Sharing sweets too, and by the look of the paper bags in both Amy and Nelly's handbags, they wouldn't go short of them.

When they arrived at the cinema they were greeted by the sight of a huge queue following the line of the building and around the corner into a side street. Oliver groaned.

'Look at all these people. We'll never get in!' Nelly gave them a packet of Liquorice Allsorts and they all munched contentedly for a while, but the children began to fidget more as time passed and there seemed little improvement in their position in the queue. Then at last the cinema emptied and the line move forward in a surge and they were in, running across the patterned tiled floor to the ticket kiosk and then through the spring doors into the darkness. Holding hands, they followed the thin beam of a torch and settled into their seats.

As their eyes grew accustomed to the poor light they recognised a few familiar heads. Megan Owen and her two grown-up daughters, Bronwen and Sian. And Bert Roberts looking around for something to complain about. Over in a corner they saw Maurice and his latest girlfriend. Oliver nudged Margaret as Maurice's arm slid around the girl's shoulders, and Tarzan was forgotten for a moment while they chuckled over the stupidity of adults.

Amy's mind was not on the film. Abbot and Costello's antics filled the cinema with laughter but she was oblivious to it. From time to time she tried to concentrate on the film and keep her mind from Prue's visit but her thoughts returned to it regardless of what was happening on the screen. The thought of Harry's double dishonesty brought an almost physical pain to her heart as she imagined him going from her to share a bed with Prue. The agony nearly made her cry out.

Her thoughts turned briefly to Freddy and his embarrassment at hearing of Prue's pregnancy. She wondered if she should speak to him. If he was going into the army as innocent as that, not even able to hear someone talking about an expected baby, then he would be in for a lot of teasing. She didn't want that. But what could she say to him? Perhaps her attempts to discuss it would only make his embarrassment greater.

She tried to think of ways of approaching the subject and persuading him to discuss it. If he was unable to talk openly about such a natural event then she had let him down. She consoled herself with the thought that he was unlikely to be as shy with his friends as with his mother, but still he needed to open out. She had never pretended with either of the children and some people had been more shocked by that than by her being an unmarried mother!

The film ended, the Tarzan film began again, and when it came to the point at which they had come in, she touched the children and ordered them to come out as quietly as they could. Oliver and Margaret and Nelly chattered all the way home on the bus, reliving the best parts of the show, and she was glad to be able to relax and allow her thoughts to dwell on how she would talk to Freddy.

He was in bed when they got home. Amy said good-night to Margaret, then tried to talk to Freddy. He was lying facing the wall on his small bed and the light from the landing shone across him. Amy did not persuade him to turn around, thinking it might be less embarrassing for him if they weren't looking at each other.

'Do you find it embarrassing to think of men and women making love and producing babies, Freddy, love?' she began. 'I only ask, because if you're going to act all shy in front of people every time the subject is mentioned, well, the army is going to be a bit hard for you. It's natural and it's something men and women enjoy. I know you're innocent at present, but when you meet someone and you love them, you'll know what I mean.'

'I wasn't upset. Just surprised, that's all.'

'You seemed upset.'

'I wasn't.' He pulled the pillow around his head. 'Mam, I don't need this and I want to go to sleep.'

'I don't want you to feel soft in front of strangers and find yourself the butt of jokes and teasing, that's all.'

'I won't.'

'Good-night then, Freddy.'

'Mam, why were you so upset when Uncle Harry died?'

'He was my brother-in-law. Why shouldn't I be sad?'

'You were more than sad.'

For a moment Amy hesitated. Freddy was so young, could he be expected to understand? But what the hell, she had always tried to be honest and it couldn't hurt anyone now.

'I loved Harry. I always have. We were to have been married once, but when I was expecting you, it – it all went wrong.'

'You mean that you and he—?'

'We loved each other, Freddy, and all that means.'

'What a mess! Don't tell me any more.' He pulled the blankets over his head and Amy closed the door and went to her own room not fully understanding the extent of the 'mess' but convinced she had only made things worse. She shrugged and began to remove her makeup. Freddy will have to learn about life by living it like the rest of us, she told her reflection.

Saturday was not Evie's favourite day. Oliver usually hung around the house and got in her way, and when Timothy wasn't in his study preparing school-work, he was always around her feet untidying the house. It seemed such an unstructured day – a phrase she had come across in a crossword recently and had adopted as her own. But today was the start of better things.

'Oliver, why don't you go and see if Margaret wants to go for a walk?'

'She's going to Mrs French for a piano lesson,' Oliver replied, thankfully putting aside the book his mother had insisted he tried to read. 'I could go and see Gran,' he suggested. 'She'll be finished her work by now.'

'No, dear, not your grandmother. I will have some friends calling this morning for coffee. I don't want you walking in on us like a tramp.' Immediately she said the word it was regretted. She tried hard to forget that her mother had married one.

'I wonder if George will come again soon?' Oliver asked. 'He did promise to call and see us as often as he could.'

'I would prefer that he didn't!' Evie said firmly. 'Your grandmother is a constant embarrassment to me, and her—husband—even more so.' She pushed Oliver's chair towards the wall so she could reach with her dustpan and brush to collect some crumbs he had dropped from his breakfast toast.

'Who's coming for coffee?' He lifted his thin legs in the air out of the way of the dangerous brush, which was darting in and out at a furious rate.

'Mrs Morgan from the school committee, and of course Mrs Norwood Bennet-Hughes.' She smiled, 'Important people, friends who can help your father in his career. It's very important to make the right sort of friends, dear, remember that.'

Oliver groaned quietly.

'I think they are rather nice, Mother, but I'd rather talk to Gran - Grandmother,' he corrected hurriedly as Evie stopped brushing and bobbed up to glare at him.

'Your grandmother is a—a—character, but not someone who should be an influence in your life.'

'What's an influence?'

Evie tried to think of a way to explain but lost patience and said with some irritation, 'Look it up in your dictionary, Oliver, that's why your father bought it for you.'

She emptied the dustpan in the bin outside and, after washing her hands, went to the shelf and handed Oliver the large, red dictionary he had been given for his eighth birthday when he had hoped for a bicycle.

'An—an—a—fluence?' Oliver struggled to remember the word and with no extra assistance from his mother, came up with affluence. 'Mother,' he called, 'does it mean that Gran is rich?'

'Oh do be quiet, Oliver. I'm busy!'

Oliver wandered upstairs and sat looking out of his bedroom window at the hill behind the house which had been ploughed with a new tractor during the week. He had watched the smoky funnel going across the field, changing it from pale yellow stubble to dark rich brown ridges of soil. Now that it was Saturday he might have been able to go and watch more closely to see how it worked, but the field was just about finished. He had been told that the bottom was traditionally left for the village bonfire celebrations the following month.

'Can I go to the field and watch the tractor if I put on my wellingtons?' he called down the stairs.

'Don't worry your mother, Oliver, can't you see she is busy?' Timothy's quiet voice came from the spare bedroom which he used as a study.

'But can I go?'

'Yes, but don't get in a mess. Don't forget to wipe your boots when you come in and be polite to your mother's guests.'

'Yes, Father.' Oliver put on a school Burberry coat which had been relegated to a play coat and, slipping his feet into the black wellingtons that stood, clean and polished by the back door, he went out.

He walked up the side of the field, running a while until

he reached the start of the ploughing. He ran faster then, trying to make the pattern of lines whirl into a moving fan like they did when he passed on a bus. He decided it didn't work because he couldn't run fast enough.

The woods at the top looked eerie and alien. The night had been stormy and rain had filled the dips at the edge of the field with muddy puddles. He splashed happily through them and watched as the mud rose higher and higher on his boots. When he reached the top of the field the misty air had gone from the trees but hovered instead around his house below him.

He knew Nelly would not be in her cottage, she would still be working for Mrs French, but he made his way there and sat for a while watching the new pullets chortling and pecking at unseen scraps, which they quickly swallowed. They were still locked inside their run and he knew that unless he waited for Nelly to return, they had better stay that way.

Perhaps he could go and meet Nelly? Margaret would be there too and he could walk home with them. He stood up, unaware of the dirt which stained the back of his coat, his belt dragging on the ground, his hands covered with soil stains where he had rested them on Nelly's garden as he sat watching the chickens. He strolled down the lane towards the main road and Mrs French's house.

When he had almost reached it, he stopped. In the garden of a neighbouring house was a gypsy woman. She wore a headscarf and a patterned shawl, her skirt was dark and long, and her feet were bare in the black shoes, the skin brown and speckled with mud like his wellingtons. She was fatter than Clara, older than Clara's granddaughter, and unknown to him. Over her arm was a large wicker basket filled with artificial flowers of every imaginable colour.

Oliver thought they were beautiful. He stepped a bit closer, sheltered from the woman's sight by a shrub growing in Mrs French's garden.

The flowers were wooden. Somehow wooden twigs had been shaved down to make the shape of many petals. He would ask Nelly, she would know how they were made. And how they were coloured. Suddenly his foot slipped on the wet ground and a voice said 'Hello, boy,' and he turned to see Clara's granddaughter watching him from the other side of the shrub. She winked a dark eye.

'Want to buy a gift for your mother, do 'ee?'

'I haven't any money,' Oliver stuttered, and ran through Mrs French's gate, colouring in embarrassment as he heard the girl's soft laughter. He knocked urgently on the back door.

Nelly opened it to him.

'Ollie! Come to wait fer Margaret, 'ave yer? You'd better take off them boots. Come inside, Mrs French won't mind you sittin' 'til Margaret's done.'

'The gypsy girl is outside, Gran,' he said as she helped him off with his boots.

'Yes, sellin' flowers an' lucky heather and Gawd knows what, tryin' to make a bit of cash to 'elp them through the winter.'

'They're pretty, those flowers. Gran, I think they're made of wood!'

'If we can escape yer mum one day, I'll take you to see Clara and she'll show you 'ow they make 'em. Like that would yer?'

'Today would be a good day,' he said hopefully. 'Mother is busy with coffee.'

'Busy with—? Oh, I sees what you means. 'Avin' people round fer coffee. Sounds posh that does, although Mrs

French does it all the time, what with 'er committees an' all.' She patted Oliver's fair head. 'Wants yer space more'n yer company, does she?'

Oliver grinned and nodded.

Through the closed door of the front room, a melody played on the piano reached them and Oliver sat listening contentedly while Nelly finished her chores. When the music stopped he felt a brief disappointment, but then the door opened and Margaret smiled in surprise at seeing him.

'Got kicked out from under Evie's feet, 'e did. I said you wouldn't mind 'im waiting fer Margaret,' Nelly shouted down the stairs.

'Hello, Oliver,' Mrs French smiled at him. 'Did you enjoy the music?'

'Oh yes,' he coloured up and bent his head. 'I thought it was lovely.'

When Oliver and Margaret left Mrs French's, the gypsy girl was waiting for them.

'Does your friend want some flowers for her mother?' she asked Oliver, coming close to him and pushing a few of the stiff flowers towards him.

'We haven't any money.'

The girl stayed close, following them as they crossed the road to Amy's shop and waiting with Oliver as Margaret went inside to deposit her music book and change into play clothes. They went without any set purpose to where Oliver lived. The girl still followed, her dark eyes darting about looking for a prospective customer for her flowers.

A large Rover car was parked outside Oliver's house and his mother was standing at the gate to welcome the occupants: two rather large women in fur coats carrying outsized leather handbags. Oliver saw to his horror that

Clara was coming out of the gate next to his. She saw him, waved and came towards him.

'Oliver! Haven't seen you for a while. Got fed up with us already? Not frightened of the dogs are you? They won't harm you. Know you for a friend they do now you've visited us a few times.'

'Wants a few flowers for his mother but he got no money,' the girl said coming closer.

Oliver saw his mother's face was wide eyed in embarrassment as her friends were surrounded by her filthy, mudsplattered son and the gypsies. Oliver looked around in horror as Clara approached him on one side and her granddaughter on the other. His mother's friends blocked his escape in front.

He darted away from the girl and tried to get between Clara and the two women standing near the car. His mother ran towards him shouting, 'Oliver! Get rid of these people at once!'

He called for Margaret to follow and ran to the fence, climbed over into the field and headed once again for the woods.

The two children sat among the trees and watched until Evie's guests had departed, then they began to walk slowly back down the newly ploughed field. To take his mind off the lecture that awaited him, Oliver thought of the word he had tried to look for in his dictionary.

'Margaret, what does a fluent, or something like that mean? It's something to do with my Gran.'

'Effluence means stuff going down a drain,' she offered. She frowned in concentration. 'I saw that on the side of a new cess pit being fitted up at Leighton's farm when Mam took me to order potatoes. As it was a new word I wrote it in my book at school.'

'It might have been that?' Oliver said frowning as deeply. 'But what is that to do with Gran?'

'She's not going down a drain!'

'No, she's too fat, she'd get stuck.' Oliver laughed at the thought and the smile lasted until he reached home and saw Evie waiting for him at the door.

Chapter Four

Freddy had been into town to buy a few extra tools to work on the garden of their new house. He had ridden in on his bicycle, strapping the long handles of the hoe and rake to the crossbar and filling his saddlebag with the rest. He had just reached the first of the houses in the village when he saw a girl struggling with a heavy basket of groceries. He could see that she was about to cross the road to the car that was waiting for her on the other side.

He stopped, and parking the bicycle against a hedge, ran to help her. She was wearing a white swagger coat with a hood and it wasn't until he reached her that she turned her face and he recognised her.

'Hello. Sheila Powell isn't it?'

'That's right. Well, don't stand there, take this basket, will you, if that's what you've come for.' Her voice was high pitched and rather shrill, but her expression did not match it. She had a friendly, inviting look in her light blue eyes, which she widened in an exciting way.

Freddy took the basket from her and she walked in front of him towards the car.

'Better put it in the boot,' she said, 'out of sight in case of thieves.'

'Thieves? Around here?' He grinned at her, his eyes large behind his glasses. 'You're not moving into the darkest pit of evil out here. Safer than town any day of the week, this village.'

'I'm not from town. I live up in the council houses, with my Gran.'

'I haven't seen you.'

'No, my parents don't let me out much.'

A voice called, and they turned to see Mr and Mrs Powell approaching. They had obviously been to see his mother.

'Come on, Sheila, get in the car, we haven't got all day to gossip.'

'But *you've* been waiting for *them*!' Freddy said.

'Strict, they are.'

'But that's unreasonable.'

Sheila bent down as if to tighten her shoe fastening and whispered, 'Meet me lunchtime tomorrow in Tolly's Park. All right?'

Freddy was so surprised he did not reply. The couple opened the door for Sheila with a barely noticable nod to him, and then settled themselves into the seats. He watched the car move away, staring after it, stunned. He had a date with Sheila Powell. Well, that will be something to tell Maurice! He puzzled over 'Tolly's Park'. He couldn't think where it was, but someone in town would know.

The following day he dressed in his best sports jacket and wore a pale green shirt and a matching tie. He caught the bus into Llangwyn and asked for directions to Tolly's Park. He had lived in the area all his life but neither he, nor any of the people he asked, had heard of it. Time passed and he began to think he had been fooled. Thank goodness he hadn't told Maurice about the date. Always best to keep things to yourself at first. Better than looking a *twpsyn*. He wandered back towards the bus stop for home.

The bus he caught was a slow one, cruising slowly

through several of the small groups of houses almost too small to be called a village. It was when the bus was reversing into a narrow entrance to a car park before turning back to the main road that he saw her. When the driver called out, 'Anyone for Tolly's' he leapt up and jumped off as the bus began to pick up speed.

Sheila was sitting on a bicycle, swinging one long, shapely leg, her skirt caught up in the saddle, her fair hair blowing lazily in the warm breeze. He looked at the inn sign, The Plough. Where did Tolly come in, he wondered?

'Sheila, Sheila, sorry I'm late,' he said, still puzzling about Tolly. 'Got the wrong bus I did.'

'What a shame. Now it's too late, I've got to get back to work. I borrowed my friend's bike specially too.' She pressed her foot on the pedal and rode past him, her figure standing out as the wind pressed her thin dress against her. 'Better luck next time. If there's a next time!' Her voice faded as she headed for town.

Freddy swore and looked about him for a notice telling him the time of the next bus. He'd probably have to wait for ages. There was no timetable and he walked to the door of the public house to ask. His eye was attracted to the notice above the entrance, 'Proprietor Edwin Tolly'. So she had confused him deliberately, he thought with irritation.

'Do they call this place Tolly's?' he asked a man who was about to enter.

'Always. It's been in the Tolly family for years, see. Never known as The Plough, except by strangers.'

Freddy began to walk into town. He walked fast, cutting across fields, reaching Llangwyn in about twenty minutes. He stopped to clean his shoes and wash his face in a stream before going to where the shops began. He hesitated then. What should he do? Walk past the shop where she worked and wait for her to see him, like a kid? Go into the shop and ask to speak to her? He decided to act like a kid and wait for her to look up and see him. Being made to look a fool once a day was enough!

He stood looking at the window display where coats and costumes in shades of green and brown were arrayed. Padding had been added to make them look more shapely—that's something Sheila doesn't need, he thought wryly. Some coats were on the floor of the window, stretched out on almost invisible threads. Others were displayed on faceless models. He examined them all, glancing into the shop occasionally for a sign of Sheila.

Time passed and his determination grew. He would wait until the shop closed if necessary. Once, he left the window to walk around to the back, making sure the shop didn't have more than the two entrances he could see—one at the front for customers and the other, marked 'Private, Staff Only', at the side.

Customers came and went, but there was no sign of Sheila. Shadows moved inside but he couldn't see clearly. The day was surprisingly warm and sunny and the reflection on the glass distorted his view. After almost two hours, the shop door opened and Sheila appeared carrying a large yellow duster. She did not speak to him, but began rubbing at a spot on the window. He moved a little closer, guessing she would be in trouble if her manageress saw her wasting time chatting.

When he was close enough to hear she said in a loud, hissing whisper, 'Give you one more chance I will, Freddy Prichard. No more mind. I'll try to get out tonight, at ten. Unless that's too late for little boys like you?'

'I'll give you little boy! Where will you be?'

'My house, number three Saint Illtyd's Road. Don't get

the wrong bus now, I won't believe you a second time.' Giving the window a final rub, she moved away. He watched as she walked on ridiculously high heels through the double glass doors and as she pushed them closed he was rewarded with a dazzling smile and a wink that startled him.

'I'm going for a bike ride, Mam,' Freddy said as Amy finished settling Margaret into bed.

'A bit late, isn't it?'

'Yes, but it's a fine night and I fancy a bit of air.'

'I'll leave you a sandwich if I go to bed before you get back, in case you're hungry.' She smiled at him. 'Don't get lost now will you?'

'See you later.' He hoped Amy hadn't noticed that he had changed into a clean shirt and was wearing his best coat and grey trousers. She'd guess he was meeting a girl.

'I hope you've cleaned your teeth,' she shouted down the stairs after him and her chuckle reached him. She had guessed!

The house in which Sheila lived was not large. It was semi-detached and exactly like all its neighbours. The gardens each had a short hedge and a small patch of grass around which was a half-heartedly planted border. Freddy loved flowers and wondered why the tenants hadn't made the small effort needed to make them colourful.

Auntie Prue's garden was still full of colour. Roses still bloomed and the dahlias were as fresh as ever, as yet untouched by a frost. He let his mind wander to the weeding that would need to be done now, trying to distract himself from the possibility that Sheila had changed her mind, or confused him with the arrangements. He was certain that the lunchtime confusion was deliberate. Calling the car park of The Plough 'Tolly's Park' was hardly a clear description. Well, if she wanted to tease, he was prepared to be patient. Perhaps she liked to test her boyfriends to see how determined they were.

He found a place close to the hedge and waited. Now he was here, looking up at the lighted and uncurtained window, he could no longer think of gardens. He glanced at the window, trying to seem casual at first in case he was being watched. But then he found he couldn't take his eyes from it, and smiled at his own foolishness. Did he really expect Sheila to come sliding down a rope of knotted sheets?

Moving forward a few steps, he looked at the side of the house where a path separated it from its neighbour. Perhaps he should wait at the back? He went on the tip of his shoes down the side wall and came out in her back garden. There he waited.

Time passed. He had no idea how long he had stood there as he couldn't see his watch in the darkness. Then, just as he was about to give up, he saw the back door slowly opening. He held his breath and tensed himself for flight. What if it was her father and he was spotted . . .? But it was a slim figure in a floating white dress. She peered around and came out into the now chilly garden.

'Sheila,' he whispered, 'over here.'

The figure seemed to glide towards him and as he took her in his arms, he was shocked to find she had nothing on but the flimsy night-dress. 'Sheila, we can't go anywhere with you dressed like this.'

'Just as far as the shed,' she whispered, kissing him and pressing him close.

She took his hand and led him down past unseen bushes and trees. Opening the door of a small wooden shed, she pulled him inside. Her body was already cold to his touch and he took off his jacket and wrapped it around her shoulder.

'If you can't warm me without lending me a coat—' she teased. She took his arms and wrapped them around her and began kissing him. His hands began to move over her, his senses whirling about as the scent of her clouded his brain. A fleeting memory of his Auntie Prue glazed his mind, and then Sheila's movements against him brought him deliciously back to the present.

'Now, Freddy,' Sheila whispered urgently and he began to loosen his clothing. Then, when he was about to completely relax into the heavenly sensations of love, she gasped, pushed him away and turned to the door.

'I've got to go. It's my dad, he'll kill me.' She pulled away and with a hurried, 'Meet me Monday lunchtime at the shop,' she ran back to the house, a ghostly figure in the darkness.

Freddy stood in the silence of the shed for a long time before accepting his disappointment and going home.

He was cycling back down Sheepy Lane when he saw Maurice. When he whistled a greeting, Maurice called for him to stop. Freddy didn't want to talk to anyone, he wanted to get home and think about Sheila in her almost invisible night-dress and her kisses and the feel of her body against his. But Maurice insisted.

'Been looking for you, Freddy. Want some work? Paid work?'

Freddy stopped, his foot on the ground, pushing slowly as Maurice reached him, to show his intention to hurry away. 'What sort of work? I help Mam in the shop most days.'

'Leighton's farm. He wants a pond filled in. Something about disease prevention. What about helping?'

'When?'

'Soon as we like. Tomorrow?'

'I've got something on in the evening,' Freddy lied.

'A girl? Is that why you're out so late?'

'Yeh.'

'Who is it then?'

'Sheila Powell.'

'A bit old for you, boy, you being only fifteen.'

'Nearly sixteen, and no, I don't think so and neither does she.'

'I bet she doesn't know you're only fifteen.'

'That's as may be, but I'm seeing her tomorrow night so apart from that you can count me in, right?' Freddy pushed hard on the pedal and left Maurice behind. 'Call for me. okay?' He didn't want to discuss Sheila with anyone, especially not Maurice Davies.

Sunday morning usually meant a late and lazy start, so it was with a shock, followed by an irritated groan, that Freddy woke to the sound of knocking on the door. He slept at the back of the house and it was from there that the knocking came. He opened his window and looked down. 'What d'you want?' he shouted, his voice sharp with annoyance. There were always customers expecting Mam to open up and serve them, even on a Sunday morning.

Maurice walked backwards until Freddy could see him. 'Work. Remember?'

Freddy closed the window and went down to let him in, calling to Amy to explain the disturbance. While he washed and dressed, Maurice made them both a cup of tea and took out a tin of biscuits.

'Got time for some toast if you like,' Maurice said and Freddy pointed to the bread-crock and the stove.

'Make it while I recover, will you?'

'Tiring night was it, with Sheila Powell?'

Freddy did not answer. He regretted mentioning the girl to Maurice. Her teasing and the secretive way she had treated his attempts to become friends, or something more, should have warned him to keep it private.

He had lain awake most of the night, wondering whether he should forget Sheila and look elsewhere for a girl-friend. She was too exotic for him. Exciting, and somehow dangerous, but at the same time unreal, and possibly a lot more trouble than he wanted. His thoughts had not been made clearer by Maurice's intrusion, although there had been nothing more than a normal interest and a bit of leg-pulling, Maurice knowing about it before anything had really begun had only added to his confusion.

It was raining when they set off for the farm, cycling past the gypsy camp where a fire burnt sluggishly and a solitary girl tended it. The girl had a shawl over her head but she allowed it to slide down to her shoulders to release the hair which hung wetly in strands. A voice called something from a *vardo* and she went back up the steps and disappeared inside.

They spent the morning working with Mr Leighton, a small, white-haired man whose thin wiry frame was deceptively strong. He worked beside them, heaving and pushing rocks and shovelling rubble and soil into the evil-smelling pond. All three wore sacks across their shoulders but the rain gradually seeped through their clothes.

Once they stopped and sheltered under the lee of an old wall that had once been the home of a shepherd, and drank from the flask of cocoa Mr Leighton had brought. At midday the elderly man threw down the fork he was using to drag the last of the rubble to the still deep pond and muttered. 'Damn, had enough of this. Call it a day? Same time tomorrow.' It was the first words he had spoken.

'Chatty old sod, isn't he?' Maurice laughed as they climbed on their bicycles to ride down the lane.

On the second night that Freddy waited outside Sheila's house, she appeared briefly at the upstairs window and shrugged as if to explain that she couldn't get out. There was a light from the landing shining behind her and Freddy could see the shape of her in a halo. He ached with longing.

The following morning, he worked with Maurice again. Mr Leighton had driven lorry loads of rubble from a nearby demolished house and was already at work, throwing bricks and stones into the stagnant water. The ground all around was too soggy for the lorry to be brought very near and the three workers heaved and struggled with the uneven pieces of broken walls and shovelfuls of gravel. Gradually the water widened as the hole was filled. At twelve, they decided to call it a day.

'Council coming tomorrow to drain off the water. Pipes'll do the work then,' Leighton explained.

'Nearly had a conversation then,' Maurice joked as they rode back down Gypsy Lane. 'In a hurry? Seeing Sheila are you?'

'Probably,' Freddy said. He stared ahead and pushed hard on the pedals although it was hardly necessary going downhill. Maurice kept up with him.

'You aren't much chattier than old Leighton!' Maurice complained. 'Tell me, what's she like? Good fun, is she?'

'Fantastic. Now shut your mouth about her, right?'

'What you so tampin' mad about? Won't she give you what you want? Shouldn't be thinking about things like that at your age, *Ach y fi*.' Maurice teased.

'Leave it go, Maurice. I don't want to talk about her.'

Freddy went home and changed his clothes. He caught

the bus into town and was waiting outside the shop when Sheila came out. It was still raining and she wore a pale mauve plastic mac but had on the impractical high-heeled shoes she had worn the previous day. She obviously didn't feel the cold, he thought foolishly, remembering her out in the night-cold garden wearing practically nothing at all.

'I've got the half day,' Sheila said, 'and Mam doesn't know. Where shall we go?'

'Somewhere out of the rain,' he said, his eyes glowing with the pleasure of walking with her. 'Pictures?'

'Pictures? Is that all you can think of for a rare afternoon treat?' She began to flounce off down the street and Freddy followed and held her back.

'Where d' you want to go then?'

'Somewhere we can be *private*,' she whispered. 'Let's get off this main road before someone sees me and tells Mam and Dad.'

There was a small arcade near and they walked through it and came to the riverbank where seats were placed at intervals. Sheila walked past two that were already occupied and pulled him to sit beside her on the third, sheltered from the rain. 'Let's sit here and decide how to spend our time,' she said, pressing herself closer to him.

'Shall we just sit here and talk? I don't know anything about you except you're smashing looking,' he said shyly.

She slid down slightly and settled her head against his shoulder. She touched his neck with her lips and, taking his hand, placed it on her knee.

'Sheila, you're driving me mad,' he murmured.

She stopped his talk with a kiss and then they were exploring each other's bodies, lost in the urgency of their loving. Sheila's eyes were dark as she gazed at him.

For an hour they stayed there, oblivious to the occasional

passer-by and the comments their embrace attracted. Then, as Freddy murmured that they should find somewhere private, Sheila sat up and adjusted her skirt. 'Freddy, I've just remembered, my half day was changed. It's tomorrow, not today! It's Monday and I've got to help with the new window display.'

While Freddy tried to adjust to the sudden change of her mood, she opened her box-shaped handbag and began to powder her face and put on fresh lipstick. She brushed her skirt and he thought she was mentally brushing away the past hour. She held out her hand to him. 'Walk me back to the shop, will you?' she said brightly. 'Don't worry, Freddy, there'll be plenty of other times. Soon we'll find a place where we can be safe from prying eyes that we can call our own special *cwtch*, our little hideaway.'

Back at the shop she carefully hung up the plastic mac she had borrowed; less chance of her being recognised that way. She ate a sandwich and retouched her makeup again before getting back to work with a secretive smile on her face.

Freddy caught the bus back to Hen Carw Parc disconsolately. When he stepped off opposite the church he saw Maurice.

'Where've you been?' he called in his usual inquisitive manner.

'To town. I've got to get back, I've promised to help Mam clean up the yard.'

'Seen Sheila?'

'Only for an hour, she's working.'

'Long way to go for only an hour. Worth it is she?'

'Look, Maurice—'

'All right, all right. I won't ask about her again, but I'd like to know what sort of girl she is, her being at least twenty and you being nearly sixteen, like.'

'She doesn't mind about me being younger.'

'Does she know?'

When Sheila left the shop that evening, it was Maurice who was waiting for her. He brushed away all her protests and insisted on taking her for a meal. She was flattered into risking her parents' anger and gave way gracefully. When the bill came to almost ten shillings, she was interested to see that Maurice took out a small bundle of pound and ten shilling notes to pay.

He was very polite and gentlemanly and insisted as walking her home. When they arrived he stood some distance away while she went inside and didn't even try to kiss her. She felt a bubble of excitement and it showed in her eyes as she tried to convince her mother that she had been talking to a girl friend and had caught the later bus.

A week later, Sheila met Freddy as he left on the carrier bike to deliver orders. She stopped and waved and he pulled over to the kerb.

'Freddy. I haven't see you for a while. Fed up with me are you?'

'No chance of that. But I thought you were bored with me.'

She stroked his hand and looked up at him, her eyes widening in the way he liked.

'Any hope of you coming out with me tonight then?' he asked.

'Don't know. It's my dad, see. Very strict he is.'

'Say you're meeting a girl from work.'

'I'd love to see you properly, just on our own without fear of being noticed. Don't you know of a place?'

'There's a barn off Gypsy Lane but it wouldn't be very comfortable.'

'Too close to the village. If we were seen, Mam and Dad would kill you.'

Freddy laughed. 'They can't keep you wrapped up in cotton wool all your life! Don't they want you to have fun? I bet they did.' Although, he thought, remembering their glum expressions, that was doubtful. 'Shall we try the barn?'

Sheila shook her head. 'No, I'll tell them I'm going to the pictures with one of the girls. At least it's dark in there.'

She went back to the shop, where she had been dropping off a few house-plants and ornaments in advance of the move, and Freddy went up the lane to Ethel Davies' to give her groceries. As he arrived, Nelly and her dogs were just leaving and she beckoned him over. 'Ere Freddy,' she whispered, 'who's Ethel knitting that baby shawl for? You must know, you bein' in the shop an' 'earin' all the gossip. She won't let on who it is an' I'm bustin' to know.'

Freddy felt himself colouring and he began to shake his head, but then changed his mind and whispered, 'Don't tell Mam I said will you?'

She crossed her heart and put on a serious expression and he smiled in spite of his embarrassment at broaching the subject. 'It's my Auntie Prue.'

'It never ain't?'

'I expect she'll be telling everyone soon, so don't let on.'

'Not me.' Her brown face wrinkled up into something resembling a walnut as she added, 'Cor, makes yer wonder that does, someone like 'er bein' capable of a bit of love.'

'Auntie Prue is all right,' he defended.

'Well there I 'ave to disagree with yer. Sorry, you bein' related an' that, but I think she's a nasty bit of work. Tarra and thanks fer tellin' me. Who'd 'ave thought it eh?' She chuckled as if he had told her the best joke in weeks.

Freddy was ashamed, but knew he had to talk about the news unless he wanted suspicion to fall on him, although, he reassured himself, who would imagine that he and Auntie Prue could have . . . He shuddered and walked on, his heart racing guiltily. He wished he hadn't said anything but he had to try to treat it as if it were nothing to do with him, difficult as that was.

Nelly was bursting to tell someone the news. She couldn't head for home and lose the chance of a good gossip and a laugh at Prue's expense. 'She owes me that for all the trouble she's made for me,' she muttered. 'Tellin' my Evie about me trips to town.'

Amy's shop was closed for lunch so she walked on up to Gypsy Lane without any particular goal in mind. She let the dogs off their ropes after they had passed the gypsy camp. The place was silent, neat and orderly, the caravans empty. Only one dog barked as they passed. Her friends must be out selling flowers, she thought, or telling a few fortunes.

The lane became steeper and she was glad to stop and rest when Mr Leighton and his horse-drawn plough came into view. She stood for a long time watching the two powerful animals and the perfectly straight furrows they left behind them. As the plough went past her she studied the process like a child, even though she had seen it many times before: the coulter slicing through the heavy ground followed by the share making the horizontal cut and the mould-board turning the slice over. 'Magic!' she applauded, waving to the man guiding the plough.

She knew it was useless to expect him to stop and talk. Talking was something he rarely did. But to her surprise and delight, he did stop, his voice calling the pair of horses loud and clear in the silent air.

'Have you seen that tramp fellow. George I think he calls himself?'

'Not fer a while, why?'

'I've got some work for him.'

'What sort of work?' she shouted, but it was too late, he had called the horses and a wave of his hand was all she had.

'Damn,' she muttered. 'I wanted to ask what was 'appenin' to 'is pond. Dozens of frogs there in the spring. Killin' 'em off 'e is. Murderer!' she shouted after him. 'What's wrong with frogs then?' she yelled, but this time she didn't even get a wave.

She climbed through the hedge and went to look at the rubble piled where the pond had been. Water still seeped out of it and a small runnel of coloured water had begun to make a channel from the pond down past the hedge and joined the stream. Thank Gawd it won't run into my stream, thought Nelly, could kill all the fish!

She walked a while longer, past fields now empty where Mr Leighton had grown his mangels and beet for cattle food. She remembered watching the corn being planted and cut, and the hay meadow with a thousand colours as flowers grew up among the grasses. 'Who needs a calendar?' she mused.

She turned back, past the gypsy camp again and down the road to Amy's shop. It would be open by now and she and Amy could have a gossip about Prue. It was then the thought came that Amy might not be amused at the knowledge of her sister's pregnancy, or the thought that Harry, who she had loved, had also loved his wife. Confused and disappointed, she turned back towards home.

She was almost at the bottom of her lane when she saw Sheila Powell. She was a little ahead of her and Nelly quickened her pace trying to think of a way to begin a conversation. Sheila glanced back but ignored Nelly, looking down the road. Nelly turned to look and saw Maurice approaching on his bike.

'Hiya, Maurice,' Nelly shouted, expecting him to stop, but Maurice rode on and stopped near the girl.

Nelly slowed her pace; this was something new. She recognised the girl who was coming to live in Amy's flat. She knew she lived at the top of the council houses with her grandmother and her parents. Flighty piece she looks, Nelly decided. Trouble, that's what her sort is. She couldn't have explained what she meant by 'her sort' or even 'trouble' except her instinct warned her that Sheila Powell would not live unnoticed in the village for long.

She watched them walking close together, then Maurice obviously offered the girl a lift and she struggled to find a comfortable place to sit on the crossbar of his bicycle, giggling flirtatiously. He took off his jacket and used that to make a cushion before she finally agreed to ride. Then, wobbling and laughing, the pair of them rode off down the road, and Nelly turned up the lane for home.

When Nelly had disappeared behind the hedges, Maurice turned the bicycle in a circle, sweeping round and around in the road near the bottom of Sheepy Lane.

'Take a short cut, shall we?' he asked.

'No fear, I know what you army types are like,' she giggled. 'Never be safe on a short cut with you!'

'Who wants to be safe?' he whispered, rubbing his cheek against hers. 'Come on, up the lane and through the fields. If it's too muddy we'll leave the bike and walk.'

'All right then, but if it's wet you'll have to carry me,' she said, pouting. 'I can't go home with mud on my shoes. Mam would need a good explanation for that!'

The lane was steep and Maurice dismounted and began pushing Sheila, still on the crossbar, one hand on the handlebars and the other across her hips. He began stroking her thigh and gradually his hand rose higher and higher. He watched her face for any sign of disapproval and saw none.

When the hill became too steep for him to push her, he helped her off and held her close against him for a moment before continuing up the lane. He stopped now and again and kissed her, the kisses becoming more and more urgent. This was going to be easy, he thought.

'What's a beautiful woman like you doing, going out with a boy like Freddy?' he asked, touching her ear with his tongue. 'Only a boy. You need a man.'

'Come on, I need to get home,' Sheila said, pulling herself free.

They reached the part where the lane forked off to Nelly's cottage. On their left were trees thickening into woodland and further up the lane were the castle ruins. Propping his bicycle against a tree, Maurice gestured towards the woods.

'Come over here a mo, I've got something for you,' he said.

'Oh yes?' she jeered.

'Yes, look.' He took a small package from his pocket and helt it tantalizingly high above her head while he walked backwards towards the trees.

'Maurice, I've got to go.' For the first time she began to look a bit worried. But as he removed the paper wrapping and revealed a red-plush jeweller's box, she pushed her anxiety aside.

'Only come into the trees a bit,' Maurice coaxed, 'Don't want anyone to see when you thank me.' He held the box at arm's length and allowed her to take it. 'All right, take it. You can thank me later. All right?'

Sheila grasped the box and slipped around behind the oak tree where his bicycle rested. Maurice stood still while she opened it. When the necklace glinted up at her, the rhinestones catching the light in a million rainbows, she gave a cry of delight and ran to him, her arms stretching up, reaching around his neck, her lips searching for his. 'It's beautiful!' she said when she had to stop for breath, her eyes shining and her head thrown back. Maurice felt a catch of his breath at her wild beauty.

'So are you,' he said gruffly. He held her firmly then, as she tried to move away from him. Her head was pressed further back, her body arched against his as he kissed her urgently, his breath heavy, his arms like a serpent's embrace.

His strength frightened her, but she responded at first, clinging to him, leaning back so he was almost carrying her in his arms. She knew she had plenty of time to make her excuses and get away.

Darkness began to close in at them, the curtain of night already thickening although the afternoon was far from spent. It filled in the gaps between the trees, drawing the evening around them making the woods their private dwelling, less vast, less public. The air quietened as with gentle twitterings birds settled. Then there was only her own breathing and her beating heart, and Maurice's louder more intense breaths catching as if he were running and had exhausted himself in a race.

Excitement at knowing she could have this effect on a man made her pulse beat with a sudden fury. She was surprised to realise that her breaths were as raw as Maurice's. She felt light-headed and was surprised to find herself first sitting, then lying in Maurice's arms, her limbs limp and helpless.

Then the kissing became frightening and this time the fear would not go away. She could hardly breathe and she pulled away both alarmed and thrilled by his strength.

Again she felt the exhilaration at her power over him and it was only when she decided it was time to stop that she realised it was too late.

Maurice was not a boy to be teased, not like all the others. She had underestimated him. All the others had accepted her unwillingness to continue, but Maurice would have to be stopped by other methods.

His hand was at the back of her head and as she opened her mouth to scream, he turned her face towards him and silenced her with his lips. He held her now so she couldn't move and began to press her down on the grass.

Then the danger reached her in a different way and the forbidden was undeniable. She relaxed and gave herself up to his experience and skill. And when he was calm and still she opened her eyes and smiled up at him, blue eyes meeting hazel, both content. Sheila thought she had found her man. Maurice knew he had made another conquest.

He walked her as far as her corner and she carried on home, her mind racing to find an excuse for her lateness. By the time she opened the door she was shaking and when her mother called to demand an explanation Sheila burst into tears, insisted she had been ill, and ran to her room.

Nelly had watched them leaving the wood as she walked to the place where she attended to her toilet. The dogs always stayed home while she made these necessary journeys, so the young couple had been unaware of her approach. She had not called out for a chat as she usually did, but had stepped back out of sight when Maurice pulled his bicycle away from the oak tree and accompanied Sheila down the lane.

'Trouble she is,' she muttered. 'I can smell it a mile off.'

In town, Freddy waited in vain for Sheila outside the cinema. He paced up and down, reading the newspaper posters reporting a crazy mixture of items, from the announcement of Father Christmas's imminent arrival on November 7th, to the towpath murderer being sentenced to death. Ronald Reagan was appearing in *Law and Order*, and special offers were being made for people to emigrate to Australia for only ten pounds travelling expenses.

An occasional firework exploded in the streets nearby and he was sad that his plans to take Sheila to the bonfire celebrations next week had to be abandoned. The sooner he was called into the army the better.

Sheila did not sleep that night. She spent it partly lying on the bed and partly sitting on a chair staring out into the darkness. Sometimes she felt the excitement of Maurice's loving over again, and sometimes she dreaded what she had begun. But whatever her emotions, she knew she could not allow it to be the first and last time. She was already making plans to see Maurice again, and deciding to use Freddy to help her.

Chapter Five

Nelly couldn't sleep. All through the night her mind had been unable to escape from the problem of the ownership of her cottage. She dressed while it was still dark, not bothering to look at the clock on the small table, lit a candle and went downstairs. The fire looked dead, but there was always a hope even when the ashes looked as pale and lifeless as now.

She lit the oil lamp and began working on the fire. Shaking the ashes through, the warmth of a few coals touched her hand and soon, with the aid of some tightly curled paper and a few sticks, she had a fine blaze going. It would be a while before the kettle would boil, she knew that. Patiently she added a few more sticks and chunks of wood, then some pieces of coal. When there was a heart to the fire, she swivelled the kettle over and prepared to go out, first to the woods and then, with the dogs, down the lane to the main road. She had no purpose in mind, just the need to walk and get away from her worries.

When Nelly's landlord had died without leaving a will and without any relatives to come and claim what he had left, Nelly had kept very quiet about her cottage. She had continued to put aside the four shillings rent each week and hoped that no distant cousin would appear one day to tell her to go. She would forget the worry for a while on occasions but it always came flooding back.

The old man had lived in a room in one of the cottages near Amy's shop and if ever anyone had known that Nelly's cottage was his, they had forgotten by now. Each week he had walked up the lane to collect Nelly's rent, stayed for a cup of tea and whatever cake was going, then returned to his room. He had died in his sleep and, apart from commiserating with Nelly on the loss of her weekly visitor, no one linked the old man with her name.

She knew that it had once been thatched, but the roof had been replaced by the old man himself with Welsh slate. The back of the house was in a dreadful state and, although Nelly had tackled it all with great enthusiasm at first, she had never tidied the back of the building. The door was nailed into place and the window blocked by a rampant Virginia creeper which covered the walls and several neglected trees. Nelly rarely went there, happily leaving it to the birds and other creatures who inhabited it. She called it her jungle. But despite the cottage's dilapidated condition, she was very happy there and the thought of losing her home was terrifying.

She had once asked Johnny to find out the legal situation but he had told her it was so complicated she had better forget it and leave it to luck. But time passed and the money in the box upstairs grew and she thought about it more and more.

It was Sunday morning, not yet six o'clock, and the roads were quiet. She had walked a short distance along the main road when she heard footsteps. She moved into the hedge, pulling the dogs with her, and waited, curious to know who was about so early. It was Maurice. She still waited, intending to give him a fright. He was certain to pass the place where she hid, she thought, he had already passed Johnny Cartwright's door and there was no one else nearby he was friendly with. But to her surprise he went up to Archie Pearce's house and began knocking on his door. He threw some stones up at the window, rattled the door and then, like Nelly, he hid. She saw then that there was a girl with him and the two of them watched while Archie stumbled out, half dressed, and looked about in a bemused way for the bus to work.

The joke was a good one and Nelly always liked a laugh, but she felt a bit sorry for Archie who was absent-minded at the best of times. She walked on, ignoring the couple giggling in a gateway, and said, ' 'Avin' a nightmare then, Archie?'

'Damn aye. I could have sworn I was knocked up like it was a Thursday.' He muttered something and went back indoors.

Later on she told Johnny, who looked at her and laughed. 'Always one for teasing, that Maurice. I'll get him back for that, shall I Nelly? I know a few tricks too.'

Nelly did not mention Sheila being with him. Somehow that spoilt the joke.

Nelly was walking back from Mrs French's a day or two later, carrying a tweed suit and a couple of dresses. Mrs French often gave her good quality clothing that had been either her own, or given to her to give to a deserving person. She knew Nelly often sold them and used the money to buy herself a few drinks but pretended not to. The woman had so little you couldn't begrudge her an evening out.

Nelly did not go straight home with her gifts but first knocked on Netta Cartwright's door.

'Your Johnny in by any chance?' she asked as her friend invited her inside.

'I think he's in the garden, sorting out the over-grown bushes at the end.' Netta went into the narrow kitchen, where a wooden board covered a bath, and called down the garden in her gentle voice, 'Johnny? Nelly would like a word.' Softly spoken as she was, her son heard her and came at once.

'Yes, Mam, I would like a cup of tea,' he said.

'All right,' Netta laughed. 'You go and talk and I'll make tea.' She turned to Nelly and said, 'Have you heard about Prue? Her being pregnant and a widow too, poor thing.'

'Yeh, I 'eard. What a thing to 'appen.' There was no sympathy in Nelly's voice. She didn't pretend to like Prue Beynon.

Johnny led her into the front room and sprawled across the couch. 'What's the trouble, Nelly?'

'It's about me 'ouse,' she whispered. 'You know, about 'ow I can get to stay in it, if anyone finds out the owner's dead.'

'I tried to find out what to do a few months ago,' Johnny said, feeling a little guilty that he had forgotten all about it since, 'but the position isn't easy to understand. Honestly, they talk in a foreign language I'm sure. I went to the library, but couldn't make head nor tail. Best forget it. How long is it now?'

'Six years.'

'There's the Citizen's Advice, but I'm afraid that once we start making enquiries and everything comes out into the open, it could mean you having to give up the place altogether. Best to leave it be. No one is going to suddenly appear and claim it after all these years. No, forget it. I'm sure that's best.'

Nelly looked doubtful, and Johnny went on, 'Tell you what, I'll have another go at looking it up in the library. Pity we can't tell Fay, smarter than the two of us put together, Fay is.'

'Thanks, Johnny. You won't mention it to anyone, will yer?'

'I promise. Don't worry, pretend it's yours. You've probably paid all it's worth in rent anyhow.'

'What shall I do about the rent?'

At that moment Netta tapped on the door and came in with a tray.

'Mam,' Johnny asked, 'if Nelly had a bit of money to spend, what d'you think she should buy?'

'A wireless,' Netta said at once. 'It would give her more pleasure than anything else I can think of.'

Johnny spread his hands in an expressive gesture of 'there you are, that's your answer' and Nelly's brown eyes sparkled.

'A wireless! Just fancy, I could hear *Ray's a Laugh*, an' *Take it From Here*, an' *Educating Archie* an' all that music!' She laughed, 'Which reminds me, can I come an' 'ear *The Goon Show* tonight, Netta?'

Nelly walked home and, after taking the dogs for a run in the woods, went upstairs and packed the clothes away in a suitcase which she hauled from under the bed, planning a trip into town to cheer herself up.

She was still uneasy. If only George would come back, she could talk it over with him and he'd know what to do.

'Better not go to town 'til after four,' she told the dogs. 'Evie'll be busy getting Oliver's tea then. It wouldn't do fer 'er to see us gettin' on a bus with me suitcase! Think the worst, she would, an' expect me to come 'ome rollin' drunk. Although,' she grinned to herself, 'that mightn't be such a bad idea!'

Packing the clothes she had been given by various people over the past weeks, she dragged the suitcase down the curved staircase to the living room. The dogs began to bark in excitement. They were usually included in a trip into town and looked up at her hopefully until she said, 'You comin'?' she was answered by a chorus of barking that made her clap her hands over her ears.

She brought some coal and wood inside, and filled the kettle and a bowl with water from the tap in the lane. She'd probably miss the Goons but that couldn't be helped.

After a wash in the bowl she went upstairs to change her clothes, discarding her old navy cardigan, which was held in place with a pair of safety pins, and putting on a tight grey dress. She was looking forward to her outing and, putting a Gracie Fields record on her wind-up gramophone, sang cheerfully as she waited for four o'clock to come.

Johnny was on the late shift and he was surprised to see Fay arriving just as he was leaving the house. She was beautiful, he thought as he watched her walk through the gate. She was wearing her favourite blue, a suit, or what his mother called 'a costume', in sky-blue, with a white blouse frilly at her neck. She wore a small hat with a veil of lace and a navy flower under the tilted side, and carried a handbag which matched her light navy shoes exactly.

She greeted him affectionately. 'Johnny, I hoped I'd catch you before you went to work. I've had an idea.' between kisses she went on, 'I'm working locally today, just short trips to Llangwyn and no further than Swansea. Why don't I take your mother with me and drop her off at the pictures? It's ages since she went anywhere and I know she'd love it. I'll treat her to tea afterwards.'

'Fay, my lovely girl, that's a great idea. Mam,' he called, and when Netta came out of the kitchen, he explained Fay's invitation to her.

Netta looked into her daughter-in law's face and saw her

anxiety. She knew Fay was tense and guessed that she was very unhappy, but this was something new. Was there something behind this invitation? All the same she smiled and patted Fay's arm affectionately.

'Fay, *fach*, that would be lovely. You and me having tea together, just the two of us. What time do you want me to be ready?'

Fay looked at her watch and shrugged. 'I don't want to rush you, that would spoil the whole thing. Say an hour?'

'Lovely.'

Netta went upstairs to select from her limited wardrobe something that wouldn't disgrace her fashion-conscious daughter-in-law. She was pleased at the invitation but still apprehensive about the real reason for it. She whispered a small prayer that Fay wasn't going to tell her the marriage was over. 'Please God, anything but that,' she murmured, her small hands pressed firmly together and her brown eyes tightly closed.

Johnny also sensed Fay's anxiety. He worried about her, knowing she did not always discuss her fears with him. When her ex-fiancé had turned up ill and injured after being presumed dead for eight years, she had kept the secret from him and tried to handle it alone, although he admitted that when she did tell him he had refused to believe her. Now there was something else, he could sense it, and he held her tightly before leaving for the bus depot. Johnny wished he could find a way to her heart and make their marriage as perfect as he dreamed it could be.

Fay admired Netta's pink dress and woollen coat.

'That looks perfect. I'll have to watch myself or you'll be ashamed to go out with me!' She opened the car door and settled the plump little lady inside.

Fay went with her to the cinema, bought her ticket, and

left her there, promising to meet her at four-thirty when the film would be finished. She stood and waved until Netta went through the dark red curtains and into the care of an usherette.

The car was parked close to the cinema and Fay ran back to it, glancing anxiously at her watch. She drove back to Hen Carw Parc and began to take boxes out of the back of the car and up to her room. Then, with a tray set for tea, she waited.

The man from the council was prompt. At three o'clock there was a knock at the door and Fay went to answer it. The official went first to look at the room she and Johnny shared, shaking his head at the lack of space, then downstairs to look at the kitchen-cum-bathroom and to drink his tea while he filled in forms.

'You'll have a good case here for re-housing, Mrs Cartwright,' he said when he had completed his questions. 'You'll be hearing from us very soon.'

At four o'clock he left, and Fay returned the boxes to the car, put some empty ones out for the dustmen and then drove to town to meet Netta. They spent a happy hour chatting, laughing and eating Kunzle Cakes and drinking tea.

Phil Davies called on Nelly before she left for town. He was carrying a can of paraffin oil for her lamp.

'Thanks, Phil, it's a treat not having to go down with me old pram wheels and bring it up.' She helped him carry it down the path and put it in the larder behind the back door. 'Stay fer a cuppa why don't yer?'

Phil shook his head. 'I'd love one, Nelly, but by the look of that suitcase you're going out. Somewhere exciting, is it?'

'Just off to town for an outin'—don't-tell-my-Evie! Get the FBI out she would. Watches me like a 'awk!'

'Not a word.' Phil rubbed the side of his nose with a finger, then said, 'What's happening with the Cartwrights then? Saw an official looking car pull up this afternoon, while Netta was out too. The man went in and must have talked to Fay for ages. Carried a clip-board he did, looked important.'

Nelly shrugged. 'Don't know, but when you finds out you'll tell me, won't yer?'

'Amy thought the man was from the council.'

'Fay's boss more like. She's an important business woman is Fay. Sees a lot of important people she does.'

'Perhaps.' Phil looked doubtful. 'Come on, Nelly I'll carry your case down to the bus. I'm going down anyway.'

They met a group of children as they turned into the lane. Two of them were struggling with a Guy Fawkes dummy made from an old suit of clothing stuffed with newspaper, and with a swede for its head.

'Nelly,' one of them pleaded, 'can we borrow your cart to take our guy around?'

'Go on then, but bring it back in good condition,' she warned. She felt in her pocket where she had put some coins ready for her bus fare. ' 'Ere, you can 'ave three pence to get you started.'

In the main road several other groups of young hopefuls were begging pennies for the guy to earn money for fireworks. Hidden by a mask but unmistakable to her, she saw Oliver.

'Does yer mother know what you're doing? Silly question!' she said. 'Don't worry Ollie, I've got a few fireworks put away for bonfire night. I've been putting a few coppers aside each week in Amy's shop. Five shillings' worth I've got, but some of that was from a win on the 'orses—don't tell-yer-mother!'

When she reached town, the rain which had been threatening all day began to fall. A wind sprang up blowing the rain into her face and making Nelly and her suitcase lose balance at every corner. Once she had sold the clothes to Mrs Greener, the case waved about worse than before and it was a relief when opening time came at the pub and she could go inside and find a seat.

The wet dogs curled up at her feet and she ordered two packets of crisps and a glass of stout. The crisps she shared with the dogs and the stout quickly disappeared. Two more glasses followed and, her damp clothes drying in the warmth of the bar-room, Nelly felt herself dozing.

When she got up to order another drink she felt cold and although she moved to sit as close to the fire as other customers would allow, she couldn't get comfortable. She watched the dart players for a while, sometimes shouting encouragement, sometimes losing track of the game, but the evening was not a success. She missed George.

The room filled up and she was warmer despite there being several people between herself and the fire. She failed to make friends with anyone, they were all in their own groups and refused to allow her to join in. Swallowing her fifth glass of stout, she went to the counter, pushing her way through the men who always huddled against the bar as if they had earned a proprietory right by long tenancy, and she bought a couple of bottles to take home.

With difficulty, and by annoying several of those standing near, Nelly opened her suitcase and slipped the bottles inside. Pulling the sleeping dogs to their feet, she headed outside.

In the doorway she met Maurice, and the girl with him was Sheila Powell.

' 'Ello Maurice. 'Ave one fer me will yer? I'm off 'ome. Got wet an' I'm feelin' a bit chilled.'

'Come and have one with us,' he invited. 'You know Sheila don't you? Coming to live above Amy's shop.'

'Yes, I know who yer are.' A grimace more than a smile accompanied the words.

'You won't let on you've seen me, will you?' Sheila said in her high voice. 'Mam thinks I'm out with the girls from the shop.'

'Old enough to do what you want, ain't yer?'

'Yes, but it's difficult living at home. It's rows all the time if I don't do what Mam and Dad say.'

'Get yourself a place, why don't yer?'

'On three pounds fifteen a week? Fat chance!'

'What about your place, Nelly. Got a room to rent for her?' Maurice asked.

'No bloody fear! I'd find meself a real 'andsome man, not a girl!' She laughed her loud laugh and pushed past them to the pavement.

The cold hit her and she bent against the wind as she hurried to the bus stop, her suitcase swinging and the bottles inside clinking. She stood back from the kerb and watched for the bus from the shelter of a shop doorway, the dogs leaning against her for warmth so that she bent and covered them with her coat.

'Back in time for *The Goon Show* with a bit of luck,' she said from between chattering teeth.

The wind began to gust, bringing showers into their inadequate shelter, and Nelly decided to have a stroll and look at the shop windows. A radio attracted her attention and she dreamed of owning one and having music and laughter all day. ' 'Eaven that would be, Bobby. But that one's electric and that wouldn't work off me oil lamp!' She returned to the bus stop as the double-decker turned the corner, splashing muddy water across the kerb, and stopped for her to get on.

'Upstairs with them dogs!' the conductor shouted.

' 'Ang on to this then.' Nelly pushed the suitcase at him and puffed her way up the stairs as the bus moved off.

She didn't go to Netta Cartwright's. She was cold and wet and hoped to get home and save the fire. She knew she had not banked it up properly, with Phil arriving and her being in a hurry because of him. Just her luck if it was out. 'Straight 'ome for us, boys,' she said, then stopped, 'We was goin' to 'ave some fish an' chips! I nearly fergot.'

Dragging the wet dogs and the ungainly suitcase, she crossed the road and joined the queue at Milly Toogood's daughter's fish shop. A soggy end to an evening out an' no mistake, she thought as the steamed-up door opened and the warmth escaped into the night.

'Don't bring them dogs in 'ere,' a voice shouted as her foot touched the step.

'Piss off then and keep yer rotten chips,' Nelly retorted, pulling the dogs back outside.

'It's bread an' fish paste for us and it'll go down a treat with a bottle of stout,' Nelly told the dogs. She began to sing defiantly as she climbed up the lane, 'She can keep 'er fish an' chips, she can keep 'er fish an' chips, I'd rather 'ave me fish paste any day.'

After the mixed emotions of the first love-making, Sheila began to meet Maurice regularly. The illicit affair had at first frightened her with its intensity, and she lay awake worrying at night. Then she had seen how other girls looked at Maurice and she began to enjoy not only the sex, but also going out with him and feeling more adult than she had felt before. She smiled when she thought of Freddy's nervous fumblings. Maurice didn't take no for an answer, but he knew what a girl wanted: someone strong and masterful, reliable and mature.

They met at exciting times; in the small hours of the morning, when it was still dark, he would bring a blanket and a flask of tea and they would share a magical picnic in the secret darkness. At night, long after her parents slept, he would come and throw a pebble at her window and they would snuggle together in the garden shed.

She told no one about the meetings, apart from hinting to her friends about the exciting man she was in love with and who was desperately in love with her. The girls at the shop had only seen Freddy and thought she was inventing the other man to cover her embarrassment at going out with a boy younger than herself. Her parents were a bit concerned at the number of times she went to the pictures with girls from the shop, but they believed her, hoping that her previous behaviour with men was past and forgotten.

The staff in the dress-shop where Sheila worked ran a Twenty Club between them. At the beginning of every twenty weeks they drew numbers from a hat and the number they drew decided which week they would have twenty pounds to spend. Sheila managed to join by telling her mother she earned a pound less than she actually did. Week seventeen was hers and she could go along to a large department store with a voucher and spend the twenty pounds collected.

On Friday morning, when the pay envelopes were handed out and everyone put their pound note into the collection, she was given her voucher and she signed the side of the list of names with a flourish. Seeing Maurice regularly was great fun, but she was desperately short of clothes. It had been all right when she had gone out occasionally straight from work with one of the girls. The green skirt and cream blouse they all had to wear was perfectly adequate, but she couldn't dress like that for Maurice. Her Twenty Club would help.

To justify the commission the manageress received from the department store, she allowed the recipient of the voucher an extra long lunch-break to spend it. With the precious piece of paper in her purse, Sheila made her way to the store to enjoy herself. There would have been a discount on any clothes she had bought in the gown-shop, but she needed other things as well as dresses. She would buy more, cheaper clothes plus a few accessories to help extend them.

She walked around the displays shaking her head at the assistants who came to help. She made a mental list of the places she and Maurice would be likely to go, extending her ideas as her hopes of a long-term affair grew. He would be so proud of her in her smart new clothes that he would speak to her mother about marriage and bring everything out into the open.

She admired a Pringle twinset but abandoned it without regret. It cost far too much and she didn't need expensive things to look good. She wanted something smart for when they went to an out-of-town pub for a drink, and something dark and practical for the visits to the woods. Her heart leapt at the memories. And she needed shoes. She ought to abandon the slim high heels she loved and choose something flat, but then she looked at them and shook her head. No need to go that far. But she did buy a pair of ballet-style shoes and two pairs of nylons, plus the thread to mend them. She chose a skirt and two men's jumpers, and the rest she spent on beads and scarves, digging into her money to buy a pretty slim gold belt with an ornamental buckle, and a wide one to wear with the men's jumpers that would almost reach the hem of her skirt.

Maurice would be so impressed. It was early days, but she knew he meant it when he talked about marriage and she firmly believed in love at first sight. Bonfire night would be so romantic and she was determined to go out with him then. She had a plan to persuade her parents she would come to no harm. Freddy would help her there.

Walking back to the shop with her parcels she was as excited as a child at Christmas. She imagined the admiration in Maurice's eyes as she wore each outfit. Her mind whirled with ideas for combining the new skirt with some blouses and the new jumpers. There was a radiant smile on her face which, when she met Freddy waiting outside the staff door, seemed to be for him.

'Freddy, what are you doing here?'

'Come to see you of course. Why else would I be standing here? Got time for a coffee?'

Sheila shook her head, her eyes full of regret. 'Sorry Freddy, really disappointed. I'm late already.'

'I came to ask if you could come with me to the bonfire party,' he said in a rush as she made to go inside.

She turned to face him, her blue eyes enormous and shining with pleasure. 'Freddy! That would be lovely!' What luck. He was falling in with her plans without even knowing it. 'I'd love to, but only if your sister Margaret will come with us.'

'Margaret? But why?'

Sheila could hardly tell him that by going with a fifteen-year-old boy and his eight-year-old sister her mother would be reassured. 'Take it or leave it. I've got to go now.'

'Give me a kiss to make up for my disappointment and I'll ask her.'

She turned her face upward for him and for a moment the kiss was less casual than she intended. Smiling, she went into the shop. Everything was working out perfectly; she would go to the bonfire with a couple of innocent kids, and ditch them to meet Maurice.

Several families had clubbed together and planned their own bonfire but the biggest was on the field behind Evie and Timothy's house. Evie had complained, of course, but to no avail. The field belonged to Leighton and had been used by the village every year since old Caradoc Owen, who was over ninety, was a boy.

But this year there was a slight change. The bonfire was being delayed from the fifth to the following Saturday. It would also be lit a few hours later than usual, so the darkness would show fireworks to their full effect. During the night of the fifth there were several parties, mostly in people's back gardens for young children, but most had saved their fireworks for the communal party.

The rain miraculously kept off for the few days before the party, and with fresh paper to start the wood burning, it was expected to go well. Early in the afternoon children began to gather, collecting further supplies of wood and chattering in excited voices. There would be potatoes cooked at the edges of the huge fire, supplied as usual by Mr Leighton. Some were stolen and eaten raw by those impatient for the festivities to begin, but most waited, just handling them and imagining the mouth-watering taste as they would receive them hot and black, singed from the ashes.

Dressed in their oldest clothes, Margaret and Oliver walked up to the council houses with Freddy. At Sheila's house Freddy knocked and waited until Mrs Powell opened the door and invited them inside.

‘It’s all right, Mrs Powell, I’ve got Margaret and Oliver here. Best we wait outside.’

The door closed again and Freddy stood with the others, trying to concentrate on the garden and identify the remains of the dying plants.

When the door opened again a darkly-dressed Sheila emerged. She wore what looked like a navy school mackintosh with a belt loosely tied around her waist, flat black shoes, and socks which came up to her knees. Her long hair fell about her shoulders, loosley tied at each side, and on her head was a dark beret. Freddy thought she looked more like a school girl than Margaret, who was wearing a short jacket and trousers. She made him feel uneasy.

Mrs Powell followed her daughter to the gate and said to Freddy, ‘Look after her now, she’s in your care.’

‘She’ll be all right with us, Mrs Powell,’ Freddy promised.

Mrs Powell stood and watched as they walked down the hill fading from her sight between street lamps until they disappeared at the corner of Hywel Rise.

Mrs Powell was a sharp-faced woman who always wore a frown. She went back into the house and stood at the window, looking down at the point at which her daughter had disappeared.

‘What’s the matter?’ Ralph Powell asked.

‘I don’t know. I’m uneasy about her. She’s been out so much lately and I know I can’t stop her but I’ve a feeling there’s a man involved somewhere.’

‘Forget it Mavis. She’s old enough now to go out without us being told everything about where she goes. She let this boy, Freddy call so you could see who she was with, what more can she do?’

‘We could go to the bonfire ourselves, make sure she is there.’

'I was hoping for a night in, listening to the wireless,' Ralph grumbled.

'We could walk down there just for a few minutes to see what's going on?'

'It's a kid's party, for goodness sake. What could be going on?'

'It was a kid's party once before, remember? I've got a feeling, that's all.'

Ralph switched off the radio and stood up with a sigh. 'Come on then. I can see I'll have no peace unless we go. Though I think you should let her alone. She's twenty-one now and all that was a long time ago.'

The trouble with Sheila had begun nine years before with a letter asking them to go and see the headmistress of her school because Sheila was 'bothering the boys'. Later, at a children's party, Sheila had undressed and danced on the table among the jellies and iced cakes, to the amusement of everyone except Mavis and Ralph Powell.

After that occasion they always met her from school and took her there. When she left to start work they continued to keep a close watch on her, meeting anyone who showed any interest in her and refusing her permission to go out with boys. Pregnancy was a constant nightmare as they couldn't watch her every moment of the day. There had been rumours about several young boys living near but these they investigated and decided were inventions.

There had only been a problem once since they had come to live with Mavis's mother, who helped keep on eye on her. Neighbours had complained that Sheila had been seen putting clothes on the line wearing only a small bra and even smaller pants. Only now, several years after that last unfortunate incident, did they feel they could leave the grandmother's house and go back to living as a family without the extra pair of eyes to watch the girl.

Mavis had been content to let Sheila go out with Freddy Prichard, knowing he was only fifteen, but had been alarmed when she saw how large he was and how grown-up he looked with his glasses and the moustache.

'He's a bit big for his age, overweight most likely, but he seems polite enough. Boys are different now. All those years without a father to guide them when the men were all taken to be soldiers. It made the girls go wild and the boys mature too quickly.'

'Yes,' Mavis agreed. 'I blame the war for our Sheila.'

'Freddy's father wasn't in the war though. He disappeared before the wedding you might say.'

'What d'you mean?'

'Amy Prichard isn't married and never has been.'

'Oh my God,' Mavis fluttered. 'Like father like son! Sheila's gone out with a seducer! Come on, let's find her before we're too late.'

'Don't be daft. There's nothing wrong with Freddy. Or his mother either. Leave Sheila be. She's twenty-one and there's nothing we can do if she means to go wild.'

'Yes there is, Ralph Powell. We can protect her like we've always done! Come on!'

Taking a coat from behind the door, she threw it at her husband and put on her own jacket, fastening it as she hurried out.

Freddy walked with Sheila, listening to her chatter about her new clothes and the excitement of having twenty pounds to spend, while Margaret and Oliver ran on ahead.

'You didn't spend it all, did you?'

'When I had a ten shilling rise last year I didn't tell Mam. Then I persuaded her I needed more cash for my bus fare and food and she let me keep an extra ten shillings and I put the money into a Twenty Club. What she doesn't know won't keep me awake nights, will it?'

'I'd have bought a new bike,' Freddy said a little wistfully. 'Not that I'll need one for a long time, I'm going into the army.'

'You're not! Fancy signing your life away. Not old enough for conscription are you? Going in proper?'

'Yes, for five years for a start.' He put an arm around her. 'Sheila, will you write to me? Be my girl? It would be great to have a picture of you to show to the other boys, and having a letter, well, I'd be proud.'

'I haven't got a photo.'

'We could get one done. Monday lunch-break. I'll meet you and we'll go to the photographers together.'

They had almost reached the field and the lane was dark, the bonfire not yet lit. People could be heard milling about, torches sent beams of light into the dark reminiscent of search lights, and children laughed and screamed. Freddy knew many of them would be dressed as Guys themselves to add to the fun; he had done so himself just a few years ago.

He pulled up the wire fencing and held it for Margaret and Oliver to slide underneath it, then held out his arms.

'Lift you over, shall I?'

'Go on, you two,' Sheila said to the waiting youngsters and Freddy's heart leapt. She was going to stay with him.

'Give the bonfire a miss, shall we?' He kissed her head. Her hair smelt fresh and sweet and a heady perfume rose from her warm body.

'Hold my coat a minute, will you?' She threw the school mackintosh at him and began to shorten her skirt, rolling it under the waistband until it was well above her shapely knees. The blouse was pulled free from the skirt and fell to the hem, like a short loose dress. Reaching into the pocket of her coat she took out a belt which she fixed around her waist, and then took her socks off. She smiled, her teeth white in the darkness.

'Sheila! You look fantastic.'

'Yeh, I suppose I do.' She reached up and kissed him lightly on the cheek then gave him a push. 'Now get lost. I'm meeting someone. Don't worry, I'll see myself home.'

'Sheila!'

She went under the fence and ran across the field. He began to run after her and as he ran, her figure was suddenly silhouetted as the fire flared into life and he lost sight of her as a hundred figures danced about in the glow.

Children were shouting in excitement, adults shouting at them to be careful. Freddy ran towards the mass of local people and recognised no one. Flickering flames distorted each face and a dozen times he saw Sheila, ran closer, and each time turned away disappointed. He went closer to the fire, but the brightness dazzled him and he walked disconsolately through the muddy field, around which groups of people were gathered, all being lectured by parents to stay close and keep well back behind the safety line.

As he watched, a line of children were arranged in a row by Bert Roberts and given a sparkler to hold. Then they sang a song which they had learnt at school. He was close enough to hear that the words sung by Arthur Toogood and some of his friends were slightly different from the school version, but he hardly took it in. He gave up looking for Sheila. She had used him again and if she wanted to find him she could easily do so.

He heard someone ask where Nelly was and the reply that she was home of course, taking care of her dogs. Milly Toogood was telling Phil Davies they had heard Fay was looking for a council house. Phil said it was nonsense, and in the gloom behind Milly, Freddy saw Sybil Tremain, who followed her friend around constantly, shake her head.

He wandered around the field like a ghost unseen, unheard and detached from the scene and the excitement. As the singing finished, the fireworks began from high up on the field close to the woods. Sparks of every colour lit the night and rockets shot up and whined for attention. Stars sparkled into life and then were gone, only to be followed by others, each vying for the loudest roar from the crowd. The fireworks threw strange shadows and made the place a magical landscape. But Freddy couldn't enjoy the spectacle and went over to join the men by the bonfire. Bert Roberts was poking at its edges and turning the potatoes set in the ashes to cook. He went and kicked a fallen log a bit closer to the flames and Bert shouted, 'Not so heavy handed, will you?'

A jacky-jumper firework was thrown among a crowd of women and Constable Harris marched up and clipped Arthur Toogood around the ear.

'What makes you think it was him?' Milly demanded.

'Who else would it be?' Constable Harris said with resounding conviction.

Sheila had met Maurice as arranged at the top of the field, far away from the three men setting off the fireworks and hidden in the extra darkness beyond the field. She tried to bring him around to talk of weddings but was interrupted by hearing her mother and father calling her name. She began to cry.

Maurice got up quickly and disappeared into the trees, whispering promises, and Sheila was found by her mother, hurriedly trying to straighten her clothes. Freddy heard her crying and when he saw her, by the light of a flaring firework, coming out of the trees, he ran forward to comfort her. But behind her, hurrying her on, were her parents.

'So it's you, Freddy Prichard! Pretending to be so innocent and all the time leading our poor girl on!' Freddy stared at them, unable to begin to explain, and he went home with their accusations ringing in his ears.

A few days later, the letter Amy had been dreading to see arrived. Phil brought it and if he guessed what it contained he said nothing. He handed her the pile of post with the official-looking envelope at the bottom of the stack and, without waiting for the usual chat, hurried on.

She handed it to Freddy and waited, fussily changing the position of tins on a shelf, while he opened it.

'It's my papers, Mam,' he said.

'I thought it must be, love,' she said, trying to keep her voice normal. 'When do you go then?'

He handed her the letter and walked away to stare out of the door.

'It isn't too late I'm sure, if you've changed your mind,' she said hesitantly.

'It is, and I haven't,' he turned to face her. 'What is there to stay for? There's nothing for me here. I have to get away.'

'Because of the gossip? About you and Sheila Powell? That will soon pass. As soon as there's something more interesting happening it will be forgotten.'

He flinched at the thought of his true reason for going—that was even more scandalous.

'I want to go, Mam.'

Something in his voice told her not to argue, but the future was beginning to look lonely and empty. She helped him pack his bag ready for his departure. She had not thought before how temporary children were.

Chapter Six

Amy opened the shop door and, seeing Nelly walking towards her, burst out laughing.

'Nelly! It isn't Coronation Day again, is it?'

Nelly patted the hat she wore into which she had fixed both the Union Jack and the red dragon of Wales. 'Prince Charles is five years old today. That's worth celebrating, ain't it?' she shouted. She came into the shop, dragging her two dogs. 'I'm just off to "do" fer Mrs French, but I thought I'd call and ask you what time you want me tomorrer. The big day, ain't it?'

'Yes, we're moving into the house at last. But without Freddy it won't be half as exciting.'

'Go on with yer. 'E'll be 'avin' leaves an' bringin' all 'is mates to visit. An' young Margaret—' she lowered her voice '—she don't know about the,' she mouthed the word 'piano', 'does she?'

'No, Nelly, I wonder if you can help with that?'

'Of course.'

'It's being delivered this afternoon. Could you go and wait for the men to bring it and make sure they put it in the right place? You know what it's like trying to be in two places at once and without Freddy to help—'

'Don't go on about it, Amy. 'E's doin' what 'e wants and that's 'ow it should be fer kids. No matter what we want for

’em, they makes up their own minds if they got any sense.’

‘You’re right. But I miss him so. I suppose I depended on him too much, made him grow up a bit quicker than was fair. It’s different with Margaret, her being a girl I suppose.’

‘You done well by them both. Now, do me a favour an’ get out a couple of flags and stick ’em on the window. Make a bit of a show fer young Charles’s birthday, will yer?’

‘All right. With all I’ve got to do and with the hundred and one things running through my mind, I’ll get out a couple of flags!’ Amy laughed. ‘Go on, get your doing done, but don’t work too hard, we’ll have a busy day tomorrow.’

‘I’ll go straight to the ’ouse from Mrs French’s, shall I, to wait fer the—’ she mouthed ‘piano’ again and when Amy nodded, went on her way, dragging Spotty on three legs away from the carrots just in time.

‘See you later,’ Amy called, aiming a kick at the dog as he slithered out of the door.

Saturday morning was not a good time for deliveries and the shop was full when Vic Honeyman poked his head around the door and shouted for Amy to open the back gate for him.

‘You’ll have to wait,’ she said. ‘I can’t come for a moment, you can see how busy I am.’ She was always flustered when she saw him. Attracted as she was, she had refused to go out with him when she had learnt from Nelly that he had a wife and three children. Since then she had made her disapproval clear. She refused to speak to him if they met, except when he brought goods from the wholesalers in town.

There had been two loves in Amy’s life and both men had been married. She swore to herself it would never happen again. For years she had believed Harry Beynon, whom she had loved all her life, would eventually leave Prue and come to live with her and her children, but he had died still married to Prue, who was expecting his child. So much for promises.

The affair with Richard French had happened when they were both unhappy, Richard because he had not heard from his son, who was fighting the enemy in Europe, and Amy because, once again, Harry had chosen Prue and not her. That brief affair had given her her beautiful and talented daughter, and the finances to start the shop.

To have a happy, honest relationship seemed beyond her, especially when a few meetings with Vic had ended with her being told about his family. Now she was never less than rude to him.

'Give me the key and I'll get them in for you.' Vic said now, pushing through the customers waiting to be served.

'Here, take the money for this cauli will you?' A woman pushed a shilling piece into his hand and he gave her a piece of newspaper from the pile cut ready.

'Five pounds of potatoes, please,' another voice demanded and without asking Amy's permission, Vic went outside and weighed the potatoes and put them into her bag. She paid and he went back inside and handed the coins to Amy.

He managed to attend to three more customers, including Oliver who had come to spend his Saturday threepence on sweets, and who spent an age deciding. Then the shop was finally empty.

'Thanks,' Amy said as he handed her the last of the money.

'Make me a cup of tea and we'll call it quits,' he grinned.

'All right. I'll have it ready when you've unloaded.'

The shop filled and emptied several times before they were able to drink the tea. While she served, Vic packed away the boxes of beans and peas and carrots in the orderly store room in the yard.

'It's so tidy out there, it's easy to see where things go. A marvel of orderliness, you are, Amy Prichard.'

'Thanks,' she said again, watching him warily, almost daring him to suggest a date.

'I hear you're moving tomorrow. Sunday's a funny day to be moving, isn't it?'

'It's easier than trying to close the shop for a day. Nelly will help me and Margaret will be out of the way. She's staying with Oliver's parents over the road while I get things straight.'

'Want any help?'

'No thanks!'

'No strings. I've got a loan of my brother's van at the moment and I could make a few journeys a bit earlier than the furniture van to get things in order. It's up to you though. I'll bring one of my kids so you won't think there's any ulterior motive,' he added.

'Now how could I think that, a happily married man like you?' she said sarcastically.

'I'm not "happily married" and you know it, but that's something different. Do you want some help or not?'

'Thanks, yes, I would be glad of an extra hand. Freddy's gone see, and it's difficult without him. Any good at putting up shelves are you?'

'Damn good.'

He arranged to call at seven the following morning. Amy spent the time between the next rush of customers straightening up the displays of vegetables, fussily rearranging the cauliflowers and cabbages, and rolling down the neck of the potato sack until everything was again as neat as she liked it, trying to find reasons to disapprove of Vic's help.

There was an entrance at the side of the shop which, being blocked with tins of biscuits and other dry goods, she never used. To get to the flat above she used the stairs inside the shop, but now the flat was to be let she had to rearrange things. The unused stairs would have to be cleared and the second staircase bolted firmly and padlocked from the shop side. She looked around her, wondering where to find space for the stock from the stairs. She sighed. Space was a problem even with the shop extended. But there was no Harry to help her this time. If only Vic were single.

He was not handsome, not like Harry, who had seemed to light up a room when he entered with his happy, glad-to-be-alive expression and the brightness of his blue eyes behind the rimless glasses he wore. Vic was pale by comparison, pale skin, pale faded blue eyes that were more grey than blue, she decided on reflection. His hair was already showing streaks of grey and was thin, too long and smelt of the cigarettes he continually smoked. She smiled to herself at the unkind description. He didn't have much going for him, did he? And yet there was gentleness and kindness in the faded eyes, and perhaps the smoking was partly due to his unhappiness at home. Whatever it was, there was a spark between them—but a spark without a chance of burning into a flame, she told herself firmly.

It was hardly light when Nelly and the dogs set off for Amy's house. She looked over at the flat before heading in the direction of the house to make sure Amy hadn't overslept. She had looked very tired the previous day, and on Sundays she usually slept late. But the lights shone in the windows.

The sun seemed unwilling to break through today and Nelly looked up uneasily at the low clouds, afraid the move would take place in heavy rain. 'An' a fat lot of good all my extra cleanin' will 'ave bin then!' she grumbled.

She opened the house door with her key and made a half-hearted attempt to clean the dogs' feet before letting them lie on the coconut matting near the sink.

'Stay put until you're dry or Amy'll be mad with yer,' she warned. She took off her old coat and set to lighting fires in the two downstairs rooms. The fireplace in the living room heated water and needed a bit of practice to get going, as the draught took the flame away from the coal and sticks if you didn't watch it.

The place was already spotless, and some second-hand carpets were down in two bedrooms and the living room. In the kitchen black and red tiles shone with Nelly's recent efforts. It was in the living room that Margaret's surprise stood waiting for her: a piano, its lid closed against the dust, the dark wood shining like new. On top of it was a new music case, an extra present from Freddy. Nelly smiled and, taking her duster, began to polish the piano again while she waited for Amy.

Out of her coat pocket she brought an ancient alarm clock and propped it up on the draining board. The van was not expected to arrive before eleven, but she wanted to be waiting, not half way through a job. She went through to the empty front room and glanced out at the garden, noticing Freddy's efforts and nodding approval, then back to the living room to polish the wooden surround to the square of carpet, humming happily to herself.

The fire was burning brightly in both rooms and the smell of polish giving the place a lived-in feeling when Nelly saw someone walk past the window and looked at the clock.

'Blimey, it must 'ave stopped!' She opened the back door and put on the kettle, then frowned as she recognised Victor Honeyman.

'What you doin' 'ere then?' she asked.

'I've borrowed a van and I'm giving Amy a hand. I've been told this is the most important.' He handed her a small box which contained a bag of biscuits, cups, and tins of sandwiches and cakes, plus a large teapot. Nelly took out the china and the food and put it all near the cooker.

'I've brought the fridge too. It's only small so I thought we could put it in place before the rest.'

He seemed to know where Amy wanted everything and busied himself fixing shelves on the wall behind the sink and bringing a cupboard from the garage to hold the fridge. Nelly watched. She did not approve of this sudden revival of his friendship with Amy and her face showed it, but Vic didn't seem to notice her hostility and had her holding screws and passing the tools, helping him to straighten the shelves and, finally, making him a cup of tea.

The cooker was an electric one and small like the fridge. He fitted it to its plug while Nelly made his tea, which she handed him with a frown.

'What does your wife think of you comin' to 'elp Amy like this?'

'She's glad to get me from under her feet. One of the kids is coming down later to see if there's anything he can do. We're like that, see, us Honeymans. It's all right, Nelly Luke, it's all above board,' he teased.

'I 'opes it is,' she said, taking his cup before he had finished and putting it in the bowl for washing.

Victor brought a second load including pot plants, a goldfish bowl and some precious ornaments, then at eleven o'clock the furniture van arrived. Amy's flat had been small and she hadn't been able to build up a home as she would have wished, so the van wasn't too full.

'Be better when the new stuff arrives,' Amy said to Nelly as the two old fireside chairs were lifted off the lorry. They stood in the window of the front room while the boxes and oddments of furniture were unloaded and set in their places. It was not until most of the large items had been brought in that Nelly noticed the two women.

'Nosy lot around 'ere,' she grumbled, pointing to where Milly Toogood watched as the van was emptied. 'Appears like magic she does. 'Er an' 'er friend.' She leaned slightly to look behind Milly and there was Sybil Tremain, as usual, standing a few paces back from Milly. 'Milly Nogood an' the Pup, I calls 'em,' Nelly said. She opened the window and called, 'The rest is comin' termorrow, about ten. Just so you won't be late an' miss something.'

'Nelly!' Amy exclaimed as the two women walked away, Sybil, as always, a few paces behind as if she were constantly trying to catch up.

'Like magic it is the way them two finds out what's goin' on.'

'If I'd known there was so much interest I'd have sold tickets!' She walked through to the living room and looked at the furniture with some dismay. 'It doesn't look much, does it Nelly?'

'When Margaret sees that piano she'll think it's the best house in Hen Carw Parc.' Nelly showed her crooked teeth in an excited laugh. 'Won't she be thrilled!'

Margaret had been sent to play with Oliver to be kept out of the way while the move was completed, but Evie had soon tired of having the children under her feet. They had attended church and she had managed to make them sit still during the sermon and had listened with pleasure to Margaret singing the hymns, coming out with a warm feeling and full of envy of Amy's talented daughter. But within minutes of getting home Evie had suggested they went for a walk.

'I want you back at one o'clock for lunch,' she said, 'Not a moment after.' And not a moment before either, she thought silently. Children were such a handful. Thank goodness she had only produced one.

They put on their wellingtons and set off down the garden and up Leighton's field. The day was cold but the rain which had threatened had moved away, the dark clouds driven by a keen wind. They were wrapped up well and soon glowing with the exuberance of youth.

They continued to climb, passing Nelly's cottage and then the castle on their left, and stopping for a while to look down at the village road snaking away far below them. There were no houses nearby now and, apart from the brickworks, the only building up here on the hillside was the Browns' dairy farm.

'Let's go and see Billie and Mary Dairy and get a drink of milk, shall we?' Margaret suggested.

There was smoke visible above the farmhouse, a tumbled column scattered by the wind as soon as it escaped from the tall chimney. As they came near, Oliver stopped Margaret's hurried progress down the steep hill and pointed. In a field ahead of them was a large ewe caught in a deep ditch. 'She won't get out of there on her own,' Oliver said.' 'D'you think we should tell Mr Leighton? She's probably his.'

'Tell Mary, she'll know what to do. She can telephone Mr Leighton.' Margaret hurried on down the sloping field. She was thirsty.

The farm looked like many others, with scattered sheds

and barns, the cobbled yards wet in the mid-November damp. But when they walked through the gate it was clear this farm was different. The sheds were newly white-washed and everywhere was newly scrubbed and sweet-smelling. The whole area lacked the usual evidence of cows, yet the Browns had a large herd of Herefords.

Mary Dairy, as she was called, ran the herd and cared for them herself. The milk was cooled, bottled, and put on to her van in crates and she delivered it around the houses of the village. Some she made into cheeses and the pale left-over skimmed milk was fed to her calves. Her brother Billie attended to the rest of the farm with seasonal help from local people who were glad to earn the odd extra shilling.

It was late morning and they could hear the sound of bottles clinking together and found Billie in the washing shed, with its large metal sinks, washing the bottles, putting them into a second sink to rinse and then draining them upside down in scrubbed crates, ready to be filled after the evening milking. He looked up and smiled at them. 'Come to help?' he asked, offering them a bottle brush with a dripping hand, 'or just for a drink of our wonderful milk?'

'We saw a ewe and she seemed to be in trouble,' Margaret said all in a rush and together they told the big man where they had seen her.

'Should we let Mr Leighton know?' Oliver asked. 'She was in a sort of ditch and couldn't get out.'

'I'll call him later and let him know, but I'll be surprised if he needs telling. Watches them sheep like they were babies, old Leighton does.'

'*Can* we help, Mr Brown?' Oliver asked.

'Go on then, carry one of them empty crates across for me and wash a couple of bottles, then we'll stop and have a drink and maybe find a biscuit or a bit of Mary's cake. How'll that be?'

He swiftly drained the bottles out of the rinsing sink and filled the crates they brought him with upturned bottles, then, wiping his hands on his brown overalls, he led them into the living room.

Billie was a tall, muscular man, his arms and chest covered with thick dark hair. But his brown eyes were gentle, and paler, Oliver noticed, now they were under the better light of the room. He took off his overalls, revealing the brown denim dungarees he wore underneath.

The children stayed a while, warming themselves near the huge fire before putting on their outdoor clothes again and setting off up the hill for home. They stopped once to wave at Billie, standing at the entrance of the washing shed waiting for Mary to return from her second round with the last of the bottles, then lost sight of him as they crossed the ridge.

Oliver was still worried about the ewe. 'It will soon be dark. Shall we go and tell Mr Leighton, in case Billie Brown forgets to call him?'

'We'll be late for dinner.' Margaret said.

'Lunch,' Oliver grinned. 'Mother calls it lunch.' They talked in an exaggerated imitation of Evie's voice for a while as they made their way towards the fields owned by Leighton. They did not have to go far out of their way. The old farmer was walking towards them before they were in sight of the village road.

'We saw this ewe—' Oliver began, but the old man just nodded and pulled two brown eggs from his pocket.

'Thanks.' He walked on with a brief nod, not even asking for confirmation of the ditch where his sheep was trapped.

'He'll wear his tongue out.' Oliver whispered with a chuckle.

In a field to their right was a solitary cow. She was all that was left of Leighton's herd. With only himself and Sidney Davies to work on the farm, he could no longer keep cattle, but he had been reluctant to part with the last one. The regular visits to the cow shaped his day and made him feel needed.

Oliver and Margaret stopped to look at the cow, but there was something about its shape that was wrong. It was cloudy now and the light was misty and unclear. Margaret thought she had seen a ghost.

Then the figure of the cow separated from the alien shadow and they saw with relief that it was the gypsy girl.

She carried a bowl and, from the way she walked, it was full of milk. Oliver and Margaret looked at each other, then back at the girl who was stealing from Mr Leighton. If Mr Leighton followed them back he would see her. Afraid to shout a warning that might be heard by the farmer, they stood still until the girl slowly pushed her way through the hedge and stood beside them. The enamel bowl was brimming with milk.

'Don't you tell,' she said warningly, her dark eyes glaring at them. ' 'Tis little enough for him to lose.'

'I—I think he might have seen you,' Oliver stuttered.

'We called to tell him about a sheep in trouble,' Margaret explained, 'he must have been able to see you.'

The girl gave an explosive sound which they guessed was an oath, and half ran, half walked down the lane, Oliver and Margaret following at a distance.

Margaret began to shiver. The lane dipped at this point and the cold settled in the hollow in a river of cold air.

'I'm freezing,' Margaret said. 'I forgot my hat and gloves, let's run.'

They ran past the gypsy girl still struggling to adjust her

pace for maximum speed and minimum spillage, and hurried down the lane to the main road. At a more sedate walk, they continued back to Evie and lunch.

A few hours later, when Constable Harris rode his bicycle up the lane to the gypsies' camp, a couple of nanny goats, borrowed in frantic haste by Clara, grazed peacefully outside the caravans.

'Now why would my girl bother to steal milk?' Clara asked reasonably, pointing to the full udders of the goats, 'Old Leighton must have been mistaken.'

Inside the *vardo*, the girl still cried from the hard slapping Clara had given her for being so stupid and dishonest. 'A good con is one thing,' she had told the girl between blows, 'telling fortunes and promising folk what they hope for is good dishonesty. But taking for no reason, that's bad dishonesty and no good will come of it.'

The removal men had gone and Amy, Victor and Nelly had stopped for a snack when Phil Davies arrived.

'Post on a Sunday?' Amy asked.

' 'E can smell a teapot and cakes faster than a fox!' Nelly laughed, taking down another cup. ' 'E usually 'as three breakfasts and on a Sunday 'e feels deprived!'

Phil laughed good-naturedly and explained, 'I came to see if you need any help, Amy. Our Maurice is on his way with a clothes line and a post. Sidney's walking down with him. Mam said you didn't have one.'

'Thanks Phil. That is kind of her. What about putting these light bulbs in for me, you're taller than me.'

Maurice and Sidney arrived with a pole carried between them and cemented it into the ground while Nelly and Amy busied themselves filling cupboards from the boxes. By late afternoon everything was straight.

It was dark when there was a knock at the door and Maurice, being nearest, answered it. A beautiful girl stood there and for a moment Maurice was too surprised to speak. In the light shining from the hall, he saw a slim, fur-wrapped figure, legs encased in boots and hands hidden by furry gloves. Her hair was almost lost in a pale fur hat, its colour blending with the wisps of hair that showed around her face. She looked at Maurice with her beautiful large eyes and as he met their gaze, the world seemed to stand still. So little of her showed from under her coat that it seemed ridiculous for him to know that she was beautiful, but he seemed able to see through the wraps to the loveliness underneath. He stuttered like a schoolboy until she smiled brilliantly and said, 'I'm Delina Honeyman. Is my father here?'

'Hello, lovey,' Vic called. 'Amy, I'd like you to meet my daughter. Come on, Maurice, let the girl come in!' Vic laughed at the effect his daughter was having. Delina came in and handed Amy a pot of miniature roses.

'From my mother,' she smiled. Vic smiled at Nelly.

At the same time that Amy and her friends were busy at the new house, called 'Heulog', which Amy had learnt meant 'Sunny', Sheila's parents were moving their possessions into the flat. Ralph walked down after seeing the furniture taken from his mother-in-law's home and by the time he reached the shop and had used the new key to open the door at the side, the place was looking organised, though rather too orderly and unwelcoming. It would take a few weeks of living there before it felt like home.

'Can I walk up to Gran's for a bit of fresh air?' Sheila asked.

'No you can't!' Mavis was sharp with her daughter these days. Ever since finding her half-dressed at the fireworks party, she had watched Sheila constantly and had even telephoned the shop to make sure she was at work, and not out gallivanting with some man.

'When you tell me what you were doing up in the woods and who you were meeting, *and* where you got the money for all the new clothes I found in your drawer, then, perhaps, you can go out again without me on your tail!'

'I told you, Mam, I saved for the clothes. What d'you think? You think I've been paid for it, don't you?'

Mavis was shocked. Such things were hardly thought of and certainly not spoken of in decent company. She was holding back tears of despair when she heard Ralph's footsteps coming up the stairs.

At seven o'clock the family sat down to eat. Then they made up the beds and unpacked the last of the boxes.

'I think I'll go to bed,' Sheila said. 'I'll take a book and read for a while.'

'I won't be long after you. I'm tired, and I have to be up early to start my new job tomorrow. Good night, dear,' said her father.

At ten the flat was quiet, but Sheila waited, listening to the small sounds that were strange to her in the new room. The traffic was not heavy but there were more cars than she had heard from the bedroom in St Illtyd's Road. Lights swished across her curtains and she wished she was out there, driving along with Maurice and leaving her parents and Hen Carw Parc for ever.

The light in her parents' bedroom clicked off and still she waited. Only when no one had stirred for a long time did she rise and tiptoe to the landing.

The only sound was the gentle snoring from her father and she went slowly down the stairs, treading at the side and holding her shoes in her hands. She was fully dressed and only needed to put her shoes on and throw a coat over he shoulders as she stepped outside. She walked softly acros the road and up Sheepy Lane to the track leading t Maurice's house.

A light showed, and looking through the unclosed curtain she saw Maurice sitting reading, beside the fire. Opposit him Ethel sat crocheting and a radio played quietly. Sh pulled a thin branch and tapped the glass with it, waving t attract Maurice's attention without disturbing his mother.

After what seemed an age he looked up, stared in surpris but did not answer her smile. Her heart thumped as sh waited for him to join her. She risked an occasional glanc feeling more conspicuous now Maurice knew she was ther and not wanting to be seen by his mother. She saw him clos his book and stretch. He said something to his mother wh nodded and went on flicking the hook in and out of th white wool.

Shivering in the cold night air, she saw him take a co from behind the door and as the door opened, heard hi say, 'Won't be long, Mam. Just a stretch before I go t bed.'

The door closed behind him and Sheila ran to him, pres ing herself against his warmth, exaggerating the shivering.

'Warm me, Maurice, warm me now.'

Nelly stayed late at Amy's. She watched Victor Honeyma and he knew that she would not go until he did. Mauri had offered to walk Delina home, and they had left togeth some time earlier. Everyone could see he was entranced b the girl, and she had seemed to find him equally fascinatin

'Tell Mam I won't be long,' Vic had called after the with a challenging smile in Nelly's direction.

Margaret came home with Timothy at seven. She want

to see her bedroom first but Amy coaxed her into the living room to fetch more cups.

'What? Already finding me a job to do,' she sighed in mock dismay, 'before I've even seen my own room?'

They all waited silently for Margaret to see her piano and were surprised to hear, not cries of delight, but tearful sobbing.

'Mam, it's beautiful,' the girl wailed. 'I wish Freddy was here to see it.'

'Freddy's already seen it,' Amy said. 'He helped me choose it. And he bought the music case for you.'

This resulted in more tears and Margaret only cheered up when she sat down to try out the piano.

Amy yawned a little later, after Margaret had played a few of her pieces, and Nelly nudged Victor Honeyman.

'Give us a lift 'ome, why don't yer?' she said firmly.

It was strange for Amy to walk to the shop the following morning and take out a key to open the door feeling rather like an intruder. The shop flat had been her home for so many years and, with first Freddy leaving, and now renting the place and going to live at 'Heulog', she had a sense of unreality. It was like finding yourself on holiday without any memory of setting off.

She unbolted and unlocked the back door with the new keys, having had to satisfy the post office over security before the changes. She moved as quietly as she could, conscious of every small sound, afraid of disturbing her new tenants.

The green grocery had arrived and was stacked against the back wall. She carried it in and began putting it outside the shop window for Constable Harris to make his usual complaints. She was filling the till, putting a selection of coins in each compartment, when the sound of footsteps came clearly through the locked door at the end of the shop near the side door. There was only oil-cloth on the stairs and Sheila's feet clattered as she hurried to catch her bus.

A few minutes later a second, more sedate set of feet followed as Ralph went outside to wait for his lift. Amy wondered if Margaret had caught her bus and wished she could have waited with her this first morning. She waited for the third set of feet but remembered that Mavis was starting her new job a little later. She was surprised therefore to hear Mavis come down and enter the shop.

'Did you know the tap drips?' she said. 'It kept us awake all night. I'd be grateful if you would get it fixed straight away.'

The visit was the first of several. Mavis asked agitatedly for an extra cupboard, a new mat for the kitchen as the one there was old and a little frayed, and even for different pillows as the ones Amy supplied were too thin. Amy sighed louder at each request but promised they would be attended to.

'Well, furnished is what it says, you know,' Mavis said and Amy just nodded patiently.

Milly Toogood was the first customer, wanting a tuppeny ha'penny stamp. 'For the football pools,' she explained. 'Settled in all right, have you? Plenty of helpers you had. All right for some, getting left a house then half the village turning out to help you move into it.'

'Yes, lucky I am.' Amy bustled around, hoping to avoid long conversation. Milly had too little to do, living with her daughter above the fish and chip shop. She did nothing all day except wander around with Sybil Tremain in tow, but she always had plenty to say, none of it riveting and Amy was always abrupt with her.

Amy stood and watched for her daughter as the bus passed and was relieved to see her red hair and gave a wave. Leaving Margaret early in the morning would not do, the girl would have to come to the shop and leave for school from there, Amy decided. The holidays were going to be difficult without Freddy to help.

She missed Freddy, but he had gone and she couldn't change that. She had leaned on him long enough, she knew that. He had to go. She shuddered at the thought that one day Margaret too would leave her. Loneliness overwhelmed her suddenly and she didn't see Phil Davies wave as he passed on the way to his mother's and a second breakfast.

The days passed and Amy settled into a routine. It was when she was carrying some vegetables outside one morning to put a display that a pair of hands lifted the heavy basket full of onions from her. She looked up to see Billie Brown's tawny eyes smiling at her.

'Let me take that, girl, you shouldn't be lifting heavy things when there's a man around to help.'

'Makes a change, a fellow being around when he's needed,' Amy retorted. 'What are you doing so far from the farm this time of the morning?'

'Your Margaret left her gloves and hat when she came over with young Oliver last Sunday. Couldn't get here before, not sure where this new house of yours is, so I waited to catch you in the shop. Sure to find you here, I thought.'

'Where else?' She straightened the sacks and boxes until she was satisfied they could not be any neater.

'They weren't a nuisance, were they? I didn't know they were going to call on you.'

'Nuisance? Damn me, no! Lovely to see a couple of youngsters about the place, tell them to call any time. Bring their mother too,' he added, touching her shoulder with his large hand. 'It's a long time since you came to see us.'

'There's never any time. Working from eight-thirty until five-thirty and then having to do the books as well as housework and cooking. Not that I'm grumbling, mind. I'm very happy with my life.'

'But lonely?'

'No I'm not! Everyone thinks because I haven't got a man to slave over I must be lonely,' she snapped.

'I only meant with Freddy going away—'

'I'm sorry, Billie. I get that remark so often that I jump before I hear the end. Yes, I miss Freddy, but he has to make his own life. I dread the day when Margaret leaves, she's only eight yet, but the time passes so quickly. It's something everyone has to face, though *you* won't! I doubt your sister will marry now and leave you.'

The side door opened and Sheila came out. She wore more than her usual amount of makeup but it failed to hide the paleness about her eyes, and the unhappy set of her mouth.

'Everything all right, Sheila?' Amy asked, hoping the girl wouldn't start to tell her her problems. She didn't like Sheila and was not in the mood for other people's worries.

'I don't feel too well, Mrs Prichard, but don't bother about me, I'll be all right.' She reached into her handbag and brought out a letter. 'Would you post this to Freddy for me, please? I've heard from him but lost his address.'

'I'll see to it lunchtime.'

Sheila said goodbye, smiling enticingly at Billie, but the gestures and the smile were automatic and she forgot him a moment later as she boarded the bus to take her to work.

'Trouble, that one,' Billie said.

'You're right. I'm tempted to burn this.' She held up the

letter. 'But, as I said before, like it or not, it's his life.'

Sheila's love for Maurice was as ardent as ever, but she sensed a cooling off in him. When they parted, she almost had to push him into agreeing to meet her again. Since she had moved into the flat, she had continued to sneak out after her parents were sleeping, but twice she had been unable to see him. She waited far into the night before walking home, her need for him a stressful ache.

Tonight she stood at the window and watched Ethel make herself a cup of cocoa, wind the clock and damp down the fire before going to bed. Sheila pressed her face against the cold pane to read the time on the clock. Almost one. The cold ate into her bones. She would give it another fifteen minutes, then go. It was already difficult to get up in the mornings, but without his loving she found it hard to sleep anyway.

How could she win Maurice over again? She wanted to be married so much, to be her own boss and not have her mother dogging her footsteps wherever she went. Not to have to get the bus into town every day and sell boring people boring dresses. Oh Maurice, she sighed silently, don't let me down.

Inside, Ethel pulled on the chain and lowered the height of the flame around the gas mantle. The room sank into darkness, and not even the fire could be seen. Sheila felt tears begin to slide down her cheeks. She had been so sure Maurice loved her. What had gone wrong?

He came at last, carrying his bicycle on his shoulder as he walked up the muddy track. She hurried towards him, longing for his warmth.

'Maurice, I'm so cold. Where have you been?'

'You shouldn't have come, Sheila. You'll make yourself ill, standing around in this weather.'

'Let's go inside.'

'No.'

She was alarmed by his attitude. He held her, but did not bend his head to kiss her. She stared at the door and moved towards it. 'I'm frozen. Let's just go in for a few moments, for me to warm up.'

'You shouldn't have come.'

'I had to. I have to talk to you.'

'It's over, Sheila. It's been fantastic fun, you're a great girl, but it's finished. Sorry.'

She drooped against him like a cut flower. He had to tighten his arms around her to prevent her falling. She pressed against him but he eased her away.

'I've tried to hint—but there's no easy way to say it.'

His thoughts were still with Delina Honeyman, who he had just left. They had been to a carol concert and his mind was bursting with the joyous music and the thrill of sharing it with Delina. He found it hard to listen to Sheila's pleadings; she was already an embarrassment to him. But the effect of meeting the charming, beautiful and gentle Delina was so devastating that he was kinder to Sheila than he would otherwise have been. Delina had released in him a new compassion and he was kinder to Sheila because of it.

'Look, I know it's hard on you now, but I'm not the sort for a long-term affair, not yet. Got no prospects, and no desire to settle down. Not for a while. After being away for five years I need time to find my feet, sort myself out, decide what I want to do with the rest of my life.

'I haven't got a job yet. Demob money's all but gone. Got to get myself sorted, see. You're best looking for someone more settled. There's a bloke somewhere just longing to find a lovely, passionate girl like you. You've got a lot to offer a man, you have, and no mistake.'

It was a long speech for him, and although it was full of clichés, it was as sincere as he could make it.

'Love me once more, Maurice, please.' Sheila pressed her eager body against his and reached for his lips. He turned away and gently pushed her from him.

'Best not. End it clean, shall we? I'll walk you back home. Right?'

'All right, but let's go up the lane and around, the long way?'

Why not, Maurice thought. It would definitely be the last time.

Phil stared at the letter. It was not for Netta Cartwright, but for Johnny. He didn't get many letters, and this one was from the council. He wasn't putting up for the council as well as Timothy Chartridge, surely? He wondered who would stand the better chance: enthusiastic Johnny, or the staid Tim. His eyes brightened at the thought of using his mother's large black kettle to steam the envelope open. Not that he ever had, but it was something he often dreamed of doing. 'Damn,' he muttered quietly, 'do anything like that and Mam would clout my ear, old as I am!' He went into his mother's kitchen and called, 'Mam, there's a letter for Johnny Cartwright this morning, from the council.'

'Be about the house, I expect, but don't say anything yet.'

'What house?'

'Well, I don't know for certain, but rumour has it that Fay's applied for the empty house up on St David's Close.'

Phil sat down and gasped. He had been keeping the news of Fay's interest in the house to himself.

'Mam, *I'm* the postman. I'm the one who's supposed to gather all the news. You hardly ever go out. How do you do it?'

'Sausage with your egg?'

Maurice came sleepily downstairs and held his hand out for a cup of tea.

'Make any more noise and the roof'll fall in,' he grumbled to Phil. 'There's loud you talk.'

'Should have been up hours ago, lazy sod,' Phil retorted. 'When are you going to get some work?'

'Got any ideas?'

'Not unless you want to try Leighton's farm with our Sidney. He's short of a man and might take you on.'

'I've already tried him and there's nothing except occasional jobs, like filling in that stinking pond.'

'What about Mary and Billie Brown then? Do they need anyone?'

'No,' Ethel said, taking a couple of sausages from the pan over the fire. 'Not much future in farming unless you work for yourself. Ask Sidney, he wishes he'd learnt a trade like our Teddy.'

'Talking about a trade, what about the building trade? Prue Beynon wanted Freddy to join the firm but he chose the army instead,' Phil said. 'Perhaps she'll have a vacancy. Especially with the baby and all.' He glared at his mother. 'Kept that to yourself for long enough, didn't you?'

'I'll go and see Prue Beynon later,' Maurice said.

'Suddenly very keen to get work, aren't you? You must be broke.' Ethel handed him a second cup of tea.

'Or wanting to settle down with some nice girl?' Phil teased. 'From what I hear you've been out with every eligible female from here to Cardiff.' He was surprised when Maurice did not retaliate. Perhaps there was a girl.

Mary Dairy and her brother arrived with the milk. They were sipping their tea and trying some of Ethel's biscuits when Bert Roberts knocked at the door. As usual, he was outraged about something.

'Call this a village,' he shouted as soon as he opened the door. 'No pub, only a tiddly little village hall, nowhere to meet, it's ridiculous.' He took a cup and saucer from the shelf and helped himself from the teapot.

'Tea's a bit strong,' he complained and Ethel nodded towards the kettle. He added some water, pulled a disapproving face and continued his tirade. 'We're having to cancel the gardening club meeting. The hall is needed for an election. Call it a church hall? It's no wonder it doesn't collapse from shame, having to listen to all those lies. Elections! Rubbish!'

'Who hit you?' Billie asked, laughing at the outraged face.

'Well it isn't right. The sooner we get a local man on the council the better. If that pompous ass Timothy Chartridge gets elected I'll be after him to get a few things done.' He didn't wait for anyone to comment but hurried on. 'See the new people are in Amy's flat. A couple from the council houses. That daughter of theirs is a bit of a tart by the look of her.'

Phil looked at his brother for a reaction. 'I've seen you with her, haven't I Maurice?'

'No, not me. Not my type at all.'

'Best for you too. Dangerous, women like that.'

'I have met a girl though,' Maurice said. 'I don't know if you've met her. She's a teacher and lives up in St David's Close. Victor Honeyman's daughter.'

Phil closed his eyes, rubbed his nose and looked thoughtful.

'Yes, I know the girl. Didn't Vic get the sack after letting Harry Beynon have goods he hadn't paid for or something?' He thought again. 'Yes, Delina she's called. Beautiful too. Works in Llangwyn Junior School.'

'That's the one, she's a lovely girl. I'll be seeing her tonight.'

Phil looked at his younger brother then at his mother and mouthed the words, 'he's smitten,' nodding wisely.

Prue had a letter that morning in answer to her complaint about Phil Davies's late deliveries. She had written to the Post Office stating that her business was suffering because he deliberately left her until last and stopped on his rounds for several cups of tea and gossip-gathering.

When the doorbell rang she was alarmed to see Phil's brother on the doorstep, but he was smiling.

'I'm busy,' she said by way of greeting. 'Was it something important?'

'Well, yes. I was wondering if you're thinking of taking on any extra staff? I know you asked Freddy and he chose the army and I thought that if you still needed someone, like . . .' The words went on and on and he wished he had rehearsed what he was going to say. He had meant to tell her how useful he would be and how reliable, but ended up sounding like a dog begging for a bone.

'You'd better come inside.' She opened the door wide and then went ahead of him to sit behind the kitchen table, to hide her swollen belly. 'I thought you had come to protest. I've written to the Post Office about your brother. His deliveries get later and later. He spends hours chattering instead of getting on with his work.' She waited for him to protest anger but he did not.

'Quite right too, Mam's always going on about it.'

Maurice guessed Prue was testing him and he very much wanted work, but he made a mental note to warn Phil. 'I think that if you take money for doing a job you should give it all you've got.'

'And working for a woman, does that offend your male ego?'

'It would just make me more protective for her interests. Men have to look after women, don't they?'

Prue stared at him and tried to sum him up. Nice looking, although a bit common. Plausible, a bit fond of exaggeration, but a slick tongue was not a disadvantage in business.

'Write me an application for the job and send any references you have and I'll let you know in a few days.' She went to rise but changed her mind, conscious of her rounded body. She stayed behind the shelter of the kitchen table, 'See yourself out, will you?'

'Thank you, Mrs Beynon, I promise I'll do a good job for you if you take me on.'

'Goodbye, Maurice.'

She sat for a while after he had gone. The fact that he had not protested at her complaint made her warm to him at once. He seemed a likeable young man, confident and chatty. Yes, he might do very well, but first she had to find out more about him. He had been away for five years and in the army too. That must change a boy and make him grow up with standards different from those of his home. She would have to make sure there was no scandal attached to him.

There was only one Junior School in Llangwyn and Maurice went there at three thirty and sat on his bike, waiting for the children to leave, and then the staff. Delina came out last of all, when he had almost given up hope and ridden home.

He reached the gate at the same time she did, pushing along on one foot, ringing his bell to attract her attention.

'Hello. So this is where you work is it?'

'Maurice, what are you doing in town?' She smiled at him, her delight in seeing him evident.

Sometimes Maurice knew it was best to play games and pretend, but not with Delina. 'Waiting, hoping to see you,' he said. 'I found out where you worked and I came along, hoping I'd chosen the right school!'

'I'm glad,' she said with equal honesty.

'Got time for a coffee?'

'Yes, but I mustn't be long, Mam will wonder where I am.'

'Right then, The Copper Kettle suit you?'

'They do lovely home-made doughnuts there. Do you like doughnuts?'

'My favourites! True!' They both laughed at the delight of discovering a mutual pleasure and, pushing his bicycle, walked to the café together.

'It was nice at your house the other evening. Your brothers gave us a good game of Monopoly, didn't they? But,' he added, 'I'm looking forward to this, talking to you just the two of us.'

They swapped details about each other's families, and talked silly talk about favourite things, but true to his word, Maurice did not try to persuade her to stay longer than half an hour. As he walked her to the bus stop he glowed with the happiness that even a simple cup of coffee and a doughnut could create in the right company. She told him she loved walking and cycling and was interested in wildlife. Maurice could think of nothing more enchanting than walking with this lovely creature beside him. When her bus left he raced after it for a while, as excited as a child who has just discovered Christmas.

He thought of the many girls he had met and from whom he had parted with very little disappointment. Delina was so different it was impossible to explain.

'It's a desire to care for her,' he told Ethel later. 'I want to look after her and protect her. I never thought I could be so unselfish, but I would do whatever was best for her.'

'I'd better start saving my butter rations for a wedding cake, had I?' Ethel asked with a smile. 'Seems you might be in a hurry to get this girl to the altar.'

'Too early to say, Mam, but I hope so, I really do.'

Johnny saw the envelope propped up on the table as soon as he arrived home from work that Monday afternoon. He picked it up and looked at the postmark. What did the council want with him? He put it down to wait for Fay to get home. They usually opened any letters that came together.

'Letter there from the council,' he said as he kissed her welcome. He felt her stiffen in his arms.

'Open it, will you' she said, 'while I take off my hat and coat?'

Johnny tore open the envelope and read the letter with a look of horror on his face. 'Fay! What have you done?' he yelled furiously. He ran up the stairs and, glaring at his wife, waved the letter in the air. 'You secretly arranged for someone to see where we live and condemn it as unfit for habitation! What d'you think Mam will think of this? Have you no thought for her at all?'

Fay was frightened. She had never seen Johnny even remotely angry with her and he had never raised his voice to her before. Even when she was being her most difficult he had never been anything but gentle and understanding.

'I knew you wouldn't agree if I asked you first,' she whispered.

'I know now, you treated Mam to the pictures and tea in town and I thought it was a generous thought, while all the time you planned for the housing inspector to look at our home and say Mam had given unfit accommodation. How could you do it, Fay?' He stared at the letter again but the words danced in front of his eyes. 'And as for us moving to St David's Close, forget it!'

Johnny stormed back downstairs and Fay shrank down on the bed. No tears came but she shivered all over and she felt sick. She had been so sure Johnny would listen to her and understand her reasons. She couldn't stay in one room any longer. The insult to Netta Cartwright was not intended, and indeed had not been a conscious thought. Thoughtless, that was what she was, thoughtless!

In despair she tried to think of what to do. Seeing Johnny so angry, she was convinced he would never forgive her. If only she had taken him or Netta into her confidence, persuaded them it was right to get a place of their own without waiting to buy a house. She could have persuaded Johnny, and Netta would have supported her, they were so good. But it was time they moved out and the house on St David's Close was the one she wanted.

Darkness came and she still sat on the edge of the bed without moving to put on the light. She heard voices downstairs and knew Johnny was telling Netta what she had done. Childishly she wished she could climb out of the window and not have to go downstairs to face them.

The smell of food wafted up the stairs but did not make her hungry, only more nauseous. She undressed, changed into a nightdress and creamed her face ready for bed. She would wait until the house was quiet before she ventured into the bathroom to clean her teeth. It was unlikely that Johnny would be coming up to sleep with her tonight.

The front door banged and the gate swung on its hinges. She looked out and saw Johnny walking away towards the church and the school. He would be going to see Maurice. Then the tears started, tears of guilt and self-pity. She curled up on the bed and allowed them to fall.

She didn't hear the bedroom door open, but a shaft of light across the bed made her look up to see Netta with a tray of sandwiches and tea.

'Come on, *fach*, you've got to eat or you won't sleep.'

As Fay began to cry again, loud and unrestrained, Netta put her arms around her.

'There, there, let it come. I know how unhappy you've been sharing this little house, and wanting your own things about you. Need to show your personality, especially being newly married. That's what makes sharing through and through difficult. You aren't a cluttery, over-crowded, ornament-strewn sort of person, and you hate people to think you are. This house is full of all the people who've lived in it, not your sort of place at all. I can see how smart you'd make a house of your own. Johnny would be so proud of the way you'd make it. No clutter at all, and there's you having to live amongst mine.'

'I'm sorry if I offended you, I didn't think.'

'I remember when I first came to live here with my mother-in-law. Gas light then of course, and her unwilling for me to change to electricity. I thought I'd help her one day and took all her photographs off the top of the chest-of-drawers and the small tables. I left a vase of flowers instead. There's a cheek I had, thinking I was helping, saving her the bother of dusting them. But she needed them all, and it was her home, not mine. I was busting to cry that day, but I didn't.'

Netta's quiet voice went on soothing Fay until she was able to drink the tea and eat a sandwich. They went downstairs and Netta said, 'Now I'm off to see Nelly. Promised for ages that I'd go and see her. Tonight seems a good night. I'll be back at eleven.'

Leaving Fay sitting beside the fire waiting for Johnny's return, Netta took a torch and set off for Nelly's cottage.

It was ten o'clock when Johnny returned. He glared at Fay and she rose to make a cup of tea which she handed to him with a shaking hand.

'I'm sorry, Johnny. I always seem to be saying that to you, don't I? But I really am ashamed of being so cruel to your mother. She doesn't deserve it. I just didn't think of how she would feel.'

He reached out but did not take the cup. Instead, he held her wrist and pulled her down beside him, the tea-cup wobbling precariously.

'Why don't you talk to me about important things? You make me feel so useless. We're married. I love you. Why do you always keep things from me?'

'I want my own way too much I suppose. I hate sharing a house. Your mother understands.'

'So would I, if you'd bothered to talk to me about it.'

'I'm sorry, I shouldn't have left you out of my plan. It's your life too.'

'We never intended it to be for ever, just until we could save for a house of our own. *Yn wir*, it's lucky we are to be able to live here. Mam is put out too, remember, just to give us a chance to save.'

'I'm ashamed of hurting her, but I promise you, I won't forget how I feel about her and you at this moment. I'll find a way of making up for what I've done.'

The tea cup still wavered about in her hand and she pulled away from him and lowered it to the floor. When she sat up again, Johnny's arms were around her and crying, laughing, they hugged each other.

'I'll never keep things from you again.'

'See you don't,' he said gruffly, kissing her with more urgency. 'Share everything in future, right?'

'Everything,' she promised with a final sob.

And as for the council house, well, perhaps you were right there. Not the way you did it mind, *Iesu mawr*, Mam would have *helped* if she'd been asked! But perhaps we were too ambitious to expect to buy quickly enough to make the temporary arrangements work. We'll take the house. But no more secrets.'

'Never again.'

When Netta got back the house was silent and she smiled and gave a sigh. A dangerous moment had passed safely. There would be other storms but, for the moment at least, the waters of their marriage were calm.

Chapter Seven

Evie was in the bathroom getting the curlers out of her short, bubble-cut hair. There was a meeting that evening and she was going with Timothy. They were to go and collect Mrs Norwood Bennet-Hughes on the way and Evie was quite excited at the prospect of travelling with such an important person. She carefully unrolled her hair and brushed out each tight roll before making smaller curls around her finger with the tail comb.

'Oliver,' she called when she heard her son come in from school. 'Come and hold the mirror for me, will you?'

'Mother, Father said he would be about half an hour,' Oliver reported. 'He has a meeting with the teachers to talk about the Christmas decorations.'

'Oh. Well, I hope it is only half an hour, I don't want us to be late calling for Mrs Norwood Bennet-Hughes.'

She handed him a mirror and stood him on a chair to hold it so that she could see the back of her head. 'Now hold still while I do this bit.' She worked away, complaining from time to time when Oliver grew tired and allowed the mirror to tilt. When she was satisfied she lifted him from his chair. 'Go and read your book. I'm leaving you with Margaret Prichard this evening, so you'll have to do your reading straight away.'

'Must I?' he pleaded. 'I'd like to start on the model ship I bought in town. Can't I read later? Perhaps at Mrs Prichard's? Margaret won't mind.'

'How can I help you if you won't help yourself?' She pushed the book into his reluctant hands and he sat back sulkily.

'It isn't fair,' he grumbled.

'That's your answer to everything you don't want to do. Don't you want to be a good reader? Are you satisfied with being the worst of your father's pupils?'

'I'm not the worst.'

'Oh, so that's all right then is it? As long as there's someone more useless than you?'

He opened the book and wandered downstairs, not seeing the pages for the tears in his eyes. He sat in a chair near the window and looked up at the hill and the woods beyond. It was dark, but he would rather be out there in the cold with Nelly than in the warm, comfortable room with a book.

When Evie came down wearing a simple, tight-waisted dress with a long full skirt that swayed about her calves, he asked her for help.

'Mother, what's this word? He pointed to a page, following her across the room as she practised walking on her new high-heeled shoes.

'Oh, Oliver! Can't you work it out for yourself? That's what reading is, looking at it and gradually understanding it, not asking the moment you get stuck!' She really believed she was helping the child, encouraging him to overcome his learning difficulties.

'Dad says it's all right to ask once,' he defended. 'How can I understand when reading the letters sound like rubbish?'

'You call him "Father", and yes, it's all right to ask

about a strange word, but you've had this book three weeks and you still can't manage it. I despair of you sometimes.'

'Can I take it to Gran—Grandmother,' he quickly amended.

Evie glanced at the clock. Where was Timothy? He had to bathe and get dressed and there was so little time.

'Can I, Mother?'

'What now, Oliver?'

'Can I take my book to Grandmother. She listens while I read and it's better then.'

'No Oliver you can't. Get changed out of your school clothes. I'll be sending you to Mrs Prichard's soon. You'll go home with her and Margaret when the shop closes.'

Oliver thankfully threw down his book and went to his room.

The meeting took place in Cardiff and was concerned with the number of houses in the area still without proper drainage. Not a subject Evie liked to think about, but she needed to know a little about it if Timothy were to become a councillor.

On the journey home Mrs Norwood Bennet-Hughes asked about the situation in their own village. At once Evie panicked. This was dangerous ground. But surely her mother wouldn't come into the discussion? She would die of shame if Mrs Norwood Bennet-Hughes heard about the place in which her own mother lived. It would ruin Timothy's chances immediately.

'Most of the farms have cesspits,' Timothy said. 'Some are already on main drainage, as is the village, except for a few isolated houses. I don't think the problem is a serious one in this area.'

'What a lovely night.' Evie said, frantically changing the subject before Timothy mentioned Nelly.

'There's my own mother-in-law, of course,' he went on, unaware of Evie's dismay. 'Her cottage is definitely—'

'Look out!' Evie squealed and the car shuddered to a halt. 'Sorry dear. I thought I saw something. It must have been a fox, we do get a lot of them around here.'

'Yes, Mother-in-law had her chickens killed by one only a few weeks ago.'

Evie began to whisper a prayer.

'You were to saying? Her cottage—?'

'Yes, Mother-in-law's cottage is one of the isolated ones. Perhaps she would be entitled to some help to get a drainage system?'

'I'm sure there are more deserving cases.' Evie's voice was little more than a squeak.

'Nonsense, my dear. Give me her address and I'll send someone along.'

'It's a quaint little place. Mother-in-law lives simply but happily, but I'm sure she would be even more content if that problem were solved.'

Timothy continued discussing Nelly and beads of sweat broke out on Evie's forehead. Surely he'd stop before telling Mrs Norwood Bennet-Hughes that Nelly used the woods for a toilet? When they had dropped her off at her large house on the outskirts of Llangwyn, Evie began to storm at Timothy.

'Well, that is definitely that! Timothy Chartridge, I can't believe how stupid you are! It's the end of any hope you had of being elected to the council. What were you thinking of? When they see how my mother—your mother-in-law—lives, they'll laugh at the idea of you being a councillor. Help others, when you can't even persuade your mother-in-law to live decently?'

'It's her life. We shouldn't allow it to affect ours.'

'How can we help it?'

'By not apologising for her and not pretending she's any different from the way she is.'

'There might be a happy end to this disaster,' Evie said more calmly. 'Once they see the place they'll probably have it condemned.'

Evie met the new tenants of Amy's flat the following day. Sheila and her mother were dragging boxes out through the front door for the dustmen to collect.

'Good afternoon,' she said, politely.

'Oh, hello. I hope it's all right to put this out early. They call tomorrow, don't they?' Mavis said. 'There's so much to get rid of now the unpacking is finished.'

'No one would dare complain, we're all used to having Amy's rubbish strewn all over the pavement,' Evie said. 'Settled in happily are you?'

'Yes, such a relief to get a place of our own again. We moved in with my mother for a time,' Mavis explained. 'My daughter was such a busy child, I needed an extra pair of hands to cope and keep her amused.' She patted Sheila's arm affectionately.

'Oh, children!' Evie said. 'Family matters are such a worry at times. Not that I have any trouble with dear Oliver, a bit lazy that's all. But you're never free are you?'

At that moment the sound of laughter filled the air and, looking across the road they saw a group, including Nelly, coming towards them. In the group were several gypsies. Evie turned swiftly away, then decided it was useless to pretend, this woman would know soon enough. She knew how impossible it was to persuade Nelly to fade into the background.

'That,' she gestured, 'is my mother.' The way she spoke encouraged sympathy.

'Oh, you poor woman.' Mavis looked interestedly at the group. 'Which one?' she asked innocently.

'That must be obvious!' Evie snapped. 'My mother isn't a gypsy!'

She glared at Nelly who, head back, laughing her loud laugh, was being dragged along as usual by those enormous dogs. With chagrin she decided that the gypsies would have been preferable.

'My father was, of course, very respectable,' she said firmly. 'He would have been horrified at the way she has let herself go since his untimely death.' She walked off head high, angry with the embarrassment Nelly had once again caused. She times her appearances to cause the most distress to me, her own daughter! Abandoning her intention to buy some items from Amy, she went home.

Nelly and her entourage of friends approached the shop door and were met by Amy, who was just beginning to bring in the vegetables from the pavement. Amy greeted them with: 'If you're buying you can stay, but if you're selling, I'm closed!'

'I've come to buy, Amy,' Nelly said, offended. 'They're on their way to sell their flowers up on the council estate an' 'ave offered to 'old me dogs while I come in.'

'Sorry, Nelly. What can I get you?'

'Big potaters fer doin' under me fire.'

'I was coming to see you when the shop closes,' Amy said, weighing some potatoes and putting them into a bag. 'Will you be in?'

'Yes, I've just finished fer Mrs French, an' I won't move far once I gets 'ome. Stay an' 'ave a baked potato, why don't yer?'

'Thanks, but I have to get back, there's still a lot to do and I've only the evenings and a Sunday.'

Clara stood in the doorway, holding back the dogs, who were straining to get inside.

'Tell your fortune, lady, if you've a touch of silver for my palm.'

Amy was about to tell her to go when she changed her mind. 'Yes,' she smiled, 'Why not? I only hope it's something good. I could do with a bit of cheering up.'

It was early-closing day and the shop was empty as most people had gone home for lunch, so Clara went in, handing the dog's ropes to another woman, who held the big basket of wooden flowers. Nelly beamed with delight and sat down on the crate of cabbages.

The till had been counted so Amy took a shilling from the paper bank bags and offered it to Clara, who frowned sadly. Amy sighed too and added eight half-crowns.

'A guinea,' she said. 'That should do it.' Clara took the money and began to study Amy's hands. She nodded, sighed, frowned and finally said, 'I see a marriage.'

'Fat chance!' Amy laughed.

'A marriage for you, not for you to attend. There's a house where there is much happiness. A baby too. I see a gurgling baby and you tending it, cooing over it, it belongs in your arms.' The hands were lowered and Clara looked up at the disbelief on Amy's face. 'A sad time of partings, but a coming together again.'

It was obvious Clara had finished and Nelly held out her soil-stained hand and asked, 'Anything fer me, Clara?'

Clara looked at the grubby, work-worn fingers and said, 'I see a visitor, a very welcome one and soon.'

'I 'ope it's George,' Nelly sighed.

Clara smiled. The news that George was on his way had reached her a few days before through the travellers, and she had waited for this convenient moment to tell her friend so it would seem she had read the news in her palm.

Amy's reading had been one of Clara's rare 'true' ones. There was to be a wedding, it was not certain how far away it was, but the wedding and the baby in Amy's arms were there. She wondered about the baby. Amy was without a man, Nelly had told her, and she was reaching an age when babies were less likely. Only time would tell.

Amy had bought herself a bicycle. It took a bit of nerve to get on it outside her house and ride to the shop but, having done it twice, she felt more confident as she rode home to collect some things she planned to give Nelly.

As she rode she thought of the gypsy's words. A marriage! Clara just meant to please her. But how wonderful it would be to belong to someone, to have a person who cared about you and looked after you. Yes, that was just a little hope put in the reading to please her. But the baby? No chance of her having another child. Unless Freddy? But no, he was too young and there wasn't anyone else. Then she remembered her sister. Prue, of course! The crafty old woman had known about Prue's baby, it was common knowledge now, and she had known that Freddy had gone into the army, hence the time of parting. The wedding was to make her think the guinea well spent.

Satisfied she had cleared up any mystery, she was smiling when she reached the house. Ah well, a fool and his money are soon parted, she reminded herself. But she did not begrudge Clara the guinea. The gypsies had a hard time and would spend the money wisely. They never had more than the necessities of life.

From her neatly stacked stock of linen she chose a pair of coloured kitchen towels, a few white tea-towels, a new floor cloth and a dishcloth and put them into the basket on her bicycle. She also took a few tins of soup and vegetables and, satisfied, set off back along the road and up the lane to call on Nelly.

She got off to push the bicycle as the lane grew steeper, and parked it against Nelly's gate.

'Get the tea on, Nelly,' she shouted, and gathering her gifts, she went down the path.

She was surprised when Nelly did not at once appear at the door. The dogs barked but did not leave the doorway. She pushed them aside to go in and was alarmed to see Nelly sitting on her big chair. She was obviously in pain.

'Clara didn't see this, did she?' Nelly said in greeting. 'I twisted me foot on a stone and went ploughin'. Me knees is full of grit an' me ankle's a bit sore.'

'I'll go to the shop and ring for the doctor.' Amy said, putting down her parcels and heading for the door, but Nelly stopped her.

'I ain't 'urt that much! Make me a cup of tea and put some of that in it will yer?' She pointed to a bottle peeping out from behind a cushion. She pulled up her dress to show the torn stockings and the cut knees.

'What are you going to do, put some gin on that too?'

'What a waste! No, I've got some ointment that'll bring out the grit a treat. It'll be good as new in a day or so.

Insisting on Nelly staying put, Amy began to tidy up the room, glad she didn't have to persuade Nelly to sit still. She gave the towels to Nelly. 'Put these out when your visitors come.'

Nelly frowned. 'Visitors?' Then she smiled. 'Ere, you don't want to take what Clara says as actual. Visitor fer me might have meant *you* was comin!'

'I mean someone from the council to talk about putting

the cottage on drainage.' Amy glanced at Nelly's face and knew she had not been told. 'Hasn't Evie been to see you?'

'I ain't spoken to 'er. Why? What's 'appened?'

When Amy had explained, Nelly looked even more troubled. She couldn't tell Amy, but she was worried about the ownership of her cottage still. If they began making enquiries, she would lose her home. She only half listened as Amy filled the larder with tins she had brought, and hardly noticed when the couch cushions were plumped up and covered with a woven bedspread.

'Do you still have those army coats on your bed?' Amy asked and when Nelly nodded absently she said. 'Take them off, and I'll bring you one of my bedcovers for a loan.'

'Thanks, Amy.'

'And Nelly, go easy on the "juice" will you? Just until after they've been. You know how daft it makes you at times.'

'All right, Amy. Thanks, you're a real pal.'

Amy left, telling Nelly to stay put and give her leg a chance to mend. 'But as soon as you're better,' she said as she walked up the path, 'get rid of those empty bottles!'

As soon as Amy was out of the way, Nelly stood up gingerly and with a few soft oaths at the pain, she put her coat on and went to see Mrs French. She would have to confide in someone and Mrs French would help if she could.

Mrs French was surprised to see Nelly back, this time without her dogs.

'Nelly? Did you forget something?'

'I got a problem and I could do with some advice. Got a moment, 'ave yer?'

'Of course. Come in.'

Nelly explained about the death of the cottage owner and the subsequent hoarding of the weekly rent. Mrs French frowned.

'I really don't know what the situation would be. I think it would belong to the Crown if there was absolutely no one to inherit. I'll ring my solicitor and without giving him any names, ask him to enquire.'

'That will cost money, won't it?'

'Don't worry. Just promise me six of your hens' eggs when they start to lay.'

When Nelly had limped away, Mrs French telephoned to make an appointment to see her solicitor the next day.

Nelly paused outside Mrs French's house, partly to rest her leg and partly to decide whether or not to go and see Netta. Then she saw a van pull up outside the Cartwrights' house and, unashamedly curious, she walked to her friend's gate and watched as Johnny opened the door and beckoned to the van driver, who was carrying a television set with the assistance of his mate.

'Blimey, Johnny! Won the pools, 'ave yer?'

'Come on in, Nelly, you can hold Mam up when she sees what we've bought her!'

Nelly forgot her aching knees and bustled in behind the delivery men.

'What's this?' Netta met them at the living room door.

'For you, Mam. From me and Fay to thank you for being so good to us.' Johnny made this speech, laughing in delight at the surprised look on his mother's gentle face.

The engineer fixed the set on a table in the corner and, with his assistant on the roof, tilting the H aerial one way and then another, fiddled with the knobs on the set until he was satisfied that the picture was as clear as he could get it.

All the time, Netta stood beside Nelly, both of them watching as the test card appeared and disappeared, stretched and shrank as the man made adjustments.

Netta offered the men tea but it was Johnny who brought in the tray. Netta couldn't take her eyes from the set.

'You can see why some call it the goggle box!' Johnny laughed, kissing his mother affectionately.

When the men finally left, Netta sat down and said in amazement, 'Well, I never did!'

'It's because of the council house,' Johnny explained. 'Fay and me, we've settled for the council house in St David's Close. Still save, we will, but not as hard.'

'Smashin' idea,' Nelly approved. 'Got a garden, 'as it?'

'Come and see! Mam's coming so you can come together.'

'Blimey, everyone is movin!' Nelly looked anxious as she remembered the cottage. 'I 'opes it ain't an omen. I've got someone comin' to look at me cottage. I don't want to be told to move.'

'Who's coming?' Johnny wanted to know.

'Somebody to do with plumbin', so Evie says.'

Johnny guessed why she was worried. 'We would start a riot if someone tried to move you. Don't think of it.'

'Just think. I might 'ave to go an' live with my Evie after all. Fate worse than death that'd be!'

There was a knock at the door and Netta tore herself away from the wonders of the screen to open it. Bert and Brenda Roberts stepped in.

'That right you got a television, Netta?'

'Yes, indeed. Johnny and Fay bought it for me. Seventy-five guineas they paid.' Netta led them into the living room and squeezed herself into a seat beside Nelly so the newcomers could have the couch. A while later, just as he was making tea for them all, Johnny answered the door again.

This time it was Phil and Catrin from next door, and Phil had sent a message to his mother.

'Don't mind if we have a look-see, do you Netta? We thought of sharing the cost and buying one for Mam now she's got the electricity, and we wondered what sort of reception we'd get.'

Netta ran out of milk and Maurice was sent back for some when he arrived with Ethel an hour later. Netta didn't see much television but she hadn't enjoyed herself so much for ages.

Nelly did not know who to expect on the day of the inspection. She sat and waited, dressed uncomfortably in a green dress which she had been given by Dorothy Williams. It was a bit tight, but by wearing a long cardigan, stretched around her ample hips, she looked fairly respectable. She wore lisle stockings held up with bands of elastic and her feet were forced into a pair of small shoes which were impossible to walk on without the occasional wobble.

On the table of the living room were the plates, cups and saucers that were usually packed away in a cupboard, and some cakes and scones which she had spread with some of her precious butter ration and covered with one of Amy's white tea towels. The dogs, much to their confusion, were tied up in the garden. Nelly had even managed to dig over the surface of the chicken run to make it look neater. Now there was nothing left to do except sit and wait, and worry.

She heard a car coming up the lane, its engine whining at the steep gradient. She stared at the gate, watching for her visitor, and was surprised to see, not a man with sheaves of papers and a worried frown, but Mrs Norwood Bennet-Hughes.

'Bloody 'ell, Evie's posh friend. Now I *know* I'm in trouble!'

'Mrs Luke?' The woman smiled and held out her hand to Nelly, who stood silently in the doorway, too afraid to speak in case she said the wrong thing. 'We are trying to discover how many homes in this area need improvements. I think your beautiful little cottage might well be one of them. May I come in?'

'Beautiful?'

'Yes, it's one of the most attractive places in the village. I've noticed it when I've passed. On the way to the castle you know, for various entertainments.'

Before she entered, she looked back and admired the chickens and asked about their predecessors who had been killed by the fox.

'I hope you have made these secure,' she said. 'It would be terrible for you if that happened again.'

'Like friends, they are,' Nelly began, but stopped for fear of offending.

The dogs were straining on their ropes to greet the visitor and Nelly was surprised when the woman went and talked to them, rubbing them behind the ears, which made the dogs look so ecstatic that they both laughed.

'Untie them if you wish,' she told Nelly, 'they won't bother me.'

'Chickens an' all?' Nelly asked, and did what was suggested.

They went inside and when Mrs Bennet-Hughes gasped with delight and began talking about the advantages of cooking on the big range, Nelly forgot her nervousness and they began to chatter like old friends. Cakes were eaten, tea drunk and the dogs lounged across the two pairs of feet, for both had taken off their shoes. The chickens walked in and Nelly crumbled a cake on the floor for them and they scratched about, their necks stretching and bobbing as if attached to their feet with invisible elastic. Mrs Bennet-Hughes stood up to leave with genuine regret.

'I'll see what can be done about the lack of a water supply,' she promised.

'I ain't got no money, Mrs 'Ughes or Bennet or whatever you calls yerself.'

'Don't worry, no one will involve you in a debt you can't pay.' Silently, she determined that Evie and Timothy would help. Nelly Luke was a dear little lady and deserved a little support from her wealthy daughter.

'I will make arrangements for someone to measure up and decide where the drains will go, but it's nothing for you to concern yourself with, my dear. Leave it all to those who are paid for it.'

The matter of drainage was nothing at all to do with Mrs Norwood Bennet-Hughes but she had been curious to visit the cottage and meet Evie's mother, and perhaps explain some of Evie's tension and snobbery. But now she had met Nelly and enjoyed their tea and chat together so much, she was determined to help all she could.

Nelly gave an enormous sigh of satisfaction when she had seen her visitor back to her car. 'A real lady, that is,' she told the dogs. 'An' Evie would never get on with 'er the way I do. Used to posh people I am, being a daily 'elp.' She went back in, still barefoot, having given up the uncomfortable shoes as soon as Mrs Bennet-Hughes had sat down. 'Come on boys, let's go an' tell Netta all about me visitor.' Shutting the chickens in and gathering the rope leads for the dogs, she set off down the lane, wearing her smart dress, the old navy coat fastened with a pin, and wellingtons. She was singing at the top of her voice.

Evie was at the corner.

'Mother, I understand Mrs Norwood Bennet-Hughes has called on you. And you dressed like that!'

' 'Ad a lovely chat we did. Real lady, an' she liked me cottage, an' she liked me cakes an' me dogs an' chickens. Real nobs ain't snobs,' she said, and laughed loudly at the rhyme. Evie shuddered.

' 'Ave you 'eard that Fay an' Johnny's movin' to a council 'ouse?' Nelly asked. 'Does that mean you'll cross *them* off your list of acceptable people now?' She laughed again. 'Snob, that's what you are.'

'You, Mother, will *not* be crossed off my list of acceptable people. You've never been on it!'

Maurice was a regular visitor to the Honeyman household. He and Delina spent every spare moment together, and their outings usually ended with an hour or so in the house on St David's Close.

He found himself taking an interest in things that he had rarely thought about before meeting Delina and when they weren't out at a concert or the cinema or for a meal somewhere in town, they spent their evenings mounting pictures for her pupils, or preparing pressed flowers and wild plants for the school.

Delina introduced him to all sorts of new pleasures – classical music especially, rather than the popular tunes he had previously loved. He looked around him and observed more birds and wild creatures and marvelled at their beauty. His eyes had been blind until Delina opened them for him with her enthusiasm for everything around her.

One evening in late November Delina brought home a collection of metal tubes of varying lengths. With Maurice and Victor's help she made a frame and looped string through holes in the top of the tubes, creating a set of musical bells to be used in the school carol concert. They had a lot of fun trying out different tunes and some worked and others did not. There was laughter and sheer enjoyment for them all except for Mrs Honeyman, who always seemed unable to join in. She would sit in her corner, hardly looking at what went on, listening to the radio turned down low, or humming to herself. For a while, Maurice was afraid she was ill, but there were times when she livened up and talked quite brightly and cheerfully. After a while Maurice observed that it was only when Victor was out that she changed.

From the few clues Delina gave, it seemed that the marriage had never been a happy one and when Victor had been accused of giving Harry Beynon goods he had not paid for, that finished it. Before that incident her sulking moods had frequently lasted for weeks at a time, but since then there had been no break. She simply did not want to speak to her husband; she was convinced he had brought shame and humiliation on them all and nothing anyone said would make her change her mind. Maurice could see that Delina kept the atmosphere at home cheerful and when she went, the household would be a very gloomy one.

The bells were packed away to be delivered to the school the following day and Maurice left for home. He said goodnight to Delina and walked down Heol Caradoc into Sheepy Lane. The air was damp and cold with the last of a rain shower. He pulled his overcoat tighter around him, tilted his trilby lower to protect his face a little, and crouched into a run. As he reached the track leading to the house the rain increased and he looked at the lights ahead of him, thankful to be in sight of the comforting warmth.

* * *

Sheila Powell sat at the window of her bedroom, looking down the village street. It was dark and although the rain had temporarily ceased, the sky was threatening. But she was determined to go out. It wouldn't be the first time she had got cold and wet waiting for Maurice.

A bus passed and in its headlights she watched a couple walking hand in hand, obviously in love. They stopped to kiss and Sheila felt envy stealing through her.

When the flat was silent and the clock showed eleven-thirty, she slipped silently down the stairs, her shoes in her hand. Pausing only to put them on, she ran across the road, anxious now that she had left it too late and Maurice would have already gone inside.

She reached the house just in time to hear him running, slipping on the muddy ground up the track leading to the house. He showed no pleasure when she greeted him, but she forced herself to ignore the harshness in his voice.

'Sheila, what are you doing here, and so late?'

'I thought I'd come for a chat.' She casually opened her coat to show him that underneath she wore only a thin night-dress.

'Go home, Sheila. You'll freeze to death standing here.'

'You can warm me if you like.'

'Go home. It's over between us, we've both agreed. You're a super girl but not for me. Don't waste your time.'

'It's that Delina, isn't it?'

'Yes.'

'She's been to see your mother, hasn't she?'

'She's been to tea, yes. Why?'

'You never took me to meet your mother. Not once. I'd have loved to come to tea.'

'I never took any of my girlfriends until Delina.' Maurice was getting a bit anxious. Sheila showed no sign of leaving and her shrill voice might wake his mother. He turned back up the track, hoping she would follow him.

'Go home now, like a good girl.'

'Good girl? Is that what you want then?'

'What I want is nothing to do with you. I don't want you!' He spoke softly but Sheila could hear the anger in his voice and stepped back in dismay.

'Maurice!'

'I'm sorry, but there it is. It was good fun but it's over. Now get home.' He pushed her towards the lane, his hand on her back until they were in sight of the road, and he watched as she crossed over. With a sigh he turned and walked slowly back up the lane.

He did not hurry. He was wondering how to explain her to Delina. Everyone who saw her thought she was a tart, and anyone seen with her would have a reputation difficult to live down. He wished he had never given in to the temptations she so blatantly offered. If Sheila talked to Delina, and he thought her quite capable of that, his future happiness could be in tatters.

Ignoring the now heavy rain he walked slowly up the track to where the dim light of the gas lamp gleamed faintly from his mother's living room. He took out his key in case the door was locked, though Ethel rarely bothered. Sheila was waiting in the porch. Her hair hung dark and damp down on to her shoulders, and her eyes looked huge in the shadows.

She had watched how slowly he walked and had climbed over the hedge after throwing her coat over it to cover the sharp twigs. Then she had run up the field, the grass wet and icy cold on her feet, her shoes abandoned at the hedge.

'One more time, Maurice, for old times' sake.'

It was tempting. The wildness of her rain-soaked hair and

pleading eyes set his body tingling with desire. With Delina things did not go any further than kisses, and it was hard to restrain himself, after years of taking what girls offered. Now, with Sheila here and willing . . .

'No. Go home. I'd—I'd only be using you.'

'Maurice, I'm so cold and wet—'

Maurice did not speak but, taking her arm, walked her back down the lane. He waited while she walked across the road and then, whistling nervously, he turned once more towards home.

Nelly and Netta had been to the cinema that evening to see *Ma and Pa Kettle*, and *The Sword and The Rose*. Nelly went back to Netta's for a cup of tea and a bite of supper and the conversation turned to the new affair between Maurice Davies and Delina Honeyman. Nelly loved a romance and this love at first sight was just perfect in her eyes. So she was surprised and disappointed, when, much later, she was out walking her dogs and saw a figure darting across the road and going into the side door of Amy's shop. Maurice was watching her, and when the door closed softly he went back up the lane, whistling cheerfully.

'Some bleedin' romance,' Nelly muttered sadly.

Chapter Eight

The day Fay and Johnny moved out of Netta's cottage and into their council house, Nelly hurried through her morning's work for Mrs French and knocked on Netta's door at one o'clock.

'I've come to see if I can do anything to 'elp,' she announced as her friend invited her inside.

'Fay has everything organised down to the last screw!' Netta laughed. 'But it would be nice to have your company. Fay and Johnny are up at the new place.'

The van arrived to pick up their few boxes almost as they spoke and, when it was loaded and the men had drunk their tea, Nelly climbed on board.

'I'll go an' see if they wants any 'elp up there, if not I'll walk back.' She held on to the side of the van and shouted with laughter when it started off and nearly dislodged her from the seat she had made for herself among the boxes.

To Nelly the place already looked surprisingly neat, but Fay, who hated even temporary disorder, was glad to see her.

'If you could give me an hour I would be very grateful. There's all the china to wash. It's been in store since I moved from Mother's house and it's filthy.' Fay showed Nelly what she wanted done and Nelly rolled her sleeves up over her fat arms enthusiastically.

'Lovely job that'll be, dearie, with plenty of 'ot water just like at Mrs French's. I'll enjoy meself.'

While Nelly washed dishes, Fay unpacked boxes and put the contents neatly away. Phil Davies dashed in, apologised for not staying to fix the curtains as promised, muttered something about a complaint and raced off on his bicycle as if a demon was chasing him.

'Fastest I've see Phil move since Leighton's bull followed him across the field!' Johnny laughed.

Nelly was full of admiration for Fay's orderliness. 'Just like Amy you are, young Fay. Gets things sorted even before you starts. Clever I calls that. I'd be in a muddle fer weeks, I would, if I had to move.' She went silent then, suddenly remembering her fear of losing her home. When she had finished the dishes, she walked sadly back to the village, though she had to smile when she saw Phil frantically running up St Illtyd's road, sweating and pushing his heavy bicycle.

'Look out, Phil,' she shouted, 'they're after you!'

'Some bugger is and that's a fact!' he puffed back.

Nelly passed Constable Harris too, but she turned away from his friendly greeting. She was a criminal, living in a house she had no right to. She couldn't look him in the eye and sidled past her eyes downcast.

She called in to report to Netta.

'Very smart it is, Netta, and your Fay, she ain't 'alf worked 'ard. All tidy like you'd never believe. An' neat? She 'ad your Johnny measurin' where to put pictures, would you believe. Not just stickin' 'em up like you an' me would. Measurin'!'

Although she enthused about Fay's organisation and neatness, the Cartwright's new home was too much like Evie's for her ever to feel at home there. Sparse was the word for it, she decided. Plain walls and very few pieces of furniture, and although it was true that they hadn't got their home complete yet, she guessed it would never have more than the downright minimum. A small table with a shepherdess statue and a bowl of flowers, which Fay had miraculously found time to arrange, were the only decoration so far and Nelly suspected it would stay that way.

She realised she had been silent too long and added quietly, 'Your Johnny's bought 'er a lovely bunch of flowers an' she's got 'em in pride of place on a polished table near the winder.' She looked at Netta who seemed a little sad. ' 'Ere, why don't we go to the pictures again?'

'I can't, really. I've promised to go and see the house once it's straight and—'

'There's a comedy on at the Plaza. Dean Martin and Jerry Lewis. Good laugh they are. An' Sidney Taffler's in the other one,' Nelly coaxed.

Netta thought for a moment and then said, 'Yes, I think I will. Better than sitting here listening to the silence.'

'Or the television!' Nelly laughed, her crooked teeth showing.

Later they met up at the bus stop after Netta had seen and admired Fay and Johnny's new home. When Nelly had walked down the lane, she wore wellingtons, which she left, poked upside down in Netta's hedge, for when she returned.

They waited in the queue for half an hour before getting inside and, to Nelly's delight, they were given a seat in the back row.

'Smashin' this is,' she chuckled, 'watchin' all the courtin' couples. Pays fer the dark, not the film, some of 'em!'

Her loud comments made one couple move and their places were taken by Maurice and Delina. Netta tried to hush Nelly, knowing how foolish young people could feel, but Nelly couldn't be stopped.

'Come fer a quick cuddle, 'ave yer? It ain't easy on a bike, is it?'

'Go away, Nelly,' Maurice groaned. He handed her a bag of toffees. 'Here, take these to keep your mouth busy.'

'That's his Delina,' she whispered loudly to Netta.

'Meet us after, Nelly, if you want a proper introduction. Shh!' hissed Maurice.

'Leave the love-birds alone,' Netta said with a soft chuckle.

'They aren't really in love. Not like your Fay an' Johnny,' Nelly confided, remembering how Maurice had met Sheila in secret.

Nelly settled down to enjoy the sweets and the film. Maurice and Delina were still there when they reached the part where they had come in, and with a pat on their shoulders and a hoarsely whispered 'Good-night', Nelly and Netta made their way along the dark row to the foyer. They wrapped their coats firmly around them before stepping out into the night to hurry to the bus stop.

Nelly knew how strange it would be for Netta to go back to an empty house for the first time in many years, so she invited herself in. 'Just fer a cuppa in case me fire's too low, got to get back then fer me dogs,' she explained unnecessarily.

Maurice and Delina waited until they were sure the two women were safely on the bus before they, too, left the cinema. They had come on their bicycles and although it was bitterly cold, they were not dismayed at the prospect of the ride home. Bicycles were their only means of transport and they were used to the discomfort.

Delina wore an old fashioned pixie hood which hugged

her head and kept the wind from her ears. It was unglamorous compared to her usual elegant clothes but Maurice found it very appealing, like everything else about her.

They walked up Sheepy Lane, pushing their bicycles, each with an arm around the other, in contented silence. Before they came to the end of the hedge-lined lane and lost their privacy, Maurice stopped and kissed her. She smiled up at him, her face a beautiful misty oval in the darkness.

'I've very happy when I'm with you, Delina,' he said. 'I want to spend every moment with you. I hate the time we're apart.' He stopped. It sounded so like he had sounded so often in the past, with so many other girls.

'I've said things like that before,' he admitted. 'I've been out with lots of girls, it seemed natural, but I do feel different about you. I want to protect you and love you and care for you always. I'd never allow any harm to come to you, Delina. You believe me?'

'I believe you've had lots of other girlfriends, Maurice, you're a good looking man,' she said, 'but I hope it's different with me.'

'You do? Does that mean—'

'Darling, I have to go now. Dad will wonder where I am.'

'Yes, of course. I don't blame him for worrying about you. Since I met you I've understood a lot more about loving and caring.'

She kissed him lightly and went on ahead, while he stood for a moment before following, running beside his bicycle before reaching her again.

'Tomorrow?' he asked.

'Tomorrow.'

When he had seen her safely into her house he didn't go back down Sheepy Lane but turned off before he reached there. It had become a regular occurence for Sheila Powell to be waiting for him. She sat in the front window of the flat, faintly silhouetted against the small table lamp, and watched for him. He had sensed her there this evening although he had not looked up.

Lifting his bicycle on to his shoulder, he climbed through the hedge and walked down the field, parallel to the lane, his shoes heavily coated with mud. Then he pushed through another hedge and into the track leading to his front door.

The moon lit his way and added a sparkle to the frost on the ground and the tree branches. He looked back up the fields and wished Delina were there to enjoy the spectacle with him. It was as if an artist's hand had touched everything with silver paint, glinting and dancing along the hedgerow.

He gave a sigh of contentment. The world was full of wonderful things and he would spend his life discovering them with Delina. He went into the back garden, avoiding the porch where Sheila often waited. He had not seen her for a few days and hoped she had at last given up on their affair.

He was puzzled and relieved that she had not approached him openly or called at his mother's house. She was still discreet, though he doubted that it was out of concern for him, more for fear of her parents' anger. She was twenty-one but was still a child in many ways. He felt a twinge of regret at the way he had used her, only to discard her abruptly when Delina came into his life.

It was late when Nelly left Netta Cartwright's, having watched an hour of television. She walked back and collected the dogs, whose greeting was ecstatic, and took them down to the main road and along to Sheepy Lane to circle around back to her cottage. It was a crisp, cold night and the moon lit her way clearly. Staying out late chatting with Netta meant she was too wide awake to sleep and a stroll with the dogs might relax her.

As she passed Netta's house, now in darkness, she felt a momentary sadness at the thought of Netta spending her evenings alone. She was used to being alone herself, but Netta had once had a husband and sons and all their friends to fill the small house, and it would be difficult to adjust.

Every morning, after visiting the woods, Nelly took the dogs out and gave them a walk through the trees and usually around the castle ruins. But this morning she rose early and went instead across the fields while there was hardly a glimmer of approaching dawn. She crossed the lane high above the gypsy camp and walked down to the farm where Mary Dairy was already filling her van with the previous night's milking for her first round.

There was a stream nearby where the boys of the village often went fishing. It was on land belonging to Billie and Mary, but the trees hid it from sight and it was only occasionally that the boys were seen and half-heartedly chased off. Mary and Billie rented out the fishing to a local hotel and so they had to discourage others.

It was rare for Nelly to walk this far but it was a beautiful morning, crisp and cold, with frost riming the grasses and the trees and bushes, spreading a counterpane of silvery white over the fields. She was tempted to wander further and further until she was in sight of the stream.

It twisted and bent half back on itself, running through meadows where sheep grazed, and around its banks grew willows, shady in summer and graceful in winter. Nelly was admiring the scene when she noticed someone standing in the water a little way off. Her face creased into a smile at the prospect of a chat, she called the dogs and slipped a rope through their collars. As she drew near the man her smile broke out into loud laughter. The figure turned and waved, and Nelly hurried to greet him.

'George! Well fancy! What are you doin' in that cold water, and almost naked too?' She couldn't stop laughing, full of delight and excitement.

George was wearing only a pair of long underpants and a long-sleeved vest, both of which streamed with water as he began climbing out of the stream. In a pile on the bank were his clothes and an old army shoulder bag which, Nelly knew, held all his worldly possessions.

'Lucky you didn't arrive sooner,' George said, jumping up and down to get warm. 'I've only just made myself respectable.' Water continued to pour from his clothes and Nelly waved a hand at him to hurry.

'Call that respectable? Come on, for Gawd's sake, get something on or you'll be frozen stiff as a board.'

George disappeared behind a willow tree which gave a little privacy. The dogs fussing around him excitedly, he discarded his vest and pants and, after wringing the water out of them, used them as an inadequate towel to dry himself. He dressed with difficulty, dragging his clothes over his still wet skin, and finally emerged dressed in trousers, a sports jacket, and a shirt and tie. As always, his black shoes were highly polished. Under the white beard his face glowed red, accentuating his clear, greeny-blue eyes.

'Nelly,' he smiled, 'you've spoilt my surprise.'

'That's a laugh, that is! What could be more surprising than me finding you prancing about like a water nymph?'

She turned away to pat the dogs, suddenly overcome by

shyness. George was a tramp she had met on one of her trips into town, and they had got married to stop Evie making her leave her cottage, but they hardly knew one another.

Sensing her unease, George chatted about where he had been since they had last met, and told her about the work he was going to do for Mr Leighton.

'I would have been here before this,' he said as they hurried back up the hill, George jigging about to get his circulation going and playing with the lively dogs, 'but I had a job of sorts, cleaning up in a small factory, and I wanted to stay until I'd saved some money before moving on.'

'Where have you been livin?' Nelly wanted to know.

'Nowhere you would enjoy. Rooms sometimes, but while I've been travelling back here, in empty houses and the occasional barn.'

Nelly could see he was shivering and needed to move faster than she could, with her painful hip.

'You go on George. The door's open, there's a fire going and the kettle's sure to be singin'. I'll follow at me own pace.'

'If you don't mind?'

'O'course I don't mind! Go on, before you freeze to death!' She watched him walking swiftly away across the field, his tall, thin figure disappearing through a distant hedge. Then she began to sing at the top of her voice.

When she reached home he was sitting in her big armchair and the fire was roaring cheerfully. She smiled contentedly; he always looked right in this room and made it seem more comfortable, somehow. It was nice to have someone of your own, even it it was only on occasions.

'Where's me cup of tea then?' she said, throwing off her heavy coat and kicking off her wellingtons.

'It's nice to be back, Nelly,' he smiled as he handed her a steaming cup.

'Stayin' long, are yer?'

'I'll be working for Leighton for a couple of weeks. He needs help raising his root crops. He's well behind and they should be in store. I've already seen him and he plans to ask someone called Maurice to give a hand too. Then, if I want it, there's plenty of work repairing the hedges and cleaning ditches. Sidney is his only help now and they're behind on all the autumn jobs.' He smiled at her as she refilled her cup. 'I won't stay here all the time though. It wouldn't be fair on you. But, if you don't mind, I'd like to stay for a couple of nights.'

'Stay as long as you like. If you can sleep in barns I'm sure you can get comfortable on my couch.'

'Thank you. Now, tell me about young Oliver.'

They chatted for most of the morning, and then George unwrapped a newspaper parcel from his bag and showed her two small fish he had caught that morning.

'I stayed in the brickworks last night and was up at dawn so I wouldn't be seen and went fishing. Then I wanted a wash before coming to see you.'

He had stayed one night at a reception centre and, although his clothes had been cleaned and he had bathed, he had been conscious of the strong smell the place left on him. The carbolic soap and the process of disinfecting his clothes were two indignities he found more and more difficult to accept. It was rarely now that he used the places designed for 'men of the road', as they were euphemistically called, preferring to find a room when he had the money. In between he would still choose a warm hay-barn rather than one of the starkly clean, almost Dickensian centres.

On arrival there, all who stayed had to strip for their

clothes to be cleaned, then bath in strong smelling water. After washing, they were given a hot meal and a night's sleep, followed by a good breakfast. They then had to do some small task to help pay for their accommodation.

George usually volunteered for work in the garden, preferring that to scrubbing the long wooden bench tables, or mopping the stone floors and white-washing the walls. The only buildings in which George felt at ease were hay-barns, and Nelly's cottage.

Although he had stayed a night in the brickworks, he could still smell the centre's strong disinfectant on his skin and on his clothes. He had tried to get rid of it by washing in the icy cold stream before putting on the new, albeit second-hand, clothes he had bought to visit Nelly.

'George, I don't like to think of you sleepin' out these frosty nights. I don't mind you stayin' here, honest I don't. The door doesn't shut so you won't find yerself locked out. Come an' go as you please. 'Ere, what d'you say we 'ave a night out at The Drovers?'

'About staying, I don't know. But the night out, yes! I've been looking forward to that and with my new clothes on we might manage not to get thrown out!'

They reminisced happily about the time last summer when a furious Evie had met them after they had gone from pub to pub and had been asked to leave by a landlord who insisted he did not serve tramps and gypsies. They went on chatting all afternoon and long into the night and fell asleep where they sat.

It was unfortunate for Evie that her first sight of George was when he was coming back from Leighton's farm the following day. She was talking to Mavis Powell when Nelly and George came down the lane with the two dogs in tow and Nelly shouted out, 'Evie, look! Yer dad's back!'

‘Your father?’ Mavis frowned at the startled look on Evie’s face. Evie had just been telling her that she had been brought up in a large London house, without explaining that she and Nelly had only one room in it.

‘Your father?’ Mavis repeated. ‘I thought you said—you gave me to understand that your father was a highly respectable man, and he looks—well—an eccentric is he?’

Evie uttered an explosive sound and in a low voice muttered fiercely, ‘That is not my father!’ and walked swiftly away.

Mavis waited to see the man, curious to meet him, but Nelly walked past without a word and hurried to catch up with her daughter.

‘Look who’s turned up!’ she shouted. ‘I found ’im bathin’ in the stream down by Billie Brown’s all but starkers. I ask you! In December!’ She laughed and George began to explain.

Mavis heard the words ‘reception centre’ and went into her front door horrified. The man was a common tramp. She wondered angrily where Evie got her airs and graces from.

When Evie went inside she called Oliver.

‘That dreadful man is back. You are not to go to see your grandmother until he is gone. D’you hear me? I forbid you to go there while that tramp person is staying there.’

‘But Mum—’

‘Mother!’ she corrected, her voice high-pitched with rage.

‘Please, Mother, can’t I even go and say hello? He is my grandfather.’

He could not have said anything worse after Evie’s encounter with Mavis Powell. ‘He is not your grandfather, Oliver and I don’t want to hear such a foolish remark again.

As if it isn't enough putting up with your grandmother, I have people laughing at me because she married a tramp! Oh the shame of it.'

'People say Gran is a character, Mother. Doesn't that mean it's all right if she does funny things like marrying someone like George?'

'Saying she's a character doesn't excuse her behaviour, Oliver. Just stay away from her until he has gone.'

'But if I see him I'll have to say hello, won't I?'

'For goodness' sake, Oliver! Can't you hear me? Are you too stupid to understand what I'm telling you?' In her anger she was more unreasonable with him than she might otherwise have been. 'We don't want you to talk to the man. He's an undesirable. He isn't your grandfather. Do not have anything to do with him. Now do you grasp what I'm telling you, you stupid boy? Now get out of my way. Read your library book, that will be more useful than thinking about that awful man.'

She went into the kitchen to unpack her shopping and Oliver heard her say to Timothy, 'As if I haven't enough to put up with, Oliver being so slow and so difficult, without my mother and her drink and her men-friends. I wish I could be shot of the lot of them! What chance do we have of leading a decent life with a family like this?'

'Don't be hard on the boy, it isn't his fault.'

'Oh, I suppose it's mine? I'm to blame for him being so thick he can't even read as well as most seven-year-olds!'

Upstairs Oliver tore up his book and poked it down the toilet pan. He was still upstairs when Nelly and George knocked on the door and asked to see him, and were turned away.

Margaret and Oliver walked up the hill wondering whether

to go and see Billie and May Brown. Although it was milder than of late, it was still tempting to head for the farmhouse and its big fireplace.

Oliver's parents had been invited to a dinner party and, although Evie disapproved of Amy, knowing she was the mother of two illegitimate children, it was very convenient to leave Oliver with her when she needed to go out. Today, as it was a Saturday, Amy had told him to come straight after lunch as Margaret would be glad of his company, and the children had set off for a walk without any real destination in mind, but their feet led them up the hill overlooking the dairy farm.

They stopped and sheltered for a while behind a small hillock and ate the chocolate Amy had given them. Oliver pointed down at the stream below them. 'That's where Gran found George,' he said. 'Fancy washing in there. It must be freezing!'

'Freddy used to fish there,' Margaret said. 'He said it was poaching but no one was likely to complain. He was caught once and Billie Brown came round to tell Mam not to let him go there again, but he stayed a while for a cup of tea and changed his mind. He said Freddy could go but always had to ask permission first, but Freddy never went again. He said he didn't want Mam soft-soaping someone so he could catch a few stupid fish.'

'What did he mean?' Oliver asked.

'Well, Mam looked at him and smiled and Freddy said she was flirting. He didn't like that at her age.'

'No, I suppose she is a bit old for that. Remember when we saw Maurice and that gypsy girl?'

'And Freddy and that awful Sheila Powell. Freddy liked her but I don't. I think she's a flirt.'

'She's quite old too,' Oliver said seriously.

'Let's walk along the bank for a while. We might see the kingfisher.'

'Or see a fish jump.'

They strolled along the high bank which had been broken by the autumn rains and hung over the water precariously. Slipping on a half-dried puddle, Margaret gave a sudden scream and slipped into the water. Oliver froze for a moment, horrified, then ran downstream, passing her before jumping in and grabbing her as she floated towards him. He lifted her out and they stood on the bank, covered in mud and slime, both shivering and crying.

'I think we should go to Brown's farm,' Oliver said between chattering teeth. 'It's nearest and I think we need to get warm as quickly as we can.'

They were still crying as, slipping and sliding in their wet shoes and trying in vain to get warm by wrapping their arms around each other, they pushed their way through hedges and ran through fields of cows and sheep. They arrived at the farmhouse just as Billie came out of the washing shed.

He didn't wait for explanations but called to his sister and they began undressing the frightened, shaking children. In a few moments they were wrapped in blankets in front of the roaring fire and drinking hot soup.

'I've rung Amy, and as soon as you've finished that food I'll drive you home,' Billie said, coaxing Margaret to take another spoonful of the home-made broth. 'She's closing the shop and going straight home. You can go there as well, Oliver as your parents are out.'

'They might not have gone yet, but I'd better go with Margaret in case, hadn't I?' Oliver said hopefully. He would rather have someone there when his parents were told what had happened. Now the sudden danger was passed and they were warm and safe, he grinned happily at

Margaret sitting opposite him in a heavy wooden armchair surrounded with cushions and blankets.

Amy was already at the house and the fire burned brightly when they arrived. She tucked the children up in bed with hot water bottles straight away.

'I'll tell your mother what happened Oliver, you brave and clever boy,' Amy's eyes glowed as she looked at him. 'She'll be that proud of your quick thinking! You stay where you are for tonight. The doctor's coming and I'm sure he'll agree that you should stay put.'

'Mother won't mind being shot of me,' Oliver said, without meaning to criticize. 'I'd like to stay, I'm so warm now.'

The doctor saw both children and declared them fit and well. 'But I'll just look in in the morning to make sure,' he said. 'Leave them where they are until then.'

'Yippee!' Oliver said. He grinned at Margaret, 'What an adventure!'

'Everyone says how clever you were, Oliver,' Margaret said seriously. 'I could have drowned and so could you. If you'd jumped straight in we could have been ages reaching each other and getting out.'

'I can swim,' Oliver said. 'I think I'm top of the class for that. I'm not stupid about everything, though Mam doesn't think it's as important as proper lessons. I haven't done any life-saving before though.'

'Goodness! How did you know what to do then?'

'I remembered floating sticks under a bridge with George and Gran. George explained about running ahead if I wanted to catch my stick and not going into the stream to try to follow it.'

'Thank you, Oliver.'

'It's all right.' He smiled again and this time she smiled back.

Downstairs, Amy began to shake as she realised how near the children had come to disaster. Billie went into the kitchen and made a pot of tea. He heaped sugar into it and stood over her while she drank.

'Thank you for what you and Mary did,' she said, trying to warm her chilled hands on the cup.

'*Diawl erioed*, woman, who wouldn't help a couple of half drowned kids? Not that they were half drowned,' he added quickly. 'Far from it. Oliver acted too quick for that. Wet they were, that's all, wet.' He watched as she drained the cup. 'Want me to stay do you, 'til the Chartridges come back?'

'Would you, Billie? I feel a bit odd. Frightened I suppose, thinking of what might have happened if she hadn't had Oliver with her. Fancy young Oliver being so sensible. He's always struck me as a fragile child, almost babyish. Far younger than Margaret, although they're almost the same age. Yet he worked out how best to save her.'

'Kids often surprise us,' he said. 'Your Freddy, he's always seemed like a man yet he's hardly sixteen. Heard from him have you?' he asked, trying to take her mind off the accident. He persuaded her to talk about how she missed him and what she had learnt about his new life through his letters, and gradually she relaxed.

When the knock came at the door, Billie answered it. Evie came in looking around for Oliver.

'Where are they?' she asked. 'In playing the piano? I didn't hear them.'

'They're in bed,' Amy said as she came into the hall.

'What?'

'He isn't ill, is he?' Timothy asked.

'No, he's fine, but they both had a soaking.' Amy explained what had happened, emphasising how well Oliver had coped with the emergency and had saved Margaret from a nasty fright, if not something worse.

'Oliver! He could have died!' Evie went white, 'I'll never let him out of my sight again.' She was very upset and Timothy had to calm her down while Billie went out to make more tea.

'Have you got anything stronger?' Billie asked, and Amy pointed to the cupboard where she kept a bottle of brandy. Evie was persuaded to sip at a glass between tears.

'It's best to leave him here tonight,' Amy said, her own fears fading in the face of Evie and Timothy's anxiety. 'The doctor said they were both perfectly all right, but he wants to see them again in the morning and they should stay in bed until then just in case.'

'In case of what?' Evie wanted to know, and the crying and panic began all over again.

Finally they looked in at the sleeping children and left for their own home. Amy smiled her thanks at Billie.

'I'm all right now. It was a help, you staying. That's one thing I'll never get used to, being on my own in a crisis.'

'Call me if ever I can help.' Billie said softly. 'I'll be glad to come, any time.'

'Thanks,' she said again. 'Come by tomorrow to see them. I think they'll want to tell the whole story over and over.' For a moment she shook again. 'Thank God they are here to tell it.'

Driving home, Evie began telling Timothy that she would only allow Oliver out when she could accompany him, but Timothy for once disagreed. He insisted that Oliver shouldn't be tied to his mother's apron strings. He had noticed Oliver's growing self-confidence and knew it would suffer a set-back if Evie made too much of the danger he had faced. He was enormously proud of Oliver's actions and did not want him punished for his remarkable calmness and good sense.

A few days later, Evie opened the door to Billie Brown.

'Called to see how Oliver is,' he said, 'and to bring him a little present for his bravery.'

'Oh, thank you. Er, you'd best come in.' Evie looked doubtfully at his disgustingly dirty wellingtons and was relieved when he slipped his large feet out of them and stood on her doormat in his thick socks. He followed her into the kitchen, lumbering after her, his large frame seeming to fill the hallway. Evie's lips tightened. She did not really approve of people coming uninvited, especially someone as big and oddly dressed as this farmer.

Oliver sat at the kitchen table eating his tea.

'Sorry to interrupt your meal,' Billie began. 'I'll come back later.'

'Don't worry, Mr Brown. It's only Oliver eating and I'm sure he won't mind being disturbed. My husband and I eat later.'

Billie wondered at a family who didn't eat together but said nothing.

'Hello, Billie. Have you come to see how I am? The doctor said I'm "perfectly fit",' Oliver recited.

'I've brought you a present, young man. Want to see it, do you?'

Oliver looked at the man's huge hands which were empty. 'Yes please.' He looked at the thick short coat Billie wore and at the torn pocket on one side. The other pockets looked very small, he thought, trying to peer into one. He hoped it wasn't something useful like a pen and pencil set.

'It's outside in the van.'

Oliver followed Billie outside and with Evie a pace

behind. In the van was a collection of chains and some wooden parts.

'What is it?' Evie asked.

'It's a swing, Mum—Mother,' Oliver said in excitement. 'These long pieces and this piece will be the frame, those are the supports and there's the seat. Is that right, Billie?'

'Well done. Just tell me where you want it and I'll get it up in no time. You'll have to help me of course,' Billie smiled.

'Thanks!' Oliver's eyes sparkled as he looked at his mother. 'Mam! What d'you think of that for a present?'

'Mother,' Evie corrected almost without thinking. 'Well, er, where did you think to put it, Mr Brown?' She sounded doubtful.

'Somewhere on the back lawn? You tell me where.'

'Well, I don't know. It will make a mark, won't it, where his feet touch? I don't think my husband would like it. He's very fussy about the grass, we've only just got it right after the neglect of the previous tenants.'

'Oh, I see. Well, sorry. I didn't think of that.' Billie shrugged and looked at the disappointed boy. 'Sorry Oliver, I'll have to think of something else. won't I?'

'Mam, er, Mother, d'you think I could have it in Gran's—Grandmother's garden? I could use it then whenever I went there, couldn't I? Would that be all right, Billie?' He spoke nervously, hoping his mother would agree to the idea without considering it too deeply.

'It's fine with me, boy. If Nelly wouldn't mind.'

'Oh no, she doesn't mind about anything.'

So Oliver visited George after all.

To reward him for his bravery in rescuing Margaret, Nelly wanted to take Oliver into town to the pictures and then to a café for tea, but Evie refused.

'It isn't good for him, all this fuss,' she said. 'We're proud of him, very proud, but now he's had all the praise and presents he needs and must go back to being an ordinary little boy.'

'Ashamed to let me take 'im, me an' 'is grandad.'

'He isn't the boy's grandfather! And yes, I would not like him to be seen out with you two in case you take him to one of your public houses! I can just imagine him sitting outside with a packet of crisps while you and that man drink yourselves stupid inside!'

Nelly walked away. There was no point arguing with Evie, but she and George did manage to arrange a small celebration. When the swing was erected, Margaret and a few of Oliver's friends from school were invited round to Nelly's garden to try it out. She and George worked hard collecting wood to make a garden fire and, with so many people involved, even Evie could not say no.

Some of the parents came, including Amy, and Billie and Mary. They ate blackened, half-cooked potatoes with the children and drank some of Nelly's home-made pop and enjoyed themselves.

The following day, while they were raking over the embers of the fire and digging the garden where dozens of feet had trampled it hard, George found a piece of wood with some Welsh letters on it. He was a more enthusiastic gardener than Nelly and, digging deeper, had unearthed several fascinating bits of debris.

Nelly stared at the wood. 'Welsh,' she announced. 'Don't understand none of that.' And it was Mary Dairy who translated for them.

'*Sŵn Y Plant*. Sound of Children,' she told them. 'It must have been the name of your cottage, Nelly.'

After that George spent long hours polishing the

neglected brass letters. 'After last night it's earned the name,' he chuckled.

George spent the next few weeks working at Leighton's farm and stayed with Nelly, sleeping on the couch each night and getting up first to attend to the fire and have the kettle singing before Nelly came downstairs.He was sad when the time came to tell her he would be leaving in a few days. He did not want to be there at Christmas. It was a time for families and whatever differences Nelly and Evie had, they were family and he did not belong.

'I'll be back in the spring,' he promised. 'I think there'll be more work with Leighton then. He's getting old and refuses to employ another man to help Sidney. He's doing too much and refuses to see it.'

'Thought of yerself fer a permanent job?' Nelly asked.

'Oh no, I'm sixty. He needs a young man. Maurice Davies, d'you know him, Sidney's young brother? He's helping out occasionally until he starts with Prue Beynon, but it's all so unreliable. Poor old chap.'

'Why don't yer stay over Christmas? You won't find much work anywhere else, will yer?'

'Thanks, Nelly, but I won't stay. I'll be back though, in the spring.'

To celebrate getting the job with Prue Beynon's business, Maurice took Delina out for a meal in a very exclusive and expensive restaurant. He didn't tell her why until they were on their way home. This time they were not on bicycles but had gone in Johnny and Fay's car, both dressed up for the occasion.

Maurice was in his new suit and brown overcoat and a trilby hat. Delina wore a slim-fitting dress in palest green wool, which made her eyes look even bluer than usual. Her coat was a fine check of blue, green and cream. Her matching shoes made her giggle as she struggled to stay upright, unused to such smart high heels.

Half-way home, Maurice stopped the car and they kissed. Maurice felt her lack of desire, knowing his was stronger, but the thought did not dismay him. It only enhanced his protective love for her. To help love blossom in her would be a wonderful thing, worth all his patience and self-restraint now. And it was a constant surprise to him how easily he could hold back from love-making. His whole attitude to Delina was different from with any other girl. When he held her in his arms he was content, prepared to wait for ever if necessary for her to waken into love.

'Delina, my darling,' he said. 'I know we've hardly known each other long enough for me to say this, but I want us to get married. I love you like I've never loved anyone before. I want us to be together for always.'

He stopped her as she was about to reply. 'No, please don't say anything yet. I want you to think about it. If you don't feel the same way I—I couldn't bear to know just yet.'

They kissed again and this time he felt a stronger response, but still he was afraid to have her answer in case she turned him down. It had been such a short time.

'Is this the reason for tonight's celebration?'

'No, I've been to see Prue Beynon and she's given me a job! And now I want to marry you. I'd always be good to you. I love you so much and getting the job makes it possible. I know I should have waited a while longer, but—'

'Maurice, I've loved you since the moment I saw you in Amy Prichard's house, when I took her those flowers.'

'I can't believe I could be so lucky,' Maurice whispered

against her cheek, soft and sensual to his touch. 'Delina, my lovely.'

'Maurice, my own darling love.'

'Let's marry soon.' He released her and stared into her beautiful eyes, 'I'll come in now and tell your parents, then we'll go and tell Mam. She'll be so pleased. We'll tell everyone. I want them all to know you're mine.'

Chapter Nine

Prue rarely went out. Although everyone now knew about her pregnancy and the talk had died down, she was still finding it difficult to face people. She was forty and pregnant for the first time. It was so ridiculous, especially in the circumstances.

When she had discovered Amy's long affair with Harry, she had stopped buying from her shop, but since then, and especially since she had learn about the baby, she had visited her sister more often and had returned her ration book to her shop. She had a special green one now that she was an expectant mother entitled to a few extras. When she needed something, she would telephone and Margaret would bring her shopping round for her. But today she wanted to talk.

She stood for a while in the landing window, watching the comings and goings in the street. She saw Nelly dragging along her two great dogs, accompanied by that tramp, who she was said to have married. They were crossing the road from the fish and chip shop with a newspaper parcel, obviously their lunch. She saw Phil Davies, who pedalled so fast on his round these days it was difficult to catch him and give him a letter for the post.

At a quarter to one, when she hoped the shop would be quiet, she put on her loose tweed coat and walked down the road. The wind was cold and she pulled the coat around her, bunching it at the front to hide her stomach. At four months she hardly showed, but she felt enormous.

'Amy, I'd like a word.'

'Come in, I'll be closing for lunch in a mo'. Stay and have some, won't you?' Amy glanced at her watch and closed the door behind her sister. 'It's almost time, I doubt if anyone will come now.' She offered Prue a chair and sat on the corner of the counter, her tight navy skirt showing a shapely leg.

'I have to go to the clinic next week, will you come?'

'Wednesday is it?' When Prue nodded Amy sighed inwardly. With Christmas approaching fast there were many jobs she had planned to do on her precious half-day. It was more difficult now she didn't live above the shop. She couldn't do the odd job in between attending to customers. Last year she had made her cake there, with customers helping to mix it. But she nodded and smiled. 'Yes, I'll come. Perhaps we can have a bite of lunch in town?'

'I really haven't the time to spare,' Prue said.

Amy sighed. Like so many people, Prue placed a great value on her own time but little on anyone else's.

'All right, I'll have a sandwich before we leave.'

She looked at her watch again and pushed the bolt on the shop door. The kettle in the corner was soon boiling and the sisters, so different in temperament and looks, sat and shared the sandwiches Amy had prepared. Prue, as always, seemed unable to begin what she had come to say, so Amy helped her.

'What did you really come to talk about, Prue?'

'I'm thinking of moving away. Perhaps before the baby is born. I can run the business from anywhere, and I thought I might live in Llangwyn.'

'Don't!' Amy said firmly. 'You might think you're

unhappy here, but at least you know us all and we know you. To start again among strangers, well, frankly, you aren't the type. You'll go deeper into your shell. Don't Prue. It would be a mistake.'

'I'm quite capable of making up my own mind.' The sharp tone irritated Amy.

'Why did you come then?'

'To tell you.'

'All right, you've told me.'

'I feel so embarrassed.'

'I know, love.' Amy forgot her impatience in her pity for her lonely sister. 'You want to walk about and face people, not hide away. Show the pregnancy proudly. You – you loved Harry, surely you're proud of carrying his baby?'

'It isn't his.'

'What?'

For a long time Amy was silent, rocked by the words, unable to believe them. She was overcome by happiness that Harry had not loved his wife as well as loving her; a selfish, honest happiness. Then the surprise of knowing that Prue had had a lover was so ludicrous that she almost wanted to laugh. She waited to speak, unable to trust her voice.

'I'll never tell anyone who the father is, so don't ask. But it wasn't Harry,' Prue said eventually.

'You can tell me.' Amy badly wanted to know who this amazing man was who had broken through the barrier of Prue's coldness and given her a child.

Prue shook her head. 'Can you understand now why I feel only guilt and not joy? I can't walk proud and boast about my baby, I can't.'

'No one knows it isn't Harry's, except you. People will only talk if you act as if there's something wrong with having your husband's child. Start going to your clubs and committees again. If you tell yourself it's Harry's, it will be easier. A child is something you've always wanted, enjoy it.'

Prue stood up and carefully shook the crumbs into a waste-paper basket. 'I wish I could.' She had a great need to tell someone her secret but there was no one. She was completely alone. Yet if Harry was alive it would have been worse. How could she have faced him with this? Even in such a mess there was some consolation.

Amy watched her sister's face carefully but hardly guessed at all her conflicting emotions.

'You carried your babies here and everyone knew you weren't married, yet no one disliked you for it.'

'Because I didn't expect pity. Nor should you.'

'But it's what I get. That or ridicule.'

'Nonsense!' Amy said, but when Prue left she watched her walk up the road anxiously. Prue was a difficult person to help. She shunned all kindnesses and her severe manner just attracted criticism. For her to have broken the rules so undeniably was hard for her to cope with. What would happen when she had the baby to care for? She'd need a lot of help, and that, Amy thought, means me!

She unbolted the shop door again and, taking a few biscuits from the glass-topped containers, began to eat them absent-mindedly. Prue had eaten most of her sandwiches. At least her appetite is all right, she thought wryly. In a corner of the shop she added fresh lipstick and a dab or two of powder and fluffed out her blonde hair. Prue was a worry that wouldn't go away, but it was business as usual for Amy.

It was still quite early when Amy arrived home after the clinic visit. She hurried from the bus stop, hoping to get a few parcels wrapped and out of the way before Margaret came in from school. When she saw someone move in her front garden she stopped anxiously. Who could it be? She moved closer and saw Vic Honeyman busily pushing some disturbed grass back into place.

'Hello, Amy. Damn, I'd hoped to finish and be away before you came. Saw you on the bus into town, so David and I planned a little surprise.'

A boy of twelve came around the corner of the house with a bucketful of soil, which he handed to his father.

'This,' Vic said proudly, 'is my son, David. He's been helping me. Off school with a cold, so I thought the fresh air would do him good.'

'But what have you been doing?' The lawn, so carefully repaired by Freddy, was now broken up and covered with soil and large footprints.

'There were some bulbs left over in the warehouse and going cheap. I scrounged some and planted them in the grass in this corner and by the hedge. They'll look a treat in the spring.' He shrugged. 'Meant to be a surprise, like I said. You'll be able to see them peeping through the grass and watch them grow and flower. Beautiful they'll look.'

'Vic, that was a lovely thing to do. Thank you. And you, David. Come in and have a cup of tea. I've bought some fancy cakes.' She was flustered and flattered by the gesture and couldn't think straight. 'To plan a lovely thing like that it's - oh I give up, I can't find the words.'

She bustled them inside and gave the matches to Victor. 'Light the fire, will you? I'll see to the kettle.' Waving her shopping bag she said, 'Secrets. Christmas secrets. I'll just go and hide them before Margaret comes in and sees them.' She ran upstairs and buried her face in her hands, smiling and glowing with pleasure at the kind thought. She spent a moment wondering about Vic's wife, who must be as generous-minded as anyone would be to have her husband

and son do such a thing. She must thank her, or at least write a note.

David was a serious boy, not unlike Delina but less fair, his brown hair more the colour of Victor's. He drank his tea and ate the mock-cream cake then took his cup, saucer and plate and washed it. Well trained, Amy noticed with a smile at Vic, who nervously smoked continuously.

'Have you heard about our Delina and young Maurice?' Victor asked. 'Getting married and before Easter too.'

'That was quick, wasn't it? He's only been home a few weeks!'

'These things sometimes are,' he said, and looked at her with such intensity that she had to look away. 'Yes,' he repeated slowly, 'these things sometimes are.'

'I'll – I'll go and thank your wife sometime soon,' Amy said hurriedly. 'I must thank her for sparing you both to plan such a lovely surprise, and for the miniature roses she sent me.'

'Yes, do that. I'd like you to meet her.'

Instead of tackling the chores she had meant to get done that afternoon, Amy sat after they had gone, wondering why she always attracted the wrong men. Married men find me irresistible, she thought, but when will I ever meet an attractive man who's free?

Oliver was aware of the disagreement between his parents and made sure his father was there when he asked if he could go for a walk with Margaret. Evie refused, saying that if the two children went out alone she wouldn't have a moment's peace of mind until they returned, safe and sound. But Timothy for once overruled her.

'Oliver,' he said, rather pompously, 'you can't expect your mother to be anything else but worried after what happened the other day, but I think it will have made you more careful, if anything. It was an effective lesson in self-preservation.'

Oliver was quiet, trying to work out whether this meant he could or could not go, and failing.

'I see,' he said, hoping that would suffice.

'So, I think you should be allowed to go.'

'Thanks. I will be careful and I promise I won't go anywhere near the river. Can we go and see Billie? He's got lots of hens. Lots and lots more than Gran.' He hardly took a breath. 'He's going to let me feed them.'

Evie made him put an extra layer of clothes on and when he left he could hardly move. He went along the road, whistling cheerfully and unwrapping himself as he went.

He called for Margaret and they walked back towards the village and up Gypsy Lane. They stopped at the gypsy camp for a while and watched as the women sat preparing vegetables for the stew beginning to heat on the open fire, and the men smoked their pipes and talked together in soft voices.

The girl leaned over the half door of Clara's *vardo*, waved to them and came over to where they stood. All three continued their walk together and Oliver, who dreamed of living a life as carefree and fascinating as George when he grew up, listened avidly while she told them the secrets of the countryside. George had taught him a lot, but the gypsies seemed even better able to survive on what they found in the wildness around the towns.

'Do you really eat hedgehogs?' Margaret asked, with obvious distaste. 'I don't think I could do that. They're such beautiful creatures.'

'Do you really call them *hotchwitchi*?' Oliver asked. '*Hotchiwitchi* cooked on a *yog*. Sounds great,' he said, using the gypsy word for an outdoor fire.

They reached the top of the hill and looked down towards Billie and Mary's farm. Here the girl stopped.

'If you're going down there I'll leave you. Don't like the farmer. Caught me stealing eggs once and gave me a hefty clout.'

'He might give you some if you ask,' Oliver said confidently, 'he's a friend of ours.'

But the girl ran off without another word.

'I don't think we'd better go any further,' Margaret said. 'We've walked so slowly and I have to get home because we're going visiting this afternoon. Sorry.'

'It's all right. I'm tired anyway. It's all these clothes Mam made me wear. If we'd fallen in the river today I'd have sunk!' They laughed together as they walked home.

Maurice was intrigued by Delina's family and anxious to behave sensitively with them. He had seen clearly the difference in Mrs Honeyman when Victor was not around and he played every scene with this in mind. He was light-hearted and amusing when the mood was right, and quiet and serious when that was the tone set by Delina's mother.

The boys seemed dull, though he knew they were good students and spent a lot of time at their books, but they didn't ever seem to have any fun. It made him wonder how much he might have achieved if Ethel had not been so easy-going but, like Mrs Honeyman, had made him spend more time at useful things instead of giving him the freedom to choose. He still loved his mother, but he began to compare her unfavourably with Delina's, and gradually her obvious disapproval of her husband influenced his opinion of Vic too. He looked at the garden, still not tidied for the winter, and remarked to Delina that her father might have been kinder if he had attended to his own place rather than

Amy's. To his surprise, Delina supported her father.

'He needs to get away from home and he appreciates a little praise. He might have deserved it, but living with Mam's constant disapproval must be hard.'

'Yes, of course,' he muttered, embarrassed by his mistake.

When Nelly went to clean for Mrs French, she usually just opened the door and called, then took off her coat and began work. But today was different. Mrs French was waiting at the gate, smiling and waving impatiently, which wasn't like Mrs French at all.

'Nelly, I have some good news for you.'

'Me?' Nelly smiled, then her face fell into a frown. 'Is it about me 'ouse?' she asked in a hoarse whisper. 'Really good news?'

They went indoors and Mrs French invited her into the living room.

'Come and sit down and I'll try to explain, although it is very complicated.'

'Oh Gawd.'

'I spoke to my solicitor and told him of your dilemma, without saying anything that could reveal who you were. He thinks you'll be perfectly all right. Apparently, the law does state that in a case of intestacy the property should go to the Crown, but it's almost certain to be handed over to the person paying the rates and with the most just claim. It would all take time, of course, and you'd have to deal with it through a solicitor. Will you let me go on and get it all settled legally for you?'

But Nelly had been growing more and more anxious throughout this recital and, at the last, her face collapsed in dismay. 'That's that then. I ain't got no money fer solicitors.' She slumped into the armchair, a picture of misery. 'I'll 'ave to live day to day, 'eart in me mouth every time I gets a letter.'

'Don't worry, Nelly. He told me that there was no actual machinery in law that would tell the Probate Office what has happened. If you continue to pay your rates and do nothing, it's possible that no one will ever know. But if you wish, and only if you want me to, I'll ask him to act for you. No,' she brushed off Nelly's protest. 'forget about the money. He's a friend and if there are any expenses, I will attend to them myself.'

'What's all that in plain English then?'

'Don't think any more about it and leave it to me.'

'Can I tell George? An' Johnny? 'E tried to find out for me an' told me to ferget it, but I feel much better about it now you've seen a solicitor. Thanks, Mrs French.'

'If I were you I'd tell no one, except your husband of course. If word got to Evie, well, with the best of intentions I'm sure, she might welcome the opportunity to report your unofficial tenancy.'

'Perish the thought. No, on second thoughts you're right an' I'll only tell George.'

'Good, that's settled. Now, would you like to start upstairs as usual?'

'Mrs French, can I come a bit later? Sorry to mess you about, you being so kind an' all, but I'd like to tell George. 'E's only up at Leighton's and I won't be more than 'alf an hour.' She grinned, her lopsided mouth opening in a way that horrified Evie and amused her friends. 'It's like winnin' the pools, this is.'

'Leave it altogether if you want. It won't hurt for once,' Mrs French offered. 'But Nelly, do be careful and don't say a word until it's all settled.' She was thinking of Nelly's occasional drinking bouts.

'Don't worry, Mrs French, dearie, I won't let it out in a celebration drink. Fear of Evie findin' out will keep me sober!'

'How much rent have you put aside, Nelly?' George asked later that evening when they sat playing the gramophone and roasting in front of a blazing fire. Nelly had been to The Drovers and brought back some bottles of stout and some crisps and they were celebrating quietly together.

'I don't know. I just put the four shillings in the box every Friday and forgets it. I could count it.'

'I think you should.' George had been doing some sums in his head and guessed she had well over fifty pounds. But when they did count it up he was delighted. It amounted to sixty-eight pounds and four shillings.

'It should go in the bank,' George said.

'You're right, I ought to put it safe, although it's unlikely I'd be robbed. Leave somethin' be'ind for me they would, when they see what I've got!'

'We'll put it in the post office,' George said. 'But first, I have an idea. Don't you think you could spend a little of it?'

'No! I daren't!'

'Well I think you should. Why not treat yourself to a wireless? It would only cost about fifteen pounds and I've got five to go towards it. I was going to buy you a special Christmas present before I left, but what could be better than helping you to get yourself a wireless?'

Nelly shook her head a few more times before George talked her round. When she finally gave way they walked up, late as it was, to tell Mr Leighton that George wouldn't be there the following morning, and strolled home making plans to go into town for a shopping spree.

Llangwyn was full of people doing their Christmas shopping and Nelly was soon as excited as a starry-eyed child. They had come early but so had everyone else. The shops were packed with mothers carrying packages of every imaginable shape. Long pieces of crêpe paper and glittering lengths of tinsel poked out of shopping baskets and the children's faces shone with excitement. In the stores there were forests of hands raised to attract the assistants' attention. Christmas trees were on sale at street corners and impromptu stalls had been set up to sell cheap gifts and wrapping paper. Nelly thought Llangwyn had never been so full, nor looked so beautiful, as she and George admired the food on sale and the wonderful toys. Nelly watched the children's faces, fascinated. She liked best the little girl whose arms rocked in a dream of owning one of the beautifully dressed dolls in a shop window.

George picked up a card game.

'Lexicon,' he shouted to Nelly above the babble of voices. 'That might be a good present for young Oliver.'

'That's a good choice, George. 'Ere, give it to me and buzz of out of the way a minute, will yer? I've seen a little somethin' I want to buy for you.'

When she had made her purchases, including a neatly boxed razor and soap for George, he made her hide while he chose a card to give her. They were laughing like children when they pushed their way back out on to the street.

On occasions they lost sight of each other in the crowds, but gradually they made their way to the shop where they intended to buy the wireless. Nelly had given George the money to carry, and watched as he carefully counted out the notes and coins. There were slight doubts in her heart when the money was slipped into the till and the wireless was theirs, still a niggle of fear that someone would knock at her door and demand the rent for the six years since she had last paid it.

The wireless cost sixteen guineas and was promised for delivery later that day.

'I don't think there's another thing I need in the world, George,' she told him as they walked to the long bus queue with their assorted parcels. 'Not a single thing.' Except for you to stay for always, she added silently, but she kept that dream to herself. She had promised never to try and persuade him to give up his freedom, but it would be nice if he was always there.

'I think we should spend the evening wrapping the presents we've bought,' George said. 'It would be a pity if young Oliver came and spoilt the surprise by seeing what we've got him.'

'I doubt we'll see 'im for a while, too busy enjoyin' the preparations I bet.'

But she was wrong.

They returned to Hen Carw Parc a little after two o'clock and they trudged up the lane with their parcels, stopping now and then to adjust the more difficult ones and rearrange their carrier bags. The sound of children's laughter reached them before they were in sight of the gate. The swing was still proving a great attraction.

'Look at that, George,' she said, as they watched Oliver and his friends milling about on her newly dug soil. '*Swn Y Plant*. What a name fer the place, eh? Sound of Children.' She laughed loudly, too happy for words.

While George unpacked their shopping and changed his

clothes, Nelly poured lemonade for the thirsty children and found them some biscuits. She and George stood in the doorway watching them, rosy-faced, enjoying their winter picnic.

By the time the wireless arrived, later that afternoon, there was a rabbit roasting in the oven beside the roaring fire, and a small bottle of gin and two of stout. It was going to be a night to remember.

They listened to the wireless all evening, and even forgot the gin. *Ray's a Laugh*, Larry Adler and music right up to midnight. The room was almost as hot as the oven in which their meal had cooked and they were full of good food and contentment. It was hard to leave her chair and go up to bed, but Nelly eventually did, leaving George comfortably ensconced on the couch against the back wall, where he would see the first light through the window facing him. Nelly was still smiling when sleep came.

They rose late the following morning when Phil Davies dragged George out of a deep sleep. He banged on the door and George sleepily opened it to find Phil standing there, holding a Christmas tree.

'Where's Nelly?' Phil asked, making for the chair closest to the fire, which he began to poke and coax into life.

'Still in bed,' George laughed. 'We stayed up late listening to that.' He pointed to the new radio.

'Best way to wake her then.' Phil turned the switch and the room was filled with the sound of a Christmas carol.

Nelly came down in a crumpled dress and an army greatcoat. She was unperturbed at seeing Phil. She patted the shiny wireless.

'What d'you think of that, then? What a Christmas we'll 'ave this year. That our tree?'

'I won't be here, Nelly,' George said quietly. 'I told you

I'm leaving in a day or so.' He handed her a cup of tea made with not quite boiling water, and sat back again on the couch.

'But Christmas Day is less than a week away.'

'I mustn't stay.' Phil sipped his tea, dying to ask questions but afraid to interfere.

Nelly fussed with the kettle, hoping for a better pot of tea than the one George had made so impatiently. She did not argue any further. She knew George was on a visit only, but each time he came she hoped he would not go away again. When they had married, she had promised never to ask him to change his life for her. Difficult as it was, especially now with Christmas so close, she kept her word.

The morning was dark and there was a drizzly rain when George packed his few belongings into his bag. Nelly gave him a separate parcel with some food for the first part of his journey and had put in her present to him too. His tidiest clothes he left with Nelly.

'Don't sell them in town,' he teased, 'I'll be back.'

'Soon, George,' Nelly said quietly, forcing a smile. 'Soon.'

She watched as he walked up the garden path, his clothes neat, his white beard a beacon in the gloom, his shoes shining like new paint. What a time of year to be wandering. Christmas would have been such fun with someone of her own to share all the small excitements. Silly things, like pulling a cracker and reading the stupid jokes. Cooking an extra special meal, and listening to the wireless. It was on now, sending music out into the bedraggled garden.

'Thanks fer me present, George,' she shouted as he disappeared behind the tall, straggly hedge.

'Enjoy it,' he called back, his voice already sounding like an echo of something fading, no longer a part of her life, only a memory.

'Come on, dogs,' she said, fixing the rope leads on Bobby and Spotty. 'Time I wasn't 'ere. Mrs French'll be wonderin'.'

She spent longer than usual cleaning Mrs French's house, finding extra jobs and giving everything an enthusiastic rub. She delayed returning to the empty cottage; this evening there wouldn't be the excitement of waiting for George to finish his day's work and come home.

The dogs tried to pull her along but her footsteps dragged. She looked across at the fish and chip shop, but no, she wasn't hungry. She wished Amy's shop was open but it was shut for lunch. Still unwilling to face her cottage she walked past the houses and the church, and the school with its windows bright with decorations. As she passed she caught the beautiful sound of children singing a well-known carol and tears came to her eyes.

George set off through the woods with a heavy heart. His thoughts were with the cottage near the edge of the trees where he knew he would be utterly content. The sense of belonging, the day spent doing work he enjoyed then strolling home to a warm welcome, a hot meal and Nelly to spend the evening with. To go to bed relaxed and drowsy to lie and look forward to another perfect day. It was hard to walk away.

Yet walk away he must. He had married Nelly as a trick so that Evie couldn't make her leave her beloved cottage; he didn't want anyone to think he was using that same trick to find himself a comfortable lodging for life. Yet he wanted so badly to stay.

If he had done something to get himself out of the mess he had made of his life, could boast of some effort to get away from the monotonous existence of moving aimlessly across the country from one dreary place to another, then he would have been able to stay and put down roots for himself in Hen Carw Parc, but he had not. It was Nelly's generosity that gave him the chance and he could not bring himself to accept it.

He lifted the shoulder bag higher and increased his pace, trying to get away before he found the temptation to return impossible to resist, but he did not travel far. He walked in a circle around the small village deciding eventually to settle somewhere close by for the first night; the place was a magnet that refused to let him go.

School had broken up for the holiday but the building was being used for rehearsals for the church carol concert. The sound of children singing usually made Nelly happy but today it only added to her sadness.

'I know I should be glad to have George for a little while now and again,' she told the dogs. 'Some never 'as even that much 'appiness, but I wish 'e could stay. Gets on so well we do.'

The children came out into the yard as the rain stopped and Nelly searched the faces in the hope of a word with Oliver.

'Hello, Gran.' He appeared at her side suddenly. 'Where's George?'

'Gone again,' she said sadly. 'You know 'ow 'e 'ates to stay anywhere fer long. 'E said to give you 'is love and 'e'll see you again in the spring. 'E said you an' 'e would go after a trout and we'd 'ave a picnic in the woods and cook it over a fire.'

'That'll be great, Gran. Pity he won't be here for Christmas though, I've made him a present.'

'Mind it for 'im.'

Nelly walked on; through tears the fields blurred and she let the dogs take her wherever they wanted to go. When she felt the rain on her face again she turned back, but still did not go up Sheepy Lane and home. Instead she went to wait for Amy to open the shop.

There was the usual rush of customers when Amy unlocked the door but today it didn't diminish. Everyone in the village seemed to want to buy or order things for the Christmas holiday. Behind the post office counter piles of parcels waited for the van to collect them. And on the walls Nelly could see various lists, some in red, some green and some blue, all telling Amy of goods on order for delivery on Christmas Eve. One list was headed 'Turkeys'.

'Never 'ad a turkey,' she said to anyone who would listen. ' 'Ad a chicken once, but I don't want one this year after all, Amy,' she raised her voice over the hubbub, 'so you can cross me name off.'

'Why, what's happened, Nelly? Spent all your money on that wireless?' Amy shouted back.

'No point, me bein' on me own again, as usual. George is gone. 'E didn't want to interfere with me plans and spoil a family Christmas,' she pulled a face as she said that, adding, 'So I'm all on me own. Don't want a chicken, not just fer me an' the dogs.'

'Come to us if you like,' Amy said at once. 'I keep on asking Prue but she's said "no" so far.'

'I'm going up to Fay and Johnny's,' Nelly's soft voice said. 'I'm sure there'd be room for one extra.'

'What about your Evie?' Someone asked and Nelly pulled a face.

'Some Christmas that'd be! Got to behave meself when I goes there.' She burped on her empty stomach and laughed loudly. 'Couldn't do that fer a start!'

She sat on a sack of dog biscuits for a while looking around at the silver-wrapped tangerines and the shiny apples, the chocolate money and the sugar mice. This was the first Christmas since rationing was brought in that people were able to buy as many sweets as they wished. They had been de-rationed only the previous February, although sugar stayed on ration until September.

Finding no excuse to stay, Nelly walked up the lane to the cottage and began the routine tasks of attending to the fire and swivelling the kettle over the heat. She began to prepare a snack, but then she sat down and allowed the tea to go cold and thought about the Christmas to come. After a while she forced herself to shake off her melancholy and brought in the tree Phil had brought for her.

'No sense in bein' miserable, boys,' she said to the dogs. 'Christmas is a celebration whatever me circumstances.'

She had no sparkling tinsel and no coloured balls for the tree but blew up a few balloons and tied them on. A couple of lengths of expanding garlands intended to loop from the ceiling were draped over its branches. The four Christmas cards she had so far received hung among the greenery and on top, having no fairy in a white dress and carrying a silver wand, she fixed a picture of the Queen. It was an unusual tree but certainly cheerful.

'If only George was 'ere to see it.'

Oliver was disappointed to hear that George had gone. He had made a small purse from red felt, and had bought two tuppeny-ha'penny stamps to go inside it. He hoped the present would result in his receiving a letter from George, delivered by Phil Davies. Now it was too late. Why hadn't he stayed?

He had been at the shop talking to Margaret and when he

got home, he went quietly through the kitchen and into the hall. He didn't call, knowing that if he did Evie would tell him to take off his shoes, change his trousers and shirt and do his reading practice. He sidled past the door to the lounge where he could hear his parents talking. Hearing the word 'secretly' he grinned and crept closer. Perhaps he would hear what was to be his Christmas present.

In fact, Evie and Timothy were discussing something much less exciting: the school funds. The school garden was a mess and some of the parents had planned to run a stall to sell home-made toys to raise money for new plants for it. Mr Evans had volunteered to make the arrangements but he had let them down.

The posters had been printed with the wrong date, he had forgotten to borrow the trestle tables from the church, and when the sale did take place, so few people came that the toys were mostly unsold. He had handed his accounts of the disaster to Timothy on the last day of term, and they made grim reading.

While Oliver listened hopefully outside the door his parents let their disappointment overflow into unreasonable anger. Evie, who could rarely be moderate about anything, at once condemned the man as an idiot.

'He is unreliable and none too bright, we both know it. He can hardly add two and two. He has cost us money we can ill afford and I wish we could get rid of him!'

Timothy's voice was lower, quieter, but he too was disappointed that all the efforts of the ladies' sewing circle had been wasted.

'There are times, dear, when I agree with you. But we can't just tell him to go. Much as we would sometimes wish to.' He pointed at the accounts with his pen. 'These totals are all wrong. It will take me hours to sort out the errors.'

Oliver did not cry. He went up the stairs and into his room, a determined and grim look on his young face. Packing a bag with a few clothes and stopping only to collect his wellingtons from the kitchen, he left the house and walked up the field to the woods beyond.

He was not certain of the way to the brickworks although Gran had pointed out the general direction in the past. But surely there would be a path and a signpost? He looked at the piece of paper in his hand and, spelling out the letters said the words aloud: The Cymer – the area in which he knew he'd find the brickworks and George. If he couldn't see a signpost he would be able to ask. He walked on confidently.

It seemed that the day had hardly become light before it began to darken again. Shadows already filled the lane and the chill of approaching night seeped through his clothes. He was frequently tempted to turn around but he was determined to find George and then both of them would go and live with Gran. She wanted him and she never called him stupid. Once he had explained to George how much he and Nelly needed him to stay, he would never go away again.

He thought he knew all about survival in the country, hadn't the gypsy girl told him how it was done? He looked at the bare branches and the few remaining berries, already difficult to see in the fading light. He had left the lane now and walked through a hillside almost bare of trees, just the occasional hawthorn dressed for winter, and a more graceful rowan here and there. Streams abounded, running silver through the ground, and he stopped once to drink, not because he was thirsty but to pretend he was able to find all he would need, playing at surviving in the wild. Water? All around me, he told himself. Food? There on the branches to be picked when I need it. But the dark was something harder to pretend about. It crept around him threateningly, hiding all that was familiar, and making him doubt which way to walk.

George had often talked to him about living rough, as he called it. The most important thing, he had said, was to find yourself a warm place to sleep. As soon as it was past mid-day, you must settle for the first likely spot you found and not be tempted to walk on in the hope of something better. Settle in it before you get cold so you'll be warm for the night hours. Settle and try and sleep in a cold place, when you haven't any body warmth, and you're in trouble.

He looked about him at the trees and the long grasses and began to feel afraid. He had passed the old castle long ago and where he now walked was new to him. He was far to the east of the council houses and no lights were visible in any direction to help him find his route. Where would he find a warm place to sleep?

Timothy walked to the school and finding it empty and locked, went to see the Reverend Barclay Bevan, who had been rehearsing the children in their carols. He looked surprised when Timothy asked about Oliver.

'I saw them off hours ago. About two o'clock, I believe. No, I didn't see who he went with, but it was probably Margaret Prichard. Come in and I'll telephone for you, to save time. So dark today it's almost like evening already.'

There was no reply.

'Of course, they would be at the shop,' Barclay Bevan smiled. 'With school finished for Christmas, Margaret would be there with her mother.' He dialled another number and was told that Margaret had not seen him since about an hour after the concert rehearsal ended.

Timothy thanked the man and hurried home. He rang everyone he could think of. No one had seen him. Evie called on Nelly, who set off at once to the castle, in case he had wandered up for a solitary game among the ruins, but she couldn't find him there.

Oliver was frightened and unsure which way to go. He would happily return home now but had no idea of the direction he had travelled. He saw a house and, although there were no lights in the windows, he knocked on the door to ask for help. But the place was empty.

The darkness was so intense now that he could barely make out the outline of the building, but he came upon a shed, its door drunkenly open across the broken concrete path. It was obviously a coal house, the smell was easily recognised. He thought of going in and trying to get himself warm but his hand touched a cobweb and he ran off in a fright.

He found the brickworks by sheer luck. He walked around the buildings, touching the walls, feeling for a space where he could shelter. He found a curve in the wall that was slightly warm to his fingers and snuggled against it, pulling his short coat around him and trying to cover his cold, thin legs.

Then he began to cry, silently at first, trying to hold back the misery and fear. But his tears increased as shapes in the darkness began to look like figures looming towards him, encroaching ominously on the space between himself and them. The old walls became giants and fearsome animals, and the night was full of terrors.

He shut his eyes tight and let out a wail that cut the silence of the bleak and lonely place. The sound of his own voice frightened him but he couldn't stop. Then he heard the sound of a twig snapping and he opened his eyes. He could just make out a figure moving towards him. His throat tightened and he gave a half strangled cry. Then a voice he knew said softly, 'Oliver, don't be frightened, it's me, George. I've come to take you home.'

Oliver could not speak. Each time he tried to explain the words exploded into deep, shuddering sobs that shook his small body.

'Don't try to talk, I'll hear all about it later. Just *cwtch* up in my jacket and get warm.'

The boy's sobs gradually subsided into a few deep sighs and he was able toG say, 'I've been looking for you, George. Nelly and I want you to stay and I want to live with you both in Gran's cottage.'

'I would love that too, Oliver. There's nothing I would like more, but I don't belong with Nelly, I can't walk into her life and spoil things for her. And as for you, you belong with your parents. They would be broken-hearted if they knew you wanted to leave them.'

'No, Mother wouldn't mind, I've heard her say so. Can we all stay together, George? Can we?'

'Let's get you home, shall we? I bet your mother is frantic with worry. She cares for you, in spite of what you think she said.'

George cuddled the boy tightly, distressed by the sobbing which even now occasionally wracked Oliver's small frame. He carried him home, covering the long miles rapidly with his keen eyes and his knowledge of the land. The sobs subsided, and he knew the boy slept. He walked quickly, anger against the boy's mother in every step.

Everyone in the village seemed to be out searching for Oliver. As George approached the first houses, every window showed a light. That was Constable Harris's idea, thinking that if the boy was anywhere near, he would be glad of a light to show him the way home.

It was past midnight, yet torches flickered in the blackness as searchers walked the hedgerows and peered into corners, calling his name, and calling to each other to stay in contact. Some were singing, the clear voices on the night air giving the impression of a scene from an opera in which the cast had lost their way and left the stage.

George walked down the field behind Evie's house and up to the open door and called out. Evie gave a scream and snatched the boy from George's arms.

'What have you done to him?' She moved the boy's head to wake him. 'Oliver, what has he done to you? Tell me.' She put the boy down and called Timothy.

Nelly, who had been waiting with her daughter for news, saw the horrified look on George's face and pushed her daughter with a roughness that surprised them both. George caught hold of Oliver, who was still sleepy and unable to stand.

'Shut your ugly mouth!' Nelly growled. 'Hug the boy, let him know you love him and are thankful 'e's safe back 'ome.'

Evie burst into tears and Timothy comforted her.

'That's enough, Mother-in-law.'

'No, it ain't enough! Call yerself a mother?' She glared at her daughter, forcing her to look her in the eye. 'Go on! Take 'im from George who found 'im and brought 'im safe back for yer.'

Nelly watched as Evie gently lifted the boy from George's arms and heard her say, 'Thank you very much,' in a low trembling whisper. She saw her daughter's shoulders shaking as she walked upstairs carrying Oliver, with Timothy following close behind her.

They quickly sent out messages to let everyone know that Oliver had been found and the house emptied. Along the main street small groups were still gathered and it was a long time before the last light went out and the village settled to sleep for what was left of the night.

Oliver had been undressed and bathed to warm him before being put into his pyjamas. Both Evie and Timothy attended to him, each unwilling to leave it to the other.

'Oliver,' Evie said, holding her son tightly, 'my dear, we've been so frightened. Where have you been? Why did you go so far on your own? Didn't you know how it would worry us, you disappearing like that, out alone in the dark? We love you so much.'

'I wanted to find George. I want to live with Gran and George. I know I'm an expense and a disappointment.'

'Oliver! What makes you think such a foolish thing? A disappointment?' Evie allowed her husband speak, she was too filled with guilt to sound convincing. What had she done to the child?

Between them they gradually unravelled the reasons for his running away, and when they felt certain he had been reassured, they put him to bed, in their bed and, one each side of him, cuddled him for the rest of the night. Neither of them slept.

In the cottage at the edge of the wood, George sat on Nelly's couch and told her how he had found Oliver.

'I heard footsteps and presumed it was another traveller, then I heard him crying. I called, hoping he would recognise my voice and not be frightened by my approach. He was so cold.'

They sat discussing the events of the night and Nelly's hopes that it might put some sense into Evie's head. At last George fell asleep where he sat and Nelly threw a blanket over him. She smiled down at the whiskered face and sighed in delight. It was a funny world, trouble bringing joy. She hummed a carol as she climbed the stairs to bed.

Chapter Ten

George had never been upstairs in Nelly's house, but the morning following the search for Oliver he rose early, revived the fire and took a cup of tea up the curved staircase into her bedroom. She sat up in her voluminous night-dress and pulled the greatcoat which served as a bedspread around her shoulders.

'Thanks, George.' She took the cup and saucer and drank gratefully.

George sat on a wicker chair near the window and said quietly. 'I wonder if Evie will let me in, if I call to see how young Oliver is?'

'Never no sayin' with my Evie. I hope she's showin' a bit of love to that boy. That's more important than what she thinks of you an' me, George.'

'My name is Henry,' he said with a smile, 'although I might not answer to it after you calling me George for so long.'

'Do you mind?'

'Not at all. I was thinking of how you suddenly made up the name when Evie challenged you and you didn't know my real name. I'm happy to be a George.'

'I forgets my name too, you know. I still calls meself Nelly Luke an' really I'm Mrs Henry Masters.' She frowned, her face crinkling and making him smile, then she added, 'No, sorry, George, but I can't think of you as a 'Enry and George it'll 'ave to be.'

'More tea?' He held his hand out for the cup.

'It's Christmas Eve, George, I've just realised. Ignoring his outstretched hand, she put the cup on the table near the battered alarm clock. 'It's a bit late for you to go, ain't it?'

'If you don't mind, perhaps I will stay a while longer.'

'Smashin!' She pushed the blankets from her and climbed out of the large bed, stretching inelegantly and reaching for the great coat. 'I'll go an' see if Amy's still got the chicken I ordered. Cancelled it I did, when you said you were goin'.'

'Not dressed like that I hope?' he laughed. He collected the cup and started to leave the room. 'Nelly, is there another bedroom?'

' 'Ardly a bedroom. It's full of all sorts of junk. We could clean it up though, if—' She hesitated, afraid to be thought in any way pressuring him. 'If you fancy a job,' she finished. 'But first,' she said casually, 'I think I'd better go an' see Amy an' order the extra grub.'

George felt in his pocket and handed her two pounds. 'Take this towards it,' he said.

'Ta, George. Fancy a chicken fer Christmas day? That's if you're stayin'.' There, it was out. She watched his face for a clue to his feelings and was relieved when he smiled.

'Thank you, Nelly. If you'll have me, I would be very pleased to spend Christmas here.'

'Thank Gawd fer that. Spoilt my Christmas proper it would, imaginin' you sleepin' rough. We'll empty the junk room for yer.'

They spent the afternoon clearing the clutter out of the back bedroom. There was no bed. The one she had had for Evie years before had ended up on a bonfire. Its metal frame was still faintly visible in the garden, under the dead tendrils of convolvulus that covered it each summer. She would look out for a second-hand one.

There were boxes containing clothes and books and magazines. Mice had nested in some of them and, as the boxes were lifted, a litter of shredded paper and cloth covered the floor.

'Seems we'll 'ave to 'ave another bonfire night, George,' Nelly laughed.

'We'll invite Oliver and his friends and make a party of it, shall we?'

In a box that had been hidden by a pile of old coats, Nelly found a set of teacups, saucers and plates. They were made of beautiful fine china and decorated in blue and dark red flowers. Nelly washed them with great care and decided to give them to Amy.

'Look good in 'er new 'ouse, they will. An' we're 'appy with the old stuff, ain't we George?'

There was nothing else of value and soon there was a large mound in the garden waiting to be set alight. They had just arranged the tea-set on the table, ready to pack and take to Amy, when Phil the postman appeared at the door.

'What's this then, expecting that Bennet-Hughes woman again?' he asked.

They stopped work and opened the cards he had brought, exclaiming over some unexpected ones. They stuck them on the over-loaded Christmas tree in the corner, much to Phil's amusement.

'That's the most unusual tree I've seen this Christmas,' he said. 'Everything on it except the envelopes the cards came in!'

'Still gallopin' about like one of Leighton's lambs, are yer? Or 'ave you got time to stop for a cuppa?' Nelly asked.

'I've finished. I left yours 'til last so I could stay and chat for a mo'.' Phil said, taking the teapot and making a brew. 'Mam wants to know if you'd like to come up on Christmas night. You know she usually has a crowd in. She'd like you to come.'

'Lovely!' Nelly's dark eyes shone. 'But I don't know if . . . ?' She looked at George, afraid to presume he was staying.

'You as well, George, if you're not leaving us again,' Phil coaxed and George smiled.

'Thank you. I'd love to accompany my wife to your party.'

'Smashin'!' Nelly laughed. She turned away to hide shyly from George's look. It was hard not to forget her promise and beg him not to leave again. ' 'Urry up with that tea, why don't yer?' she said to Phil. 'I thought you'd changed from a snail into a grey 'ound!'

Phil noticed the piles of clothing from the cleared room upstairs that had been thrown into a corner.

'It's all rubbish to be thrown into the bin,' Nelly explained.

'I might be able to find a use for some of it,' Phil surprised them by saying. He rubbed the side of his nose and smiled secretively. 'Not a word, mind. It's for a bit of fun at Mam's party.' He sorted through the dresses and shirts and packed a few items into a paper carrier.

Leaving the two men still talking, Nelly went down to see Oliver. She did not go down Sheepy Lane, which would have been quickest, but turned left out of her gate and walked first to Netta Cartwright's where her friend was half-heartedly draping a few garlands around the walls of the living room.

'It's very strange, this,' Netta sighed, 'not having anyone

here for Christmas. I don't know what to be doing with myself. I'm going to Fay and Johnny's for the whole of the holiday and I can't accept that I have nothing to do.'

'None of the boys home then?'

'No. All far away and not in need of me, Nelly.'

'Johnny will want to show off his new wife and 'er cookin'. It's their first Christmas for Gawd's sake!' Nelly spoke a bit sharply. 'Don't begrudge 'im that, do yer?'

'No no, not a bit. I just wish I had something to do, that's all.'

'There'll be plenty to do when you get to their 'ouse, I bet yer.'

'Washing up?' Netta said sadly.

' 'Ere, you comin' to Ethel's on Christmas night?'

'Yes, I don't think Johnny would miss that.'

'I'm takin' a few scones, got some stale milk an' with a bit of jam. You takin' anythin', like a few mince pies?'

Nelly went on to visit Evie, leaving Netta busily gathering the ingredients for making pastry.

Evie was smiling! Nelly looked for the reason; it could surely not be for her? But there was no one else. She followed her daughter into the house, expecting the smile to fade, and found Oliver and Timothy playing a game of whist in the living room. They were laughing too. Nelly felt her heart expand with happiness. Oliver was positively glowing.

'You've been teaching my son a few skills without me knowing it,' Timothy said in his quiet voice, but Nelly sensed no criticism. She waited for him to explain.

'I began to teach him whist and he's winning every game. He tells me you and he, and George, play quite often.'

'E's a clever boy, didn't Clara say so?' Nelly hesitated, glancing at Evie in alarm. The mention of the gypsies might be enough to spoil the happy mood, but Evie ignored the comment.

Nelly watched for a while, cheering when Oliver won a trick and booing at Timothy's rare successes. There were no unpleasant effects from his hours in the cold and, from what she could see, many good ones.

'George is stayin' a while longer,' she announced and again waited for the outburst that did not come. 'Ethel 'as invited us both to 'er party. Nice that'll be.'

'We're going to a party too,' Evie said.

'Smashin'. You'll enjoy that, Oliver.'

'Oliver won't be coming. It's for adults.'

Evie stared at Nelly defiantly, sensing that her mother disapproved of her leaving her son so soon after his attempt to run away from her. She moved slightly and placed a hand on Oliver's shoulder. Timothy and Oliver seemed unaware of the silent battle between the two women.

'What's 'appening to Oliver?' Nelly demanded, her dark eyes full of pent up rage.

'I haven't made an arrangement yet. I'm sure Amy and Margaret would love to have him.'

'So would George an' me. We'd gladly give up the party.'

'No, Mother, that isn't possible.'

'Amy can't look after 'im. She's goin' to Ethel's too.' There was victory in Nelly's voice.

'We'll see. I'll telephone her.'

'Do it now, why don't yer?'

It was obvious from the responses Evie made that Nelly was right. When the receiver was replaced, Evie looked at Nelly angrily.

'I didn't arrange it!' she said defiantly.

So it was agreed that Oliver would go with Margaret and Amy to Ethel's on Christmas night. Nelly went home jubilant. 'What a Christmas this is goin' to be!' she shouted as she went back into the cottage and told George the good news.

Christmas Day began in much the usual way, with the fire to see to and breakfast to prepare, the dogs to walk and the chickens to feed. Nelly felt an unusual urge to attend church and she and George slipped into the back pew and sang and listened with the rest, leaving just before the service ended.

They walked arm in arm through the winter woodland, the dogs about their feet, then back to the chicken roasting in the oven. The afternoon was spent listening to the wireless which was broadcasting a Christmas programme of excerpts from all Nelly's favourite comedies. They listened avidly to the description of the Queen's journey to Barbados and New Zealand and concentrated carefully on the Queen's speech which followed. Finally they slept, sated with food and drink, until the room had grown dark and the fire gave only an occasional flicker.

Ethel's house was full of activity. Besides the last-minute cooking and setting out of food, Johnny and Phil were organising a few entertainments. Ethel could hear their muffled laughter but didn't try to discover the reason for it. Best let them get on with it.

Maurice had surprised and disappointed her by going to Delina's family for Christmas dinner. It was unheard-of not to have all the family together—that is, until marriage changed things. Maurice and Delina had only just got engaged. The hurt took some of the pleasure out of the day, though they had both promised to be there for the evening gathering.

The room was not large, and there were not enough seats for the crowd expected and, to add to the squash, Phil and Johnny insisted on bringing in a small table and a stool which they placed in a corner and draped with material that looked suspiciously like the skirts of ancient dresses. Ethel was in no doubt that someone was going to be teased and tormented for the amusement of others. She thought about her future daughter-in-law and wondered how the quiet, gentle young girl would cope with the uninhibited fun about to begin. She hoped her introduction to the Davies family would not affect her love for Maurice. It wasn't really true that you married a man and not his family, different upbringings and inherited attitudes and beliefs were often inseparable. From what she had heard, the Honeymans were not noted for their lively sense of humour.

The prospect of Christmas in her new house had excited Amy but the reality had been disappointing. Freddy had not come home and the atmosphere of warmth and comfort she had hoped for had not materialised. The house had too many empty spaces and didn't fit easily around her. The decorations seemed sparse and hollow and even the tree with its new baubles was like a new hat worn with a shabby coat. Nothing felt right.

Working every day had made settling in a more prolonged affair and the place was still not as welcoming as a home should be. It would wrap itself around her eventually, she knew that, but she had depended on the Christmas period to give her that feeling of belonging. With Freddy absent, the feeling still evaded her.

Prue did not stay very long once the meal had been cleared and although Amy understood how difficult this first Christmas must be for her, without Harry to cook for and make all the extra touches for, she was unable to hide a sigh of relief when her sister left.

During the afternoon she played some of the new games they had been given with her daughter, and they passed the hours in a relaxed and contented mood. As darkness came and they drew the curtains and heaped extra coal on the fire, she was glad they were going out. The prospect of the evening at home seemed long and lonely, even though Margaret was with her.

In Fay and Johnny's smart new home, the hours passed slowly for Netta. The meal had been excellent and the welcome as warm as she could have wished, but Netta couldn't help watching the clock, which tormented her with its slowness. After so many years of arranging everything for the busiest day in the year, she felt lost and sat fidgeting. Joining in the occasional bursts of conversation, and watching the clock hands drag themselves around, she wished she had invited Nelly and George to dinner with her.

Making the excuse that the fire would need attention and she did not want to go back to a cold house, she made her escape and went home, to sit in her quiet living room and sip tea and wonder, not for the first time, whether all her future Christmases would be as empty.

At Evie and Timothy's Oliver played with the pieces of Meccano which Nelly had bought for him in a second-hand shop. Through the morning and for most of the afternoon he concentrated on making a working model of a crane. Timothy lent a hand and Oliver occasionally had to revise his father's help. He was completely absorbed and the day sped by. It came as a surprise when he saw Evie beginning to dress for her party. He wondered if the party he and Margaret were going to would be as boring as it sounded.

Maurice spent most of Christmas Day with the Honeymans. He and Delina had decided to marry in April and the initial discussions had begun. He was rather anxious when Mrs Honeyman mentioned the number of bridesmaids, and the choir and bells, and the large reception which would be held in the hotel in town.

'But won't that be expensive?' he said hesitantly. He knew Victor had been a delivery man all his working life. How could such a large wedding even be considered?

'Leave that to me,' Mrs Honeyman said, smiling at her daughter.

Maurice looked about him and wondered if, somewhere in the distant past, Mrs Honeyman had been wealthy. Certainly not since she had married Victor, he guessed. The furniture in their house was heavy and old, but had once been beautiful, perhaps a remnant of better days, and certainly of a much larger home than this council house near Hen Carw Parc. The cutlery was large and heavily patterned and the glasses, although they weren't in full sets, were crystal.

The house always lacked brightness in spite of some of the beautiful things it contained. He wondered how such surroundings had managed to produce a beauty like Delina. Even now at Christmas time there were no frills, only a rather bare tree in a corner.

The boys were dressed in grey trousers and grey pullovers, and Mrs Honeyman wore a loose, dark green dress without anything to disperse the gloom. Only Victor had made a defiant gesture and wore sand-coloured trousers and a yellow pullover. But it was Delina who shone. Her dress was simple, but Maurice guessed it was very expensive. It was a fitted style with a high neckline and she wore it with a thin silver belt. A necklace of silver and earrings to match were her only jewellery but she looked lovely. He thought with sudden guilt that the house would be a gloomy one indeed, once he had taken from it the jewel which was Delina.

After they had eaten a light meal of cold turkey and salad, they walked down the hill and through the muddy path to Ethel's house, where a different sort of celebration awaited them. Maurice hoped Delina would not be embarrassed at the lively crowd and the nonsense that his mother attracted, not realising his thoughts matched Ethel's exactly.

Amy had left for Ethel's early. She could not stay another moment in the quiet house and as soon as Oliver had arrived she had taken both children for a walk through the village, around the back lane past the shop, and up through the fields, with only the street lights behind them to guide their feet. Then, back to the road and up the lane to pass Nelly's cottage. They walked by the trees at the edge of the wood, Amy's torch flickering on the bare branches and the thicker profile of the firs.

She had no real purpose in mind, just a need to get away from the walls that seemed to enclose her and cut her off from the rest of the living world. Margaret and Oliver thought it great fun and they ran about her, pretending to be afraid of the dark.

Sudden voices behind them gave them a real fright until they recognised Nelly's loud laugh. Amy called and waited for the couple to catch them up, so it was a crowd who were the first arrivals at Ethel's that Christmas evening.

Preparing for the invasion to come, Ethel had settled on a high chair near the door to the back kitchen as rising from a lower chair was painful. So the first arrivals made for the couch to settle comfortably before the crush.

George stood behind Nelly, unsure of how well he would be received. He knew that everyone in the village referred to him as 'The Tramp' and he was afraid that people would be uneasy in his company. He leaned against the wall, prepared to watch and take little part in the proceedings.

Constable Harris arrived soon after them and brought a flagon of beer.

'Budge up Nelly,' he urged, 'there's room for one more on that couch.'

Billie and Mary Brown came, and as Constable Harris squeezed in beside Nelly and Amy, Billie groaned in disappointment.

'Big man I am,' he complained, 'got to have a bit of couch or I'll fill the room so's no one else'll get in.'

He went to stand near George and when old Mr Leighton arrived with Sidney, Nelly was pleased to hear the four men in lively conversation. She turned her head so she could hear what was being said. They were discussing the advantages of electric fences, with Billie in favour and Mr Leighton arguing about the difficulty of watering the animals between the narrow sections of the fields.

'What a conversation fer Christmas,' she shouted. 'You should be talkin' about angels an' 'eavenly choirs. Not electrocutin' cows!'

'Lord,' someone joked, 'what an idea!'

'*The cattle were lowing, the baby's awake, but the little lord Jesus no crying did make—*' Billie began and others joined in one by one until everyone was singing. The words varied as people forgot the original ones but no one minded the occasional mistake.

Margaret stood on the table and sang a solo that touched everyone's heart, her clear and pure voice filling the room with a carol that Monica French had written and taught her during her music lessons. Nelly tried to coax Oliver to sing but he shook his head and slumped down in his seat, so she sang a song herself.

'Not a carol,' she explained, 'I can't never remember the words.' Without leaving her seat she sang, 'By A Babbling Brook', only just reaching the high notes and making Amy and Constable Harris cringe and cover their ears. Billie Brown quickly handed her a beer, but whether to refresh her or to stop her no one was sure.

A table in the corner was hung with material that Nelly recognised from the bundle Phil had taken. It was causing a lot of comment but no explanations were offered. A stool was set behind it. Who could it be for? All Johnny would tell them was that at ten o'clock they would have their questions answered, when their special guest arrived.

Johnny began singing a song that could go on for ever, 'Did You Ever See Such A Funny Thing Before' and after fifteen verses, each more embarrassing than the last, Ethel stopped it as she heard the beginning of the verse about brother Morgan and his organ. There were cries of disappointment.

'None of that sort of thing when Delina gets here, mind,' Ethel warned. If she ever does, she thought bitterly. 'Come on, Fay love, pass these plates around, will you? Perhaps a bit of grub will stop them singing disgusting songs and frightening the cats.' She passed a pile of plates and Fay and Johnny began to distribute them among the forest of hands eagerly waiting for the food. There were huge platters of sandwiches, some of egg and others filled with brawn which Ethel had made. There were vegetable pasties flavoured with Oxo and brushed with egg to improve the look of the low-fat pastry.

Ethel watched the food disappear and refilled the plates with cakes. Nelly had brought some scones and there was fruit cake in a large slab, which Ethel called 'cut-and-come-again cake'. Amy had sent some iced fancies, and from the oven beside the fire Netta's hot mince pies appeared.

Ethel watched to make sure no one was forgotten, and all the time her dark eyes glanced repeatedly to the door, waiting for Maurice and Delina. She had been so certain they would have been among the first to arrive. Their engagement was just as much a cause for celebration here as at the Honeymans'.

She shivered at the possibility that she was going to be excluded from all the joy and excitement of the wedding preparations. Even her offer to make the cake had been refused.

'Shall I go and fetch them, Mam?' Phil suggested, seeing the look in her eyes and guessing the cause. He was angry with his younger brother. 'Thoughtless sod, I bet he's forgotten the time.'

'No, give him a while longer,' Ethel said. 'Better he doesn't come than if he comes on sufferance.'

Phil clenched his teeth. He would have strong words with Maurice over this. And the surprise he and Johnny had arranged would start as soon as the food was cleared whether Maurice was there or not! 'Thoughtless, inconsiderate sod,' he said aloud.

Bert Roberts's head bobbed up prepared to argue. 'Who, me? What d'you mean?'

'Why, what you been up to then?' Nelly asked.

Speculation on what guilty secret had made Bert think himself accused kept everyone entertained until Sidney took out his mandolin and the singing started again. Then, when Johnny gave him a signal, he strummed loudly to gain silence. Fay smiled at Johnny and raised an eyebrow in question but he shook his head, refusing to tell her what was about to happen.

'Our visitor has arrived and Phil will go and welcome her,' Johnny announced. Then Phil caused an uproar by pulling the chain on the gas light and putting it out completely. But Ethel had been forwarned and carried a small oil-lamp in from the kitchen where it had been lit in readiness. In its ghostly light they saw that the empty stool behind the draped table was now occupied.

A gypsy woman sat there dressed in flowing garments which smelt of mildew and damp. Her long hair almost covered the lean, long-nosed face, and when she spoke she had a high-pitched, wheezing voice.

'Like she sat on somethin' 'ot!' Nelly said to Oliver.

'I want you to pass this crystal ball among you and make sure everyone touches it,' the woman said, handing a glass ball to Billie who was nearest.

Ethel watched as each person touched the glass ball and wondered what a psychiatrist would make of them all. Some held it lovingly, wrapping both hands around its cool surface, while others hurriedly passed it on, perhaps afraid to leave an impression on it and give away a secret. Bert refused to handle it at all, and in the indistinct lighting, Ethel was almost certain that Fay had her fingers crossed.

The ball was returned to the gypsy and as she was about to speak, Johnny whispered something to her, and gestured towards the front door. The gypsy stood and with a theatrical waving of arms, said, 'I heard someone approaching, someone who will want to borrow a cup of sugar.' They all looked at the door expectantly. There was a knock, Johnny opened the door and Milly Toogood was there. Inevitably, behind her was Sybil Tremain.

'Come to borrow a cup of sugar?' Nelly shouted.

'No, a cup of flour.' Milly stepped back from the gale of laughter and applause but was dragged inside by Johnny.

There was a re-shuffle to find room for the newcomers and this time Billie Brown was quick to sit beside Amy. He sat on the edge of his seat to protect her from the crush. Many of those who were lucky enough to have found a chair were regretting it, being sat on, leaned against and stifled under the press of people as the gypsy began again.

The room was quiet as the woman studied the glass ball intently, and some of her audience began to squirm uneasily, not knowing what to expect. But the mood was spoilt again when Delina and Maurice finally arrived. They were immediately hushed and stood in the doorway of the kitchen while the gypsy began to speak.

'I see we have present a man who has just got a ring put through his nose.' Everyone laughed and pointed at Maurice.

'Somebody here is continually flouting authority,' the gypsy continued, and in a pause, everyone looked at his neighbour for a clue. 'This person defies someone wearing a uniform and representing the law. I see baskets of potatoes and carrots and even the occasional onion!'

The gypsy went on to tease most of the people present. Nelly was referred to as the football wife, with her husband sometimes home, sometimes away.

Nelly watched the gypsy for a hint of her real identity and when she rubbed the side of her nose with a gloved hand she stood up and laughed, pointing a finger, she called out 'Phil Davies, you silly old fool!'

The crowd began to quieten down, splitting up into small groups, subdued by the food and drink and the heat of the overcrowded room. Fay struggled to reach Delina.

'When are you and Maurice getting married?' she asked.

'Early in April, we think,' Delina told her.

'And we're going to have a horse and carriage, what d'you think of that, Fay?' Maurice shouted from where he was cuffing Phil and helping to dispose of the smelly clothes. 'And a real splash do at the hotel in town.'

'Splash do!' Delina laughed. 'A reception at the Royal Hotel!'

'Bridesmaids?' Fay coaxed.

'There will be six, three from my family and three from Maurice's we hope. I won't tell you what colour though.'

'You haven't known him long,' Fay said. 'Are you sure you can put up with him?' She joked, but there was a serious question behind the smile.

'Oh yes. We both knew straight away.'

'You're different from how I imagined Maurice's wife would be. Your education for a start,' Fay insisted.

'We'll both change and grow together, I'm sure of it.'

'Change Maurice you mean?'

'Don't we all choose a husband and then set about trying to change him?' Ethel Davies laughed. But Delina shook her head firmly.

'There's nothing I've learnt about Maurice that I would want to change.'

'For Gawd's sake lock her up 'til April, Maurice, so she don't find out what you're really like!' Nelly shouted.

Talk of the forthcoming wedding evoked memories of

weddings past and the mood became maudlin, the occasional singing sentimental. Nelly tried to sing 'By a Babbling Brook' again and Billie shut her up with a glass of beer once more. More and more outrageous jokes were aimed at the engaged couple, and Maurice sang his own version of 'Men of Harlech', which began: 'Men of Vigour grow much bigger . . .'

'Are you sure you can cope with this?' Fay asked Delina, who had blushed at the sauciness of the words.

'There's more than one way to live, it's a mistake to expect everyone to behave the way you're used to behaving.'

Amy listened to the hum of a dozen conversations around her and in the crowded room felt lonely. It was not that she lacked attention. Billie Brown seemed to spend all his evening making her comfortable and seeing that she needed nothing.

'I'll walk down home with you when you go, keep an eye,' he said now, as she began to stir.

'There's no need, Billie, I'm used to looking after myself. Go you with Mary, you can't let her walk home alone while you come with me!'

'We've got the tractor outside,' he said and that caused a laugh.

'That's no vehicle for courtin', Billie,' Johnny said.

'Who's courting?' Amy snapped. She hated it when people teased her about finding herself a man. It was a relief when the door opened and Vic Honeyman pushed his way in. Constable Harris went outside to the *tŷ bach*, the little house, at the bottom of the garden, and Vic slipped into his place beside Amy.

'I came to see if Maurice was sober enough to walk Delina home,' he explained. 'I can't have her wandering about at this time of night on her own.'

'I'm not drunk, just a bit silly,' Maurice called, having heard his words.

'Then I can walk you and Margaret back,' Vic said.

'It's all right, I just offered,' Billie said and Amy was amused at all the attention she was getting.

Sidney brought out his mandolin again and, to everyone's surprise, George sang 'Bless This House' in a wonderful bass voice. Nelly was overcome by the beauty of it.

'What a voice,' she gasped at Amy. 'It's like milky cocoa on a cold winter's night.'

As a few people began to leave, the men settled to play cards. The crib board was brought out along with ha' pennies and pennies. The women made tea and began to tackle the chaos in the back kitchen. At four, the house was finally quiet and Nelly and George, who were among the last to leave, wandered home through the lane, stopping to go into the wood for a few last private moments, and singing all the way.

They opened the door and the dogs rushed out into the garden. Without bothering to close it again, Nelly climbed the stairs to bed and George sprawled happily on the couch.

Amy and Margaret and Oliver walked home accompanied part of the way by Billie and Mary on their tractor. Vic waved them goodbye thankfully at the end of Gypsy Lane and took Amy's arm for the rest of the way. They too sang all the way, but Amy didn't invite Vic into the house. Still singing, he wandered slowly back through the village and up the lane to the council estate. Passing Delina and Maurice in the porch, he called goodnight and went to bed.

The new year of 1954 began with everyone in a contented state. George was working regularly for Mr Leighton and apparently enjoying it. Oliver seemed much more relaxed and able to talk more easily with Evie.

The shock of his running away had only made a slight difference in her attitude towards him. She still felt a deep disappointment that he was not a brilliant student, but she did try harder not to let her regrets show. She spent more time with him and coaxed him to read without sending him to his room to struggle alone. She would never have admitted it to Nelly, but she had begun to allow him to choose simpler books to built his confidence. She praised him more, holding back the criticisms which still came too readily to her lips.

Amy was growing used to being without Freddy, who had written to tell her he would soon be home for a week's leave. Billie called occasionally to see if she needed a strong arm, and Vic sometimes called with one of his sons as chaperone. Margaret had passed her first music exam and was already progressing towards the next. She seemed to call in to see Mrs French more often and Amy guessed the friendship was good for both of them and didn't mind. The shop, although quieter than before Christmas, was doing well and with the extra income from renting the flat, Amy was well content.

Nelly worked three mornings each week, plus a few hours for Amy in the new house. The promised work in the Powells' flat had not materialised. She had called a few times but had been told that the place was being decorated and would she call again, later, when things were straight? The money was not as urgent now that George was earning, but she still wanted the extra cash. She wanted to buy George a new bed.

'Is that Mrs Powell in?' she asked Amy one morning.

'I think so. I heard someone moving about, but I don't think it was Mrs Powell. Go and knock on the front door.'

Nelly ignored the suggestion. It was blowing a gale and

cold enough to make your head feel as if it were splitting. Instead she went up the stairs inside the shop which Amy had once used to get to the flat above and raised her hand to knock on the door before shouting to see if there was anyone in. But a strange noise stopped her. She pressed her ear to the crack and listened, then crept back downstairs to Amy.

'Come 'ere an' listen to this. What d'you think it is?'

Amy listened then said, 'Someone being sick by the sound of it. Perhaps Mavis is off work and ill. D'you think I should go up and see if she wants a doctor?'

'No, I expect she went out on the razzle last night an' is sufferin' because of it,' Nelly whispered back.

Amy smiled. 'Don't judge everyone by yourself, Nelly Luke!'

They crept back down.

A while later, Amy heard footsteps on the stairs and saw Sheila go out. The girl wore a lot of makeup as usual, but Amy thought she looked pale. She wondered if she should offer some help but Sheila walked across to the bus stop and a customer came in and the incident was forgotten.

When Margaret came home from school, Amy asked her to go and see her Auntie Prue. 'She hasn't sent me an order this week, and there's no reply when I 'phone. Perhaps the 'phone is out of order. Go and see, will you love?'

When Margaret returned she looked puzzled.

'I knocked at the back door and at the front, Mam, but she didn't answer and I know she was in. I saw the curtains move.'

Amy, taking Margaret with her, went to see Prue as soon as she could close the shop. She shouted through the letterbox that she would not go away until the door was opened.

'Prue? Answer this door at once!' She banged loudly,

knowing how Prue hated to attract attention or cause a scene. 'Answer this door!' She continued banging for several minutes. 'I'll get the police, mind,' she warned. Her determination was rewarded at last by a pale and ill-looking Prue opening the door.

'For goodness' sake, Amy, be quiet. You'll have everyone gawping at me!'

'So what? Now, what's the matter with you, locking yourself in and not bothering to answer the 'phone? Worried sick I was, thinking you were ill. Are you ill? You don't look too good.' Amy was shocked by her sister's appearance but pretended not to have noticed the unkempt hair and the untidy clothes.

'I'm all right. A bit depressed, that's all. I haven't felt like going out.'

'You look as if you haven't been eating either!' Amy turned to Margaret. 'Will you fetch me some fish and chips, love? Sorry to ask you, but I think it's best if I stay with Auntie Prue. All right?'

'All right,' Margaret sighed, 'if I must.'

Amy saw her daughter to the door and handed her some money. 'I think she's ill, love, and I might have to send for the doctor.'

'You needn't get any for me, I'm not hungry,' Prue called, following them into the hall.

Amy stood over Prue while she ate the meal and then went upstairs to collect a few clothes. 'You're coming back with us, for tonight at least. No arguing. Either that or I'll call an ambulance now this minute, and send you to hospital.'

Unusually submissive, Prue agreed.

She was packed into bed with hot water bottles and a couple of aspirin. Within minutes she was asleep. Amy was still undecided whether to ring for the doctor, but eventually judged it best to wait until morning.

'Thanks for your help, love,' she smiled at Margaret.

'D'you think, if I kept my foot on the soft pedal, I could practice for a while?'

Of course. I doubt if Auntie Prue would wake even if you played as loudly as you can. I don't think she's been to bed for ages.'

At Prue's house there had been blankets thrown on the couch in the normally orderly lounge, and upstairs the bed was freshly made up, but there was no sign of bed linen in the washing basket.

Prue stayed for three days, but when she heard that Freddy was coming home she insisted on leaving.

'It's nothing to do with not wanting to see Freddy,' she explained, 'but there are things I have to check on in the business. Maurice is doing well, but he isn't experienced enough yet for me to leave him for days on end.' Her voice was sharp and Amy thought her health much improved. Her previous weariness and tractability had been worrying.

'All right, you can go home, but only if you promise to get someone to call in every morning to see if you're all right. Mrs French will call, I'm sure. I'll come every day after the shop closes. And, you must promise always to answer the 'phone.'

'All right! All this fuss!'

'Auntie Prue is near to being her normal self again,' Amy said to Margaret a little later, 'but she does need watching. Depression can be very dangerous.'

'What's depression, Mam?'

'Not caring what happens to you and thinking you aren't important,' Amy replied. Saying the words aloud seemed to increase her anxiety about Prue. She wondered if things would be better or worse once the baby arrived. She thought she would close early one day and take her shopping for baby clothes. Perhaps that would cheer her up.

Through the coldest, wettest weeks of the new year, Delina and Maurice walked, talked, and delighted in everything they discovered about each other. New flowers shot up among the bedraggled grasses and rotting leaves and seemed a symbol of the new life beginning for them: celandines and snowdrops and the spears of wild daffodils, and later, carpets of white and blue violets delighted their eyes in the wood above Nelly's cottage.

They watched redwings finishing off the last of the berries and fieldfare in flocks on the ploughed fields. Finches worked in pairs in preparation for breeding and hunted for nest sites as leaves opened to give them privacy. Everything was so beautiful, Maurice could not believe it had all been there unnoticed all his life and it had needed Delina to show it to him.

They spent their evenings either with the Honeymans or with Ethel, but gradually they began to stay more often in Ethel's small cottage, where every evening developed into a party, with half the village finding an excuse to call. Ethel's open house was strange at first to Delina but, as she had opened his eyes to the countryside about him, so he had shown her the fun of being involved in a lively, happy neighbourhood.

Ethel had wondered at first about the expense of the large wedding Mrs Honeyman was planning for the young couple, but it gradually became obvious that Mrs Honeyman had come from a rich family and had married beneath her when she married Victor.

'She keeps it all from Victor,' Maurice had confided one

day. 'Now the wedding is a chance to show everyone what she's made of. She put all her money aside for the children, apparently. They're all very clever. The boys will go to university, like the mother did. Yes, they're clever. Dull, mind,' he added with a frown, 'all except Delina and Vic, but clever.' He sounded as if he was not sure being clever was a good thing.

'So all the arrangements are going well?' Ethel said one evening when Delina had brought the inevitable lists out of her handbag.

'The only problem is where we're going to live,' Delina said. 'I've made enquiries at school and looked in all the papers but the only thing I've found is a couple of rooms in a house not far from Mam and Dad. It's not ideal, but it will do for a start.'

'It's how I started, and how I finished, really,' Ethel smiled. 'I came here as a bride to live with my in-laws, and here I still am forty-three years on. I know young people want a place of their own, but I've been so happy here I wouldn't change a single thing in my life. Except this old rheumatism which slows me up something terrible.'

Phil arrived then and when he heard about the two rooms, asked for the address.

'That's Mrs Rees,' he said, frowning in concentration as he visualised the houses in St Illtyd's Road. 'She's Sheila Powell's grandmother – you know, Sheila Powell who lives above Amy's shop.'

Maurice felt his face stiffen with shock. That was the last place he wanted to live! Anything to do with Sheila was unwise. She hadn't bothered him for a while, but he knew that the slightest excuse would bring her back.

'Isn't it a bit far?' he said. 'Surely there's somewhere down on the main road? We'll ask Amy to put a card in her window asking for rooms. There's sure to be someone who'll be glad to earn a bit of rent.'

To his relief, Delina agreed. Still, Maurice did wonder if it might not be better to look in Llangwyn. He could easily travel to work from there, and it would be nearer school for Delina too, and further away from Sheila Powell.

Sidney came with some eggs and some illegal cream made by Mr Leighton, and he was followed by Catrin and Netta who had come to offer rations for the cake making.

'No need, Delina's mother has it all in hand,' Ethel said, trying not to sound disappointed.

'Delina and her mother came to see me and Rita about the girls being bridesmaids. Delyth is quite excited, but we aren't too sure about Megan. Being only four she's a bit worried about it. The new dress appeals though,' he laughed. 'Six bridesmaids she's having, that will cost a bit.' He looked at his future sister-in-law. 'Your dad a millionaire, is he?'

'No, but my mother's family have agreed to pay for my wedding. I'm the only girl and it's their one chance to make a grand occasion of it.'

When the house was quiet again, Ethel sat and smiled happily. To have Maurice home and settled and so obviously in love was a dream come true. She had been so afraid he might not come back to Hen Carw Parc after his years in the army. She picked up the tea cosy she was crocheting and her fingers began to work swiftly. She would finish it by tomorrow and give it to Delina to add to her rapidly growing 'bottom drawer', ready for their new home.

She wondered why Maurice had not wanted to look at the rooms in St Illtyd's Road. Perhaps it was too close to an ex-girlfriend, she chuckled. He certainly went out with a few when he first came home. Phil always let her know what he was up to – and probably exaggerated much of it to make me laugh too, she thought as she snapped the wool and reached for a needle to finish off the tea cosy.

Freddy had been given a lift most of the way home when he came on leave that March. It meant he had to walk a few miles, but the prospect of seeing his mother and Margaret made the journey effortless. He had a rucksack on his back and a small canvas bag in his hand. He whistled as he came towards the village from the direction of Llangwyn, the early morning sun bright behind him.

He heard a bus approaching from the opposite direction and wondered if Johnny would be driving it, but smiled when he was near enough to see that it was the forestry bus, waiting for Archie Pearce as usual. Nothing changes, he thought as Archie rushed out of his house and, half-dressed, clambered into the bus where the impatient driver revved the engine into snorts of disapproval.

The village was still quiet, and he looked up at the closed curtains in the flat above the shop, remembering Sheila, disappointed that in spite of her promises she hadn't written. He watched the curtains as he passed, hoping to see her look out, but they remained closed. He shrugged. His disappointment had not faded, but he realised she was nothing more than a dream. Girls like Sheila were for a quick fling but not for anything permanent.

Amy gave a scream of delight when he opened the back door of 'Heulog', dropped his bags and opened his arms to her.

'Mam, it's great to be home again.' He hugged her and shouted as Margaret ran in and hugged them both. Then they all talked at once. He congratulated Margaret on her exam result, and they discussed the news of Maurice's wedding.

'Delina?' he asked with a frown. 'I thought—' He hesitated. Better not mention Sheila if Maurice was marrying someone else, but Sheila and he had seemed so close—

'I did write and tell you,' Amy laughed. 'Didn't you read my letters?'

Amy had to leave as soon as they had eaten breakfast. Thursday was a busy day with a lot of people wanting their weekly orders.

'I'll come with you,' Freddy suggested. 'I'll give you a hand, then go and see Maurice. Working at Leighton's is he?'

'No! Working for your Auntie Prue. I told you that, too.'

'We've moved a couple of times and I think some of your letters must have got lost. I don't remember hearing about Maurice's job or his wedding.'

'It happened suddenly. Love at first sight,' Amy said. 'It'll be quite soon, early April I believe. Will you be able to get home for it?'

'I'll try. Not very likely though.'

'Sheila Powell asked for your address, didn't she, Mam?' Margaret said.

'I haven't heard from her.' His blue eyes seemed to brighten, Amy noticed, as he added, 'Perhaps that one went astray too. I'd better ask her.'

They walked to the shop, Freddy pushing his bicycle with Margaret on the crossbar. There seemed to be so much to talk about after his absence, letters only touched the surface of the news.

The village was waking up as they neared the shop. Nelly was standing with her dogs, waiting for Amy to open up, Milly Toogood's daughter was cleaning her shop, a few people waited for the bus to Llangwyn. Freddy's heart seemed to stop when he saw Sheila run across the road and stand in the queue of people, but he only waved and didn't go to talk to her. There was no point really, first she had teased him and she then had made it clear what she thought of him. He wondered vaguely how she felt about Maurice getting married. Was she upset? Or did she look on every affair as short-lived anyway? He thought he would ask her if she had written though. A letter and a photograph of a girl like her wouldn't do his image any harm with his new friends.

'Know her well, do you?' Margaret had seen the brief salute. 'Fancies herself she does.'

'She's very pretty.'

'Shop assistant she is, but she calls herself a saleswoman and calls the shop a saloon.'

'Salon,' Amy laughingly corrected.

Amy forgot all about Sheila and her parents as her work filled every moment, but as the time came for her to close, she heard Mrs Powell coming down the stairs. She walked past the window, tutting at the boxes still outside, and entered the shop, her eyes glaring angrily.

'Now what?' Amy muttered. 'Something else wrong with the flat?'

'I need to talk to you urgently.' Mavis said.

'I haven't much time. I have to finish here then go home to cook—'

'This is more important than cooking!'

'Oh?'

'Our daughter is pregnant, and I believe your son is responsible.'

Chapter Eleven

Amy reeled with shock as she took in Mavis's words and it was a moment before she could reply. Denial, ridicule, disbelief all passed through her mind and for a moment she even thought of the words of the gypsy, who had seen her caring for a baby. No, not Freddy, it couldn't be.

'Freddy is barely sixteen,' she said at last.

'He's a man. And he's the only one I've even seen with Sheila. She denies it of course, won't say who the father is, but she's a simple girl, an innocent child, and I can't let him get away with it. Why should he? In this life you pay for what you do. Break the rules and you have to accept the consequences.'

The shrill voice went on and on, while Amy wondered what to do. Best to say as little as possible, except to deny it, she decided.

'I'm sure you're mistaken. If Sheila herself won't blame Freddy, why should you presume he's responsible? I'll talk to him,' she went on quickly, refusing to allow Mavis to interrupt and turn the conversation into a slanging match. 'I'll talk to him and we'll discuss it again. If necessary.' She ushered the woman out of the shop and pulled down the blind. She pushed the bolt across with unnecessary force, overcome by anger.

Amy stood for a long time in the silent shop, her nerves

jangling and her hands tightly clenched. How could she deal with this? For a moment a wave of self-pity overwhelmed her. She was always alone. Everything important or worrying had to be faced alone. She thought of Harry and wondered what his advice would be.

Deny it, his voice seemed to whisper in her ear and she frowned. Would she accept anyone else's advice about her son if there were someone to discuss it with? No. There had been so many times before when she had faced things alone. She was too used to making her own decisions.

Remembering her own lonely pregnancies she felt a pang of sympathy for Sheila, but refused to allow that to cloud concern for her son. Sheila must be secondary, but she knew she would make sure, so far as she could, that the child was cared for properly and lovingly. Babies are the innocent ones, not the girls like Sheila. Or herself.

It was late when she finished cashing the till and doing the books and when she left Freddy and Margaret were waiting for her.

'Thought we'd walk back to meet you, Mam,' Freddy said, taking the basket of groceries she carried.

Amy stared at him. He was taller, and seemed to have filled out since the army had taken him from her. He was a man and, she guessed, quite capable of making love to a woman. She tried to pretend, tried to think of him as a child, who wanted nothing more than a day's fishing to be happy. But walking beside him, hardly reaching his broad shoulders, it was impossible to deny his adulthood.

Margaret was laughing, trying to guide the wheels of the bicycle through puddles, when Freddy caught sight of Amy's face and saw her distress.

'Something wrong, Mam?'

'I'll tell you later,' she said quickly.

'I see,' Margaret said. 'That means it doesn't include me!' She skipped ahead, leaving Freddy and her mother alone.

'Mind the road and walk, don't run.' Amy warned as they reached the place where the road narrowed.

'What is it, Mam?' Freddy asked again.

'Mavis Powell came to see me.'

'More complaints about the flat?'

'No. About you.'

'Me?' His eyes behind the glasses clouded. 'What have I done?'

'Sheila is pregnant and she says you are the father.' The words came out quickly.

'Not true, Mam.'

Amy looked up at him and sighed with relief. She believed him completely. 'Thank goodness for that. I'd hate to see you mixed up with that one, she seems like nothing but trouble to me.'

'Sheila's all right. I've been out with her once or twice but we never – there's no chance I'm the father of her baby. I promise you that.'

'There's a load off my mind. I'll talk to her tomorrow and tell her to look somewhere else for her scapegoat. Fancy her thinking that a young boy like you would—Well, at least that has set my mind easy.'

Too young, Freddy thought as he passed his Auntie Prue's house. He couldn't look across, afraid to see her and be reminded of the terrible thing he had done. That pregnancy must be obvious now and he felt a shiver of dismay pass through him from head to foot. If Mam only knew how easily Auntie Prue could prove he was not too young!

* * *

How gossip filtered so quickly through the village was always a source of amazement to Amy, and the news of Sheila's pregnancy seemed to spread faster than normal. The only two who seemed unaware of the gossip were Delina and Maurice, who were oblivious to everyone but each other. Everyone else who came into the shop spoke of it, but the fact that Freddy's name was included worried and annoyed Amy.

'No! Freddy is not the father and I'll sue anyone heard repeating that he is!' She flared up, when the third person congratulated her on the prospect of being a grandmother.

She ran up to the flat, and when there was no reply, pushed a note under the door warning them not to spread untrue rumours about her son. Ralph and Mavis came into the shop and, without waiting for it to empty, insisted that Freddy must accept responsibility.

'There's no mention of her being even seen with anyone else,' Mavis screeched at Freddy. 'You were seen with her in the park, outside her shop, walking in the lanes, and standing outside the house late at night, calling for her to come out. And her in her night-dress too. No one else has ever been seen with her except you. And don't forget her father and I saw her half undressed at the bonfire party and who did she go with? You!'

'There were others,' Freddy confided to Amy after several days of this. 'One of them was Maurice and I can't tell anyone that, can I, not with him and Delina getting married in a few weeks' time.'

'I think you must, Freddy. I doubt if Maurice was the only one. She's the sort of girl who likes men and would never settle for only one. Neighbours who live next door to her grandmother complained about her walking about half naked, and—'

'I don't want to hear, right Mam? I only know I didn't make her pregnant.'

'Then tell someone about Maurice and any other boys you know about. Please, Freddy. You can't have your life spoilt because of loyalty to Maurice Davies, friend or not.'

'You tell Mrs Powell, Mam. I know it's cheating, but it won't be so bad if it isn't me who says it.'

Mavis Powell hadn't been to work for days. In fact, the way she felt, it was unlikely she would ever work again. She saw Sheila off to the bus, and Ralph out to meet his friend who gave him a lift, then sat with another pot of tea, wondering what to do to make Freddy face up to what he had done. She was still sitting, unwashed and with her hair uncombed when there was a knock at the door.

She fastened her dressing-gown and ran her fingers ineffectually through her hair before going downstairs to answer it. Probably Phil Davies, the post, she thought. But it was Amy, smartly dressed in a costume of pale beige, with a green jumper, a plastic mac over her arm, emerald and diamanté earings dangling and sparkling in the morning sun. She made Mavis feel scruffy. She straightened the gown around her and began to apologise for her appearance.

'I'm sorry, but I've—'

'Don't worry, this won't take long.'

Amy pushed her way in and waited impatiently for the woman to go back up the stairs. She looked so determined that Mavis went without a word of protest. In the living room the dishes still sat on the table, and the ashes lay where they had fallen from last night's fire.

'I'm sorry about—' Mavis began again.

'Freddy is not the father of Sheila's child and he is far

from the only man your daughter has been seeing. I have three other names for you. No doubt you'll find plenty more!' Amy stood at the door of the room, and Mavis was foolishly reminded of a mother cat defending her young.

'Maurice Davies is one,' Amy continued 'and I'll bet that once you stop trying to implicate my Freddy, you'll find plenty who have seen Sheila and Maurice together. Pete Evans and Gerry Williams are two more for you to be going on with. With a reputation like Sheila's, there'll be plenty more. And don't try to stick this on Maurice Davies either. He's getting married in a few weeks to a decent young woman so he's not likely to fall for your threats! Accept what she is and make the best of it, that's my advice!'

'And you're a fine one to give advice, with your record!' Mavis retaliated at last.

'Just don't spread any more lies about my son or I'll complain to the police. Right?'

Amy stormed down the stairs and walked around to the back entrance of the shop. Her hands were shaking as she unlocked the door. At lunchtime she saw Mavis catching a bus into town. That evening, Mavis and Sheila alighted from the bus and walked up the lane towards Ethel's. Amy shrugged. Well, what did it matter if they were pestered for a while? It would give her and Freddy a break.

Rumours spread fast, and the knowledge that Ethel was disappointed that she was not able to make Maurice's wedding cake was a topic of conversation in several gatherings. When it was suggested that she might make a second one for all the friends who would call at the house, Ethel was delighted.

In March 1954 fats were still on ration, but Ethel was determined that Maurice should have the best possible cake and her many friends helped out. Rations of butter came in slowly and steadily. Nelly gave her two ounces two weeks in a row, and Phil's wife, Catrin, mixed half butter and half margarine to make her contribution.

Amy received her supplies in bulk and when she had weighed out the small pats into greaseproof paper, she gave the butter-smeared sheets that had wrapped the fifty-six pound slab to Ethel. Many others gradually swelled her collection.

One tin was already made and packed away in Ethel's cool larder. The second was in the oven sending tantalizing smells through the house.

'Soya flour will have to do for the marzipan layer,' she was explaining to Delina as they washed the basins and bowls she had been using. The big mixing bowl still stood on the scrubbed wooden table when Maurice came home from work. He came in, sniffing appreciatively and taking in the scene. After kissing Delina and his mother he picked up the bowl and, like a child, began to clean it with his fingers.

'Marvellous, Mam. Deeelicious! I can't wait.'

There was a mock battle underway as Ethel tried to take the bowl for washing, when through the open door they saw visitors coming. This was hardly unusual, the house was rarely empty, but unless they had come to bring a gift, as so many of the villagers had done, they couldn't think why Mavis Powell and her daughter were visiting.

'I'll go and change out of my suit, Mam,' Maurice escaped up the stairs and sat on his bed, meaning to wait until Sheila and her mother had gone. Trouble was, with Mam people usually stayed and stayed. Never let a visitor go without a cup of tea and a bite to eat, would Mam.

When he heard his mother calling him down he groaned.

He hadn't seen Sheila for weeks and hoped never to see her again. But there, he was so happy, he could spare a few moments for her. She had probably brought him a present. Swiftly changing into a pair of tan trousers and a brown sports jacket, he ran downstairs, knowing that if Delina knew of his affair with Sheila it would be difficult for her to understand. He took a few breaths to calm himself before going in. He sat down next to Delina and held her hand firmly.

Sheila sat close to her mother and her fair head was bent, not looking at anyone. Fear began to twist his insides.

'What is it, mam?' he asked. Ethel shook her head.

'I don't know. They wanted to talk to you, Maurice.'

'My daughter is expecting a baby and she says you are the father.' Mavis said, loudly and forcefully. Sheila burst into tears. Maurice turned to Delina, pleading with her silently not to believe it.

'I don't think that's true, Sheila,' he said. 'What makes you say such a thing?'

The girl continued to cry softly. Ethel made a move to go and comfort her as Mavis was sitting coldly by, but seeing the stricken expression on her son's face she held back.

'Sheila?' Maurice said, determined to bluff, even if it meant humiliating the girl. 'What are you talking about? Why are you saying this? Lies won't get you out of your difficulties.'

Sheila stood up then and stepped towards him.

'I'm sorry, Maurice. I really tried not to say. I really did. But Mam got it out of me. I didn't want to tell about us. I know you don't really love me, not now, since you met Delina and abandoned me.'

Nothing could have been more telling, and Delina gasped in horror. She looked from Maurice to the girl and back to

Maurice. 'It's true, isn't it?' she said, staring down at the table. 'You have given this girl a baby.'

'Wait a minute, let the condemned man speak!' Maurice blustered. But Sheila, standing wiping her tears away, added, 'Maurice, I'm so frightened. I had to tell Mam about the baby coming. I couldn't cope without help. I'm sorry you had to be named. I did try to keep it our secret.'

Delina pulled her hand free from Maurice's and his shoulders drooped in despair.

'Don't leave me, Delina, please. I love you,' he whispered, but Delina's eyes were moist and accusing as she stood up and walked away, to sit close to Ethel.

'You'll have to give the child a name,' she said through trembling lips. 'It's an innocent child and is entitled to your name.'

'No, I can't marry Sheila. I love you. How can you even suggest it?' Maurice stood up but was stopped by Ethel's hand. He slumped back into his seat.

'I'm sorry Maurice,' Sheila whispered. 'I tried to keep our affair a secret, but—'

Delina sat unmoving, her pale face drawn with shock, her blue eyes brimming with unshed tears.

'They'll have to marry,' Mavis insisted. She looked at Ethel, who was sitting stony-faced, her dark eyes troubled. 'It's your grandchild my daughter is carrying. Can you send her away to have your grandchild without it's having a name? Can you?'

Ethel thought of the unborn child, and she already wanted it and loved it as part of her family. She could not bear the thought of losing anything so precious. But then her deep dark eyes looked at Maurice who was staring at Delina with such unhappiness on his young face. He was only twenty-three and he loved Delina so much.

They sat through most of the evening, Ethel occasionally making tea or coffee, and since Mavis and Sheila had arrived there were miraculously no other callers. At eleven-thirty Victor arrived to see what had happened to his daughter.

'We were worried, see,' he said almost apologetically. 'It's not like Delina to be so late without telling us first. Very considerate she is and we—' his voice tapered off when he saw the serious faces. 'What's happened? Not burnt the cake you're making?' He looked at the cake which had been taken from the oven and which now stood ignored on the small table. 'Damn, Ethel, that smells good.'

'Dad,' Delina said in a small voice. 'Take me home please. There isn't going to be a wedding.'

'What? But—tell me what's happened.' He hugged Delina who had run to him, and looked at Maurice for an explanation. But it was Mavis who replied.

'Maurice has got my daughter pregnant, Mr Honeyman, and he has to do the right thing.'

'How can it be the right thing when I don't love Sheila? It's Delina I love and what went before is nothing to do with that. Damn it all, man, we're getting married in a couple of weeks!' Maurice's outburst was received in silent disapproval by Delina.

'Maurice, whatever you decide about Sheila and your baby, I won't marry you. I can't, knowing that somewhere in the world there's a child who was refused a name.'

'Delina!'

'I'll fetch my coat, Mrs Davies. I think it's behind the back door.' She went through to the back kitchen where she had so recently washed up the baking tins and bowls from the preparation of her wedding cake. She took her coat from its peg and went through to the living room and, without a glance at Maurice, walked past him out into the dark, cold night.

Vic gave an embarrassed good-night to the room in general and no one in particular, unable to look at Maurice's stricken face. The door closed behind them and Maurice was stopped from going after them by Ethel. On the wall, the old clock struck twelve. It had been a long night.

Sheila and Mavis left, saying they would be back with Ralph the next morning. Maurice sat on as if unaware of their leaving. His face was curled and twisted in an agony of wretchedness. Ethel went to bed, but Maurice stayed up until dawn crept through the closed curtains and told him the worst day in his life was over.

Plans whirled crazily through his head. If Delina had not refused to go on with the wedding he would have been as generous as he could to Sheila, given her an allowance for the child. They could have worked something out. But he knew without a doubt that Delina meant what she said. There was no point in trying to see her and persuade her to reconsider. It was over.

At six-thirty he went into the back kitchen and washed. Then he put on his suit ready to go to work. His mind was made up. He would marry Sheila, but that was all he would do.

The sad little ceremony took place near the end of March on a cold, gusty afternoon. Maurice made his vows without any intention of keeping them. Sheila tried to hold his hand but he found it impossible to touch her. She had destroyed his wonderful new life before it had begun. He was filled with such hatred and bitterness, he thought it must show on the photographs that came from the clicking cameras around them.

Sheila wore a plain cream dress and carried a white prayer book with a small spray of flowers marking the page of the marriage service. Maurice wore the suit he used for the office, the buttonhole the Powells had sent up had been thrown on to the kitchen table and left there to die, like his hope of a happy future.

A few people from the village stood to greet them as they left the Register Office and Nelly was one of those preparing to throw confetti, but the look on Maurice's face stopped her.

Johnny and Fay drove them back to Ethel's, and the newly-wed couple waited in silence for the rest to arrive. They ate the cake which Ethel had iced with less than her usual enthusiasm, accepted the good wishes of all who had come in tones more appropriate to a funeral, and as soon as was reasonably polite, dressed to leave.

Leaving the rest to enjoy the party food which Ethel and Mavis had prepared, Maurice took his bride back to her grandmother's house and the rooms where he was expected to make a home and a life with Sheila.

At Ethel's, the party remained sober and subdued until Mavis and Ralph left, but then the atmosphere became more cheerful as everyone tried to cheer Ethel up. They all tried to give her a few happy moments to remember of the day her youngest son married.

The following day, Sheila woke to find a note from Maurice telling her he was leaving. He had risen early, cycled into Swansea and caught a train to London, from where he would shortly leave to start a new life in Australia, alone.

* * *

Talk about the unfortunate affair filled every corner of the village for days and a constant stream of callers filled Ethel's kitchen, all bent on cheering her up. Unkindly, most of the blame went not on Sheila and Maurice, but on Mavis and Ralph as the villagers didn't fully understand the difficulties they had had with their flighty daughter.

Ethel was devastated. Of her four sons, Maurice was the youngest and still her 'baby'. He had needed her protection and guidance, and she had failed him. Now he was gone and it was unlikely she would ever see him again. It was difficult not to hate Sheila and her mother.

Mavis gave up her part-time job in Woolworths and seemed hardly to leave the flat. She came down to the shop when it was at its quietest, bought what she needed, and scuttled back upstairs like a terrified dormouse, so in need of shelter and safety she could think of nothing else.

One morning, while Amy was putting out the vegetables and preparing the shop of her first customers, she heard a knock at the door and, lifting the blind to scold whoever it was for coming too early, she saw Mavis. She was wrapped in an all-concealing loose coat with a hood. She opened the door to her and dropped the blind again in case anyone else had the same idea. Really, she thought, if I opened twenty-three hours a day there would still be someone not suited!

'I'm not really open yet,' she said.

'I know. I wanted to ask you something and as it's private, I thought you wouldn't mind me coming early.'

'What is it?' Amy's voice was sharp, expecting to be told of something more needed for the flat.

'It's about a job. I wondered if you needed someone to help, part time. Any hours you like.'

Amy was surprised. Having hidden herself away for weeks, it seemed an unlikely thing for Mavis to do.

'Well, I have been thinking of taking someone on, but I haven't made up my mind yet,' she extemporised, giving herself time to consider. She wasn't sure she could stand having Mavis around her for hours on end, and she remembered the untidy state of the living room that day she had called unannounced.

'I am experienced in shop work and I need to—' Mavis hesitated then began again. 'I know what people think of me and Sheila for what we did to Maurice, but I can't hide for ever. I thought that by facing everyone and letting them say what they think until they get fed up with saying it, well, it seems the only way if we don't move right away from Hen Carw Parc.'

'That's remarkably brave,' Amy said. 'Will you be able to cope? Some people can be very nasty. I'm not thrilled with your behaviour myself, mind.'

'I'll concentrate on doing a good job for you. That will make it easier.'

'Right then,' Amy said, 'you can start now. Go on, get yourself tidied up a bit. Shoes, not slippers, and get a bit of makeup on. Does wonders to know you look your best in situations like this."

'But I wasn't thinking of—'

'Now!'

Nelly was utterly content. George had been to see Leighton again and was working at the farm regularly. He still hadn't said he would stay. He still felt uneasy about the way he had found himself a home and did not want anyone to think that had been his plan all along. But each week he said, 'Perhaps I could stay another week?'

'Or two?' Nelly would coax and they would laugh and continue to enjoy their simple life in the cottage at the edge of the wood.

They often sat up late at night and watched the fox wander around their garden, and listen as the vixen called her shrill bark, as eerie as the hoot of the owl who often sat on the branch of a fir tree close by.

The gypsies had gone, leaving only the pale yellow patches on the grass to show for their winter sojourn. Even these were fading fast in the strengthening sun and soon the strong new growth would hide the fact they had ever stayed. Nelly was not sorry to see them leave. She would miss having Clara to talk to, but their departure meant the beginning of better weather and the end of the long dark nights. The new season was upon them with the promise of flowers and fresh new leaves, and her old gnarled apple tree blossomed for spring as beautifully as ever.

Flowers had always marked the seasons for Nelly and she and George delighted in each new discovery as the leaves unfolded and buds stretched themselves and burst into colour. Snowdrops and tiny wild daffodils appeared in secret parts of the wood, and on banks where the sun slipped through the green umbrella the gold of celandines spread like a priceless carpet.

Nelly and George were unaware that their footsteps had been followed by Maurice and his lovely Delina, and that the same happy memories of seasons passing and colours changing were held in the hearts of the young couple with more sadness than joy.

Coming back from an early walk one morning, a dog fox crossed Nelly's path and Bobby and Spotty gave chase. Nelly waited patiently until they returned, panting and looking a bit foolish. She was still laughing and patting the dogs at the gate when Phil arrived. He was hot, having rushed through his rounds.

'Put the kettle on then,' he panted, waving a letter as she opened the gate.

'A letter for me?' Nelly held out a hand.

Phil put it behind his back, then walked down the path behind her and sat on the chair near the open door.

'Kettle first, then I might give it to you,' he teased. 'And what about a bit of cake? Starvin' I am. Catrin doesn't feed me proper you know.'

'I shouldn't think she needs to with all you gets on your rounds!' Nelly moved the kettle over the fire and put tea in the brown pot. Phil gave her the letter and waited hopefully for her to open it.

'Looks official,' he said.

'Yes, I'll leave it fer George to see to. Smashin' it is, 'avin' someone to talk things over with. I don't know 'ow long 'e'll stay but I hopes it's fer ever. Sharin's so good after bein' on me own fer so long.'

Phil dug deep into his sack and produced a newspaper-wrapped parcel. 'Mam sent this,' he said. 'They might make a meal. Must be off now, the secret watcher is sure to be on duty. Late I am. It's your fault, Nelly, forcin' me to stay for that second cup.'

Nelly unwrapped the parcel and waved her thanks, smiling her crooked smile at the kind gesture. It was sprout tops, enough for her and George to have with their potatoes and gravy that evening. Roll on Friday, she sighed, when there would be a bit of meat.

George was late and the letter sat on the mantelpiece while they ate their meal. It wasn't until they were sitting in the garden in the fading light, listening to the last murmurings of the birds and the occasional shuffle of wild creatures in the grass, that Nelly mentioned it.

George read it with the aid of a torch, unwilling to go

inside and miss the last moments of the dying day.

'They're going to connect your cottage to the mains, Nelly. You'll have a tap in the house at last. What d'you think of that?'

'Oh my Gawd! 'Ow am I goin' to pay for that?' She stood up and began pacing around the garden, trying to think how she could prevent the work being done. 'It's that Evie's doin'. She's at the bottom of this, tryin' to get me out of 'ere. Oh, George, I thought she'd settled for peace and quiet at last. Now this!' She screwed the letter up and almost threw it away.

'Don't destroy the letter, Nelly, that won't do any good. I think we should go and see Evie and Tim. See if they know anything about this before we accuse them.'

'But it's bound to cost money and I ain't got none!'

'Let's go now and see what Evie has to say.'

Nelly went to collect her coat, discarding the idea of dressing with care as she tried to do these days when visiting her daughter. She threw on the old navy coat she used for gardening and waited while George built up the fire.

'An we'll take the dogs,' she said defiantly. 'No good bein' thoughtful in the 'ope she'll be kinder. Come on dogs, and save some piddle for Evie's front door!'

Oliver was in bed when they arrived and the table was set for two.

'What's this then?' Nelly asked when they were shown into the living room. 'Don't you share with young Oliver? Or does 'e 'ave bread an' scrape while you eats the meat ration?'

'Hush, Nelly,' George warned, 'save the big guns until later, eh?'

'What did you want, Mother? As you see, Timothy and I are about to dine.'

'It's about this.' Nelly thrust the letter at her and added, 'Seems you're tryin' to get me thrown out, again! Where d'you think I'd find the money to pay fer a lavatory – supposin' I wanted one, which I don't?'

Timothy came down the stairs, having settled Oliver to sleep with a story.

'Hush, Mother-in-law, you'll wake your grandson.'

'I want to know why you got me involved in this expense if it ain't a plot to get me out of me cottage?'

'Evie,' Timothy said in his quiet voice, 'you tell her.'

Nelly looked at George with a suspicious frown.

'Timothy and I,' Evie began, 'have arranged to pay for certain improvements to your cottage.'

'You – blimey, you never 'ave!'

'When Mrs Norwood Bennet-Hughes saw your cottage, she convinced me that you deserved some assistance and with the council getting the drains in, we have agreed to pay the rest.'

'I don't know what to say.'

' "Thank you" might be nice,' Evie said sarcastically.

'Thank you.' Nelly spoke as if in a dream. Then her usual distrust of her daughter returned and she said, 'I ain't promisin' to use it, mind.'

They stood discussing the arrangements for a while, Nelly's eyes glowing with the surprise. As she prepared to leave, she turned to Evie and asked, 'Oh, can you lend us a couple of cups and saucers? I'm a bit short an' I'll 'ave to make tea fer the workmen. Nice that'll be, a bit of company while George is working.'

'Remember you're a married woman,' George joked, but Evie and Timothy did not laugh.

Mavis found the first few days in the shop very difficult.

Some spoke to her in a friendly way, but asked questions about Sheila that she found embarrassing. Others refused to allow her to serve them and waited until Amy was free. Amy treated them all in her matter of fact way and gradually things changed. Sheila returned to live at home and the events faded in importance.

Victor Honeyman called at the shop with goods one Wednesday and suggested that he and his sons might come to give Amy a hand with her garden. His interest in her was obvious, but he always brought one of the boys when he called at the house so no scandal attached itself to either of them. But he was becoming a regular visitor at 'Heulog'.

A few of Amy's customers would stop by when out for a walk and stay for a cup of tea. Nelly went each week to clean and she and George called with bunches of wild flowers when their walks took them in that direction. Billie Brown also visited occasionally, usually arriving on his tractor. Nelly teased Amy about her men-friends and how easily she managed to get work done.

'It's not 'avin' your 'Arry around to do things,' she said in a conspiratorial whisper. 'Most people knew 'ow it was between yer and stayed clear. Now, well, them gypsies might be right an' you'll be findin' yerself a handsome 'usband one day soon.'

'When Mavis accused Freddy of making Sheila pregnant I thought they were right about me looking after a baby,' she confessed, 'but only for a moment, mind. I knew Freddy wasn't likely to be responsible. He's a bit young anyway, but I'm sure he'd respect a girl too much for that.'

'Well, 'uman nature being what it is . . .' Nelly said and Amy thought it best not to ask what she meant.

Amy called daily on Prue but as the weeks passed Prue seemed to become more withdrawn. Amy tried asking others to call, including the vicar's wife, but Prue would answer the door to no one but her sister, or to Margaret when she brought groceries.

Nelly still glared as she passed the house, her dislike for Prue no less because she was expecting a child, but she was stopped one morning by loud knocking on the window and, going to investigate, found Prue in the kitchen, sitting on a chair and seemingly unable to move.

'I've tried to ring Amy,' she gasped, 'but there was no reply either at home or the shop.'

'On her way, I expect. 'Ere, I'll ring the doctor. Amy would do that seein' you like this anyway, then I'll go over the shop. She's bound to be there by then.'

Nelly's hands shook as she dialled the Doctor's number and when it connected, she shouted into the 'phone, 'Come an' see Mrs Beynon, an' don't be too long about it. She's in trouble.' She answered a few questions, mostly with 'Gawd knows', before putting the 'phone down then dialling the shop. This time Amy answered and said she would come at once.

The shop was not yet open and Amy ran up the inside stairs and knocked on the sealed door.

'Mavis, can you come for a while? It's an emergency. My sister is ill.' After a moment's delay, Mavis came down and Amy ran down the road to Prue.

The doctor arrived just as she reached the door and they went in together. The doctor gave a brief examination and rang for an ambulance. Nelly and Amy waited quietly, Nelly offering a silent prayer, and an apology for all the nasty things she had said about the woman.

'You go with 'er an' stay as long as you want,' she told Amy. 'I'll see to your Margaret, don't worry.'

Amy looked white and scared. Prue was rambling

deliriously, her skin grey and moist. Nelly thought Amy looked only a little better than the sick woman, her blue eyes shadowed with worry.

'I'll meet Margaret from school an' she can stay with me or with Evie an' Tim if she'd rather, 'til you gets back.'

'Thanks, Nelly.'

Amy was trembling now. Prue looked so deathly ill and old. She was like a stranger, her thin face distorted with pain and the pale blue eyes staring and wild. 'I'm afraid she'll never get over this,' Amy whispered.

'Don't think that,' the doctor comforted. 'Once the baby arrives, things usually settle down very quickly.'

'But you don't understand. She didn't want it, not at her age. It won't be that easy, not for Prue.'

Amy was proved right. The baby was born that day, a tiny scrap of a girl hardly bigger than one of Margaret's dolls. Almost six weeks premature, it seemed impossible for her to survive. But as the weeks passed, the doll grew and became a beautiful, fair-haired baby. She had a small mouth and surprisingly full cheeks with a nose pert and tiny in the perfect face. Amy adored her.

On a hospital visit a few weeks later, Amy was approached by a nurse and told the doctor wanted to see her. She was taken along corridors and into a large ward with rows of beds, whose occupants followed her progress with mild curiosity. Near Prue's bed, in which she still spent a lot of her day, the doctor waited.

'Nothing wrong with the baby, is there?' Amy asked at once.

'The baby's fine. In fact, I think she's strong enough to go home in a week or so. That is, she would be able to, but—' he nodded his head to where Prue was lying, dozing, her thin face sagging at the mouth and looking less like

Prue than ever. 'I'm afraid your sister is far from well. In fact, with your permission, I would like to transfer her to a different hospital, just for a while, to see if a different kind of treatment would help her.'

'A mental hospital?' The words that had been hiding away at the back of Amy's mind came out like a cry.

The doctor nodded. 'We think it's best. With luck she will respond quickly to treatment and soon be home. But in the meantime, is it possible that you could care for little Sian?'

'Of course.'

A million fears filled her mind as she made her way home. How could she possibly run a house, a shop, and look after Margaret properly as well as care for this tiny infant? She didn't know how. She only knew she would.

When she stepped off the bus outside 'Heulog', Nelly and George were walking past, the big dogs straining on their leads: leather ones now, a present from George.

'I'm going to have an addition to my family,' she said in greeting.

'Not Prue? Coming home is she?'

'I'm afraid not. She's still very ill. I've been asked to have little Sian.' She smiled, 'I don't know how I'll manage, with the shop and all, but I couldn't refuse. I couldn't see Prue's baby going to strangers, could I?'

'When is she comin'? I'm lookin' forward to seein' 'er. Pretty is she? Or like your Prue, Gawd 'elp 'er,' she couldn't resist adding.

'She's lovely, and if she reminds me of anyone, it's of Freddy when he was a baby. Fair, blue-eyed and so tiny.'

'Seems the gypsies were right about you having a baby to care for,' George said. 'Nelly told me of their predictions.'

'Typical of my life!' Amy laughed. 'Another baby and

still no husband! That part of her fortune-telling hasn't come true!'

'Not yet,' Nelly said, and she gestured to where a tractor was puffing along the road driven by Billie Brown, who was waving enthusiastically.

'Not yet.'